Flora Flowerdew and the

Secret of the Sarcophagus

FLORA FLOWERDEW VICTORIAN MYSTERIES
BOOK THREE

AMANDA MCCABE

OLIVER-HEBER BOOKS

PUBLISHER'S NOTE: This is a work of fiction. Names, characters, places, and incidents either are the product of the author's imagination or are used fictitiously. Any resemblance to actual persons, living or dead, business establishments, events, or locales is entirely coincidental.

Flora Flowerdew and the Secret of the Sarcophagus 2025 Copyright © Amanda McCabe

Published by Oliver-Heber Books

0 9 8 7 6 5 4 3 2 1

One

WINTER, 1889

The winter of 1889 held London in an icy grip, its bony fingers squeezing the life out of every home and shop and theater and party. It was impossible even to look forward to Christmas, with its lively singsongs at the piano, plum puddings, and pantos, when no one could stand to venture out of their heavy-knit shawls and away from their own firesides.

A gray-green fog muffled all the brick and pale stone buildings; even Buck Palace was enveloped. The usual clatter of traffic sounded distant and eerie. The world was now only peopled by ghosts and secrets, which usually boded well for Flora Flowerdew's business, which was conducting séances and winkling secrets out of the dead to pass to the living.

Alas, it was not. Even those ghosts were hunkered down in their comparatively warm nooks in the Great Beyond, and she hadn't had a booking for a séance in weeks.

Flora herself was certainly not immune to the bone-aching chill. She sat in the little office at the back of her Kensington flat, wrapped in no less than three shawls, hands tucked into fingerless gloves her maid Mary had knit for her, trying to make sense of the accounts. No matter which way she turned them, squinted at them, started again, the image was the same—not promising. At all. Madame Flowerdew's brief fame when she found the Duke of Everton's diamonds was fading in the icy atmosphere.

She slumped back in her chair with a huff, disturbing her Pomeranian, Chou-Chou, ensconced in her little velvet bed under the desk. Chou-Chou sneezed, sighed, and shook out her caramel-colored ruff before turning around and lying down again. She stared up balefully at Flora from her amber eyes.

"Sorry, duckie," Flora said, her "Madame Flowerdew" plummy accent fading back into good old Florrie Gubbin, chorus girl and not-bad-but-not-good actress before she learned the rare arts of summoning the dead—and getting the living to pay dearly for it. "It looks like it'll be broxy on the table soon if we can't raise up some clients."

Chou-Chou wrinkled up her dainty nose in disgust at the thought of eating cheap, diseased sheep, and burrowed back under her fur-edged blanket.

"I do quite agree."

Flora kicked up her booted feet as she studied the room around her. The flat was her pride and joy, bought and paid for all herself after years of scrimping and saving and bustling about town, learning everything she could, working all hours.

It wasn't a large place, but it *was* pretty, and best of all, it was in a very respectable neighborhood of tidy houses and flats, little gardens, and pretty shops. It paid the wages for her friend and maid Mary, kept Chou-Chou in roast beef and marrow toast, and bought Flora the colorful gowns and fine, feathered hats she adored (when she wasn't draped in Madame Flowerdew's black crepe and veils). After the diamonds, and then the purloined letters case, there had been a flood of new clients, full of urgent questions about lost wills and buried jewels. But the winter seemed to have choked off the supply of afterlife seekers, just as it had the London supplies of coal and candles.

She slammed the ledger shut. She hadn't even heard from the old, dead dukie lately. He was probably busy with his celestial bridge games with Prince Albert. She didn't really miss the irascible, bossy old coot, though he could certainly be happy in throwing a ghostly friend or two her way. But she *did* miss his lovely grandson.

Ah, Benedict. She kicked her feet just a bit faster as she thought of him. Benedict. The Duke of Everton. After their adventure at Windermere Abbey, she hadn't seen much of him. She heard he was starting to make his way in politics a bit, journeying between his London house and the estate at Thornhill. Squiring a few earls' daughters and rich merchants' nieces about to balls and teas and operas. Not that she blamed him one bit. Thornhill was crumbling around him ... he needed money double-quick.

She, more than anyone, understood that sometimes a person had to do what they had to do to survive. A young, handsome, golden-hearted but utterly impecunious duke with a crumbling estate had to make hard choices just like a chorus girl did. She'd seen his name in the gossip rags, matched with American heiresses and English earls' daughters.

But she was just human, and a girl could daydream about kissing a blond, broad-shouldered Apollo in the moonlight, couldn't she? She closed her eyes, and remembered their little jaunt to the South of France to seek a thief. That achingly blue sky, the scent of roses in the warm, salty-sea breeze, the heat of the sun on her skin. The touch of his hand as he led her down a garden path ...

It was certainly a long way from a London pea-souper, and that was the veriest truth.

Flora opened her eyes, and scowled to see she was still in her stuffy, smoky office, the fog still swirling beyond her window. She caught a glimpse of herself in an oval mirror hung across from the desk. She looked like an ogre, wrapped in several knitted shawls and her red hair tousled!

"I look like the old granny in a fairy story," she muttered, and unwound two of the shawls. Only to put them back when the cold air tickled her neck. No duke would look twice at her, even if she'd been an heiress.

"We'll just have to find another ghost or two, CC," she told the dubious pup. "Drag them out of their cozy ether. Or maybe I'll get out my spangled tights again, and trot on down to the Gaiety Theater."

Chou-Chou snorted loudly, and Flora laughed. "Too right you are. No one would hire such a long-in-the-tooth chorus girl. I can't even remember the words to *Daddy Wouldn't Buy Me a Bow Wow*. Maybe Evie could use a proof-reader." Evie Finnegan was now a writer at the *Evening Star* newspaper, though they'd met back when Flora was at the Gaiety and Evie was penning theater reviews and scandal bits. Now she specialized in crime, and had been very helpful. Flora thought she might rather like chasing through the streets like Evie, tracking down criminals. Or maybe she could be a stage manager, get back in the theater business. Or open a modiste shop, pretend to be French, and sell ladies ribbons and silks.

Whatever she did next, Flora feared her adventuring days with Benedict were behind her.

She abandoned the disappointing accounts, and went to add a shovel of precious extra coal to the fire. Lined up on the carved mantel were souvenirs of the adventures she'd found on her recent shenanigans with the duke and her friends, bibelots from Cornwall and Nice and the circus tents they'd visited together in Picadilly. Reminders of fun.

Mary suddenly rushed in, making Chou-Chou sit up in interest. Wherever Mary went, a tea tray usually followed. There was no tray this evening, but there *was* a small parcel.

Mary had once been a dresser at the Gaiety, and left with Flora to start this spirit-contact business. She was a compact, dark-haired, no-nonsense Cockney, whose ability to spot con men and flim-flams was invaluable, as was her loud laughter at any joke. Flora couldn't do without her. Her eyes glittered with excitement at something unexpected in those days of being cooped up in the flat, and Flora remembered that Mary missed excitement, too.

"What's that, Mary?" Flora asked, hoping for chocolates. Or maybe emeralds from a very grateful ghost-seeker. "Does someone need a séance?"

"It's from Lady Hastings."

Now Flora was *really* interested. Imogen, Lady Hastings, was Benedict's great-aunt, a woman who'd had a most adventurous life, and always brought new mysteries with her when she appeared. "Oh, I do hope it's a conundrum from another old suitor of hers!" Their visit to Windermere Abbey had been for Imogen to retrieve scandalous papers from her past. They found much more than they'd bargained for.

She took the little parcel to her desk and quickly opened it. On top was a sheet of thick, expensive pale-green stationery, scented with jasmine and headed with a gilded, embossed coronet with the initials IH. The slanted, spiky handwriting was darker green. No ordinary black on white for Imogen!

"*My dearest Flora,*" she read aloud to Mary and Chou-Chou. "*How I have missed you! I'm quite aching to hear of your latest encounters with the Beyond. I myself have been traveling in Italy, and returned to find this quite alarming package waiting for me, along with the appalling weather. You are the only one who can help me make sense of it all. Sir George Crosbie was a dear beau of mine once upon a time ...*"

5

"I knew it!" Mary exclaimed. "Her ladyship must have been in on the hanky-panky with every handsome bloke in Europe back then."

Flora laughed and went on with the letter. *"Though I have not seen him in an age. Perhaps you have heard of him? He became quite the renowned archaeologist, though when I knew him, he was a secretary at the British Museum. You may have met with some of his discoveries in their spirit forms. He is dear Benedict's godfather, friends with his father, the great explorer. I know little beyond what I read of his work at the Temple of Nephthys at Luxor, and that he recently married a lady much his junior, a viscount's daughter. Imagine my shock to receive this letter and book! Well, my dear, just take a look for yourself..."*

Flora took up the second note in the parcel, this one scribbled in pencil on a torn, stained bit of sketch paper.

"My beautiful Imogen. My Habiba, Great of Praises. If you are reading this, I have surely departed this earthly plane to lay my soul at the mercy of Anubis. Unknown to Maspero at the Egyptian Museum, I am sending something special to London in my next shipment, a Dynasty XVIII sarcophagus to the British Museum. Thompson will receive it and know what to do with it. I trust you will, too. You were always the bravest, boldest of women, my goddess of glowing wisdom. Though fate has kept us apart, I have always known we are connected as Isis and Osiris and cannot be parted. I beg you, I need your help now more than ever. We shall meet again in the Duat, and hear of all our adventures. Good-bye, my darling."

"Cor blimey," Mary sighed as Flora finished reading. "No one has ever felt passionate love for me for centuries. Or at all, really. Though there were those four months with Alfie that one year ..."

"Me, neither," Flora murmured. She remembered an old love or two, that bloke at the pub behind the Gaiety, a sweetie who'd owned an apothecary shop, a circus

6

strong-man. None of them at all like Benedict. "But is he really gone from the earthly plane now? How? And why tell Lady Imogen? What's this sarcophagus got to do with it?" She studied the paper again. "No date on it."

"Maybe that book in the parcel says."

Flora tore away the rough brown wrappings and found a diary, bound in faded red leather, stained with water and sand, embossed with the initials GC.

A note of more green stationery fastened on top said *"This appears to be Sir George's last journal from his dig at the temple of Nephthys, but I fear I know little of reading hieroglyphs. I thought we might perhaps work at it together, if you can spare an evening or two from your busy work. In the meantime, Ben and I are invited to a mummy unwrapping party at the British Museum—and it features the very sarcophagus dear Georgie speaks of! I am sure it will give us a clue, and we shall hear of his fate (if indeed he has met his fate), though such events do give me the shudders. The dead should rest! Can you come? Thursday next? No one is more helpful and more fun in a mystery than you. Ben and I can call for you in my carriage at eight, if that suits. In the meantime, see what you can make of this diary. I am quite at sixes and sevens. Your dear friend, Imogen Hastings."*

"Well," Mary said gleefully. "I knew Lady H would come through for us! An adventure at last."

"One would hope so. But I admit I'm a bit flummoxed by it all." Flora did feel a flutter of excitement at this hint of something bright and enticing in the cold days, yet she wondered what was really going on behind such a cryptic message. A mummy-unwrapping party had definite possibilities. Lots of spirits must be lingering there, just aching to get their messages out!

And maybe Benedict would be there, too. She wasn't sure if she longed for that—or dreaded it.

She tapped the paper against the desk as she turned

it over in her mind. It would surely be the sensible thing to tell Lady Hastings she was too busy. Nearly falling out of that tower at Windermere Abbey hadn't been much fun, after all. Yet, just like everyone else in London, Flora was quite fascinated by Egypt, by the tales of daring archaeologists uncovering the past from beneath the covering sands and brought it to life again. Gods and goddesses, powerful families, sun-struck days by the green Nile.

She reached for the water-warped journal and flickered through the stained pages, the quick sketches of strange little images. Lozenges filled with beetles, a lady in a blue robe bending over a seated man, birds, squiggles, vases. A rather alarming scene of someone getting their head lopped off. Short, abbreviated notes. And— was that a bloodstain? Or a blob of raspberry jam? This was clearly no ordinary document, no diary listing daily meals and chores. That ember of excitement caught inside of her, and she knew it wouldn't be denied. It never had before.

She pushed back her chair and went to the window. The fog was rolling in, casting everything in endless gray. But in her mind, she saw a blazing butter-yellow sun, shining down on temples and pyramids and obelisks, massive statues of crowned pharaohs and sphinxes, lines of camels meandering through the drifting sands. An oasis of palm trees and glittering water, white minarets sparkling in the distance. A place of danger and romance, far from the foggy streets. She'd always longed to see it all.

Surely an evening at the British Museum would be the next best thing. And Benedict might be there. Chou-Chou whimpered as if to urge Flora onward.

She glanced down at the book in her hand. *If you are reading this, I have certainly left this earthly plane.* Excitement and danger—they were always there when Benedict was nearby, whether she liked it or not.

"Shall we go, then?" Mary asked.

Flora clutched the book close, like a rope to swing them up out of dreariness, and laughed. "What d'you think, Mary?"

Mary clapped her hands in delight, as Chou-Chou barked and twirled. "I think a little fun might be coming our way!"

Chou-Chou threw back her head and howled.

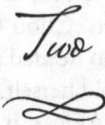

Two

Something wasn't right.

Flora opened her eyes, and found herself staring up not at her own looped and be-ribboned taffeta bed canopy, but at a night sky. And what an astonishing night sky! Endless, sparkling stars like diamonds and pearls on a dome of purple-black velvet sky. A crescent of amber moon, its edges bright and sharp, almost so alive she could reach out and brush it with her fingertips.

For an instant, she was so enchanted, so caught by a star shooting past in a flare of sparks, that it didn't strike her she was *outside*. A warm breeze brushed over her skin, scented with heady white flowers, and she had a flash of panic she'd been lifted from her bed and dropped far away. Some new, not-funny ghostly trick?

She tried to sit up, out of breath, yet something held her down. She turned her head and saw stone pillars rising up to either side, carved with signs or words she couldn't read in the moonlight. A building, then, roofless, open to the sky.

Panic rose up in her like a cold wave. *Calm, my daughter,* a voice whispered around her. *Ra shall soon sail his sun-boat across the sky, and all will be well again.*

11

But for now, silence.

Flora realized it all had to be a dream. Astral projection was not one of Madame Flowerdew's supernatural gifts—not that Madame Flowerdew really *had* any supernatural gifts. It was Chou-Chou who seemed to summon the ghosts who needed their help.

Just a dream, she told herself. *Might as well enjoy it.*

Whatever "it" was. At least it was warm there.

Once she took a deep breath, let her limbs relax, she lifted her arm as if to brush the stars. She saw bracelets on her wrists, gold and turquoise. Not hers, but she coveted them in her magpie heart. She decided to see if she could sit up.

She could, or rather she seemed to levitate, and peeked over a low wall. She saw gardens, palms and flowers lining walkways, a reflecting pool that showed the shimmering outline of the wall, the sky. And there was a figure, standing very still beside the moonlight-rippled pool. A man, but she couldn't make out his features, only the outline of his tall, lean figure. He wore a gauzy, pale robe, his long, waving hair falling over his shoulders. Something urged Flora to go to him, some irresistible force in her feet. A sense of excitement, yearning, yet also an icy edge of fear. Something wonderful waited there, she was sure, but also a terrible menace lurked just beyond.

Something warm and soft brushed her hand, startling her, and she glanced down to see a cat beside her. Long and sinuous, glossy black fur that blended into the night shadows. Except for a pair of amber eyes, staring up at her, unblinking. Chou-Chou's eyes.

You are not meant to be here yet. Begone. Its voice was only in Flora's head, yet she knew it belonged to the cat. Full of authority, not to be disobeyed, but so calm and gentle ...

Flora's eyes flew open, and then she *did* see her own

canopy. It was dark in the chamber, yet she made out the outline of her own, familiar furniture, the lace-draped dressing table, the armchair by the grate with her discarded shawls tossed over it, and the carved posters of her bed. The room was cold, the fire simmering low after all its valiant efforts to ward off the freezing fog. She sat up, gathering her satin quilt as her eyes adjusted to the gloom.

She felt the heat of that other night tugging at her, the mystery of that man by the pool. She heard a tiny "chuff," a snore, and saw Chou-Chou asleep on her back atop her velvet cushion. Her paws waved in the air as if she, too, dreamed. Maybe she imagined she was the cat. Whatever had just happened, Chou-Chou wasn't fussed.

Flora leaned back on her pillows and tried to take another deep breath, to shake off those feelings of longing and dread. Yet they lingered until Ra did indeed sail his sun-boat across the London sky.

～

Quite against all her natural inclinations to stay in bed and keep the blankets over her head until a much more sensible hour, Flora set out early to catch the omnibus to her friend Evie Finnegan's office at the *Evening Star* newspaper. If she didn't, Evie could very well go out tracking down thieves and murderers for some exciting story, and then Flora would never find her.

Despite the earliness and the bone-chilling cold, Flora was happy to be outside after the long days cooped up indoors, the strange dream that still seemed to hold onto her with gossamer ties. She felt a bounce in her steps as she made her way down the street. She had a new task, a new purpose!

New clothes. No Madame Flowerdew black, no

13

layers of thick knitted shawls. She paused to study herself in a shop window, backed by white flurries of snow. Her red hair shone warmly against all that gray-white, but her eyes were dark-rimmed with the sleepless hours after the dream-cat came to her. Yes, she needed some answers, or her complexion would suffer!

Her attention wandered over the displays arranged before her, and just as she did every day, she marveled that *this* was where she lived. A neighborhood of clean streets—usually, when not blanketed with soot-darkened snow. Neat carriages bounced past, well-lit shops and cafes, and pretty windows full of hats and books and bolts of fabric.

So different from where she came from, fetid, lightless courts stinking of boiled cabbage and garbage, beggars and prostitutes on every corner, crowded rooms where disease and violence flourished. She'd fought so hard to get away from being poor, abandoned Florrie who everyone knew would grow up to be one of those lightskirts on the corner, a shilling a toss. She'd gone from the foundling home to selling vegetables, to being the orange seller in the lobby of the Follies to dancing there herself, until she met Madame Duvall and learned to sell a good séance. All those years of escaping into reading penny dreadfuls (at least the foundling home taught her to read and write) had paid off.

And she knew she was never, ever going back, no matter what she had to do.

She remembered her errand, and whirled around to hurry for the omnibus before if clanged off on its way.

She disembarked at the end of Evie's street. Unlike her own cozy, domestic lanes, this was all business. Tall brick buildings, blackened and faceless, lined up next to pubs and a coffee house or two where deals could be struck. Everyone who passed, muffled in great-coats and scarves, was in a great hurry to be someplace important. Do something important. It made her rush along, too.

The *Evening Star* was not one of the finest newspapers in London; they rather specialized in gory murder and mayhem and scandal. But Evie liked it there, as they were the only ones who let her write about crime and Westminster politics instead of relegating her to the ladies' pages of tea parties and deb balls. Flora loved to visit, to let the raw noise and life fill her up.

There was always the clatter of printers, the constant clack-clack of typewriters, shouts and curses. Flora dodged around newsboys and typesetters in their stained aprons, a few secretaries in crisp shirtwaists, and dashed up a set of narrow backstairs. The cold of the day was banished there. Stuffy air smelled thick with ink, paper, dust, and cigarette smoke. It felt like backstage at the theater, all commotion and clamor and Big Personalities. She'd once loved it, until it got old and exhausting.

She always marveled that Evie could not only manage to work amid it all day every day, but positively thrived there, feeding on the excitement.

She knocked at a door at the end of a corridor, and waited for Evie's bark of "Well, come in already! I don't have all day, do I?"

Flora laughed, and pushed the door open. Evie wasn't expecting her that day, but she wouldn't have stood on ceremony in any case. They'd been friends since the Follies days, when Flora danced and Evie wrote reviews of the performances (such as they were; Follies girls mostly kicked their legs and spun about). They were both older now, and Evie, at least, was wiser.

Evie sat as usual behind her battered old desk, piled high with paper and books. Her booted feet were propped up, her heavy tweed skirt muddied at the hem. Flora wondered if she'd already been out chasing up a good story.

Evie grinned when she saw it was Flora. She put aside the lorgnette she used to examine small print, tucked her pencil into her loose knot of auburn hair, and plucked the cigarette from the corner of her mouth to put it out in the overflowing ashtray.

"Flora, luv! Just who I need to see. What do you know about that strangling backstage at the Merring Theater?"

Flora shoved a pile of old newspapers from the only other chair and sat down, careful of her fur-edged skirts. "Only what I read yesterday in the *Globe*. A stage manager infatuated with a chorus girl, everything getting out of hand. Blood, shrieks, all that."

"Bloody 'ell. I can't believe the *Globe* got there first! I need a good break on that one." She leaned forward over her desk. "But I can tell from that look in your eyes that you have *some* kind of story. Something exciting happening on the ghostly plane?"

"Very possibly. You know how Egypt is all the rage right now ..."

"Do I ever! Even our receptionist insists on wearing a headdress *a la Egypt*. Whenever we have stories of cursed tombs the papers sell like oatcakes. They'd like me to cover some mummy-unwrapping folderol at the British Museum, should be good fun."

"That's perfect! This should make you happy, then." She quickly told Evie about Lady Hastings and her old *amour* Sir George, the dig at the temple of Nephthys, the letter and diary. She took the battered volume out her reticule and passed it over for a look.

Evie flickered through the stained pages, her expression avid. If there was anything Evie loved more than her work, or Daisy, her actress love, it was ancient curses. "Whenever your duke and his fascinating family come around, Flora, something interesting is sure to follow."

"He's not *my* duke," Flora murmured, feeling a blush heating her redhead's pale cheeks. As if she was a giggly schoolgirl and not an ancient spirit medium. "But I do agree that interesting happenings follow him about."

"Which is why he *should* be yours," Evie said stoutly. "You're two peas in a pod. Full of adventure. No milk-and-water deb would do for him."

Flora sadly shook her head. If only the world worked that way. "I'd be a terrible duchess. I'd never know how to run a great house, or how to curtsy properly to the queen." But surely other people could be happy in their love lives! "How is Daisy, by the way?"

"Pfft," Evie said, pulling the pencil from her hair and pushing it back again, mussing the knot. "You know actresses. Always rushing here and there. She's rehearsing a new show right now, *Watch Out for Uncle Arthur*, or something like that. So, I have lots of extra time on my hands. How can I help? If there's a story about Sir George Crosbie ..."

"I think there might be, with such a dramatic letter to Imogen. You're going to this mummy thingamie at the museum; we can pool our observations there and get people to talk to us. You must know a lot about this Temple of Nephthys and Sir George. Is he still among the living?"

"As far as I know. Everyone's been agog at his findings at that temple, you know. They say it's dedicated by a pharaoh to his dead love, lots of heartbroken scenes in tomb paintings, very romantic. It's been a big story. I'm sure we would have heard if he perished." She pushed back her chair and shot to her feet. "Come one, let's have a wee peek at the archives."

"Oooh, the archives!" Flora clapped her hands. She always loved it when they got to dig about in the shelves of the archives—it was like a treasure hunt of old stories and scandals. You never knew what was lurking there, all those goodies on crumbling paper. She eagerly followed Evie down the stairs to the dark basement, lined with shelves to the ceiling.

Evie lit a lamp to cast a small glow into the shadows,

17

and started opening creaking old drawers and cabinets. Flora tucked away her tidy gloves and hurried to help.

"Here's some of the articles about the discovery of the Temple of Nephthys," Evie said, blowing dust off a thick folder.

Flora flickered through the crumbling pages. Gushing columns about the romance of it all, descriptions of statues and paintings, blurry images of halls and pylons. Swooning descriptions of how handsome and dashing Sir George was. "What about his family? Anything here about them?"

"One son, I think. He works with his father, but I doubt he's so dashing or renowned."

"The sons usually aren't." And sometimes the sons were an improvement. Flora thought of Benedict's adventurer father, who was weak in matters of duty and the heart; his blustery grandfather who had insisted on dull duty above all. Yes, sometimes blood had nothing to do with character. "I think Lady Hastings said Sir George is married now?"

Evie gave a bark of laughter. "Second wife. A viscount's daughter, I think he had something to do with Egyptology, too. *Much* younger, of course. Harriet? Henrietta? Quite a beauty, I think I've heard, but in fragile health. She never comes back to England and this damp air."

"Smart lady." Flora shuddered to remember the icy winds howling outside, and her dream of a balmy, flower-scented night and black cats. "Oh, I say, look at this. Interesting. It talks about a disagreement between Sir George and another archaeologist. A quarrel about how the dig is being run, where the artifacts are sent, but he doesn't name names.

"Fascinating!" Evie exclaimed, reading over Flora's shoulder. "That's sure to cause some bad blood. Archaeologists are a ruthless lot, anyway. They'd cut their own granny's throat to claim a find like the temple."

"What's come of it recently?"

Evie shrugged. "Nothing yet, that I've heard of. You know how these bureaucratic quicksands go, even at the Society of Antiquaries—they swallow up, inch by slow, painful inch. And they all hate each other. I'm sure we can winkle out more at the Museum."

Three

F lora fought against the cold wind blowing and made her way through the tall iron gates tipped with dull gilding along Great Russell Street. She dashed up the stone steps to the British Museum. The gray day seemed to magnify the museum's grand solemnity with the dozens of columns of Portland stone, and the hurrying, hunched scholars rushing past on their way to the Reading Room with arms piled with books. She held onto her tilted green felt hat to stare up at the "Progress of Civilization" pediment above the doors, and felt a quiet sense of awe come down over her.

When she was a child, constantly searching for places out of the cold, for any kind of refuge, she'd longed to see inside those walls, sure there must be magic waiting within. She still felt sure of that when she looked at it all, at the quiet certainness of learning, the beauty of ages, and she wasn't at all sure she should be there.

But she was here now, and she had to go forward. She followed a line of those scholars, jostled by a few harried nannies with noisy charges to entertain in the foul weather, and made her way into the vestibule, between rows of yet more columns. Usually, she would go see the Elgin Marbles or some of the Roman jewelry, but today she had a different mission. She went straight to the Egyptian Sculpture Gallery, away from the faint light radiating from the iron-veined glass dome of the Reading Room, and found herself facing the impassive stare of a towering onyx pharaoh, beckoning her into the column-lined, shadowed galleries. A whispering guide directed her toward the collection of Sir George that was on display.

It was quieter there, except for the echoes of those restless children running toward the ever-beckoning mummy cases. She thought of the artifacts found in Sir George's temple, the carved statues and gilded perfume jars, painted shards, and beaded necklaces. It was all so intriguing. Hanging behind a case was a row of watercolors, which the label said had been painted by Sir George's late first wife, images of the temple as it was now, with crumbling pillars, and how it must have been thousands of years ago. Shining and bright.

A sudden image flashed through her mind, towering pillars bathed in moonlight, a silent figure beside a star-reflected pool. Her dream. Yet it seemed so real there in the painting! She could smell the white flowers, feel the tingling sense of anticipation and fear that overcame her at the sight of that dream-man.

Something soft and warm, fleeting, brushed against her hand, warm through her gloves, and made her skirt sway. She jumped, and could have vowed she heard an echoing "mrrrow" before all went still again.

"You are admiring the Temple of Nephthys, I see," she heard a voice say. Not some dream voice in her head, a *real* voice, and Flora jumped back again, afraid she'd come too near the case and a museum employee was going to scold her.

She spun around, and found a young man watching her. He wore a somber, dark suit like a clerk, with the overly-long hair of a student who had no time for fashion, yet he didn't scowl at her. He had a shy smile, an avid gleam in his brown eyes behind oval spectacles, and he looked rather appealing. Like some wide-eyed lad who managed to sneak in the backstage door to stare at all the behind-the-scenes secrets.

"I—yes. It all seems most fascinating," Flora said. She gestured to the watercolor, the selection of gold and turquoise jewelry. "So, that is the Temple of Nephthys? Sir George Crosbie's dig site?"

His eyes widened even more, and he shifted his weight back and forth like a puppy ready to run ahead. "Yes, indeed! You know of it, then?"

"I know *of* it, of course. Who does not? Do you study it, then, Mr. ..."

"Mr. Ottway. Theodore Ottway. I work there! Or at least, I soon shall. I have been working in the restoration studios here at the Museum since I left Cambridge, but received word last month that Sir George requires more assistance for the rest of the season, so I am going out there soon. I am so terribly excited!" He tilted his head as he studied Flora, suddenly shy, an admiring gleam in his eyes. "Are you a scholar of Egypt yourself? You do have the look of one, Mrs. ..."

"Miss Flora Flowerdew. How flattering of you, Mr. Ottway! But I fear I am only an interested amateur, as so many people are." In London, spirit mediums were taking advantage of the Egyptian craze in many ways, bringing in Egyptian gods and goddesses, ancient spirits that visited to impart the wisdom of centuries. But surely someone like Mr. Ottway was not interested in *those* aspects of Egypt. It was a great stroke of luck to run into someone connected to Sir George's own temple. "I should so much love to hear more about it all."

His shoulders squared with pride. "Oh, indeed! I have been following the progress at the Temple of Nephthys ever since it was first discovered. I was a student at Cambridge then, and it made me change my focus at university from theology to Egyptology, despite my parents' doubts. Who could do otherwise once they saw this glorious temple? Shall I give you a small tour of the holdings here?"

"I should enjoy that very much, thank you, Mr. Ottway. But I should not wish to take you from your duties."

"Not at all. One of my first duties is to share this knowledge and beauty!" He glanced about them, as if seeking the finest examples to show off to her. "I am afraid we don't have a great deal displayed right here, of course, Miss Flowerdew. And I must say, what an enchanting name! The work at the temple is still proceeding, and much remains in Egypt, both at the Egyptian Museum in Cairo and in Sir George's own care. Everyone just felt that, with the interest in the Temple, whatever can be seen now should be. It's so important."

"And I am so grateful." Arrested by a beautiful little object, Flora stopped to study it. It was a carved bottle, pale-blue stone, topped with a cat-shaped stopper. The cat sat erect, staring straight at her with a small, darker blue stone. "What is this? It's quite beautiful."

Mr. Ottway beamed at her. "One of my very favorites! A bottle for holding precious scented oil, lapis, depicting the cat Bastet with the eye of Horus. As I'm sure you've read, Miss Flowerdew, the temple—which is not large at all by Egyptian standards, just four main chambers and some storage areas, dedicated to the worship of Nephthys, goddess of the mourning and the night—was probably built by a high government official, who served one of the Amenhoteps in the XVIII Dynasty. Some people say it was the pharaoh himself, out of grief for a lost love, but there is no such evidence of that yet. The official is the most likely builder."

Flora studied an elaborate collar of gold, faience, carnelian, and turquoise, its five layers of beads fastened with a gold head of Horus. "It would seem he was well-rewarded for his work, if this was his."

Mr. Ottway laughed, and a red flush stained his cheeks as if he was somewhat embarrassed. "They do say it was the official's beautiful daughter who was the love of the pharaoh. That would account for the lavish sums spent on its building, if so. Perhaps I shall find out for sure, once I am there!"

Flora tried not to giggle, thinking of the lavish sums they said their own Prince of Wales spent on his many mistresses. "I daresay it might have curried some favor. Look at Mrs. Cornwallis-West's house! It's no shabby pile, is it? The more things change ..."

His blush deepened to a brick color, and he coughed. "Erm—yes. Quite. Yet you can see that the daughter, if she was real, had a special devotion to the goddess Nephthys. The wall paintings you can see in these sketches are most detailed and elaborate, the colors astonishingly well-preserved, perhaps due to the remote location or the fact that it seems to have been mostly undisturbed over the centuries." He showed her an array of sketches, copies of wall art depicting a goddess in a headdress of a disk and a pair of horns beneath a moon, ringed with unreadable text. "This is Nephthys, goddess of spirits and the underworld; the temple was dedicated to her, to those who mourn their loved ones."

One in particular caught Flora's attention, the goddess in a chariot pulled by hawks. "Fascinating," she murmured. "The sense of movement and emotion in this one! We can actually sense it all, even now." She thought of a play she'd recently seen, *A Priest of the Nile*, filled with intrigue, romance, dastardly deeds, gods who swooped in to save their foolish acolytes in a burst of stage-smoke. It had been thrilling, but not nearly as much as a glimpse of the real thing.

Mr. Ottway beamed even brighter, if that was possible. He stared at Flora adoringly, and she realized she should be a bit worried. She didn't need a puppyish adoration just then. "You are so right. I can't wait to see it all myself. Sir George's wife—his late wife, I mean—did all these sketches. Her artistry and insight were quite invaluable. Such a loss to the project when she died ... so tragic."

Flora remembered that Sir George was now on his third wife, a much younger lady of fragile health. "Does Sir George's new wife not wish to assist in the work?"

Mr. Ottway glanced away. "I—I understand she prefers to own a shop. Selling, er, gowns and such, maybe. The last Lady Crosbie was from a family of archaeologists herself, the Pattersons. So very sad." He lowered his voice and added, "It's said the Pattersons are not best happy that Sir George would wed again so soon after the—the events."

"Events?" Flora whispered back. She wondered if this family, the Pattersons, had some hand in Sir George's worries.

"Lady Crosbie—it seems she was unhappy. She may have, only *may* have, mind you, taken her own life. In the inner chamber of the Temple, the god's sanctuary."

Flora was shocked. "I had no idea. I've not read anything of it. I should never have brought up something so indelicate!" Poor Sir George. Maybe the grief of it all had something to do with his current anxieties. Yet he *had* married again quickly. And what about the first Lady Crosbie?

"It was not wished for it to be generally known, of course. I think it was above a year and a half ago now."

"And then Sir George married again." Perhaps that was why the former Lady Crosbie had been so unhappy, suspecting her husband of having a new love even before she died. Flora had seen such things too many times to count, the scoundrels.

Mr. Ottway gestured to one sketch, a scene of the sanctuary chamber. The goddess of darkness, Nephthys, looking down at it all with stone eyes. "It does give a certain poignancy to it, doesn't it, Miss Flowerdew?

This is Lady Crosbie's rendering of the myth of Nephthys and her brothers, both of whom she married and who fought over her most bitterly. It's a wall painting found in the chamber, though I fear the story is rather indelicate."

Flora bit back a grin. "I do not mind indelicacy, Mr. Ottway, when it's historical."

He coughed. "Well, Nephthys, you see, had no children by her husband-brother Seth. She fell in love with Isis's husband Osiris, who was also their brother—confusing, isn't it? Thus she conceived her son Anubis, the jackal-headed one. But Seth was jealous, and murdered and dismembered Osiris, much to the mourning of Isis and Nephthys. They wept and gathered him up in hopes of resurrection. Maybe Lady Crosbie did the same. Here you can see the goddess as a hawk, her wings outstretched in protection."

"Love lost, no matter how scandalous, I see. How very sad, Mr. Ottway. A heart that can mourn for so long must have been a true and passionate one indeed."

He gazed at her even more adoringly. "I can see you definitely have a touch of Egyptian spirit about you, Miss Flowerdew. They believe our loved ones are with us eternally, as long as we remember and mourn them. It must be marvelous to possess such a love."

Flora feared he was standing rather too close, perhaps beginning to see things about her that weren't there. She turned and walked on toward the next case. "You must know Sir George himself, then? Since you are to work with him."

"I fear I have never met him," Mr. Ottway answered, hurrying to keep up with her. "It will be such a great honor!"

Flora thought of Sir George's letter to Imogen. Maybe he was no longer there to be met at all. "Then as far as you know, he is quite well?"

His brow wrinkled in confusion. "Oh, yes. Word of

27

any accident or illness might be a bit slow to reach London, but we have heard nothing amiss. Why would you ask, Miss Flowerdew?"

Flora airily waved her hand. "Oh, I suppose we here in England must imagine there are dangers aplenty in the deserts! Fevers and, er, snakes and such. Cobras hidden in baskets." Or possibly that was only in the novels Flora loved to read, the penny stories of adventure and doom. "But then again, so many people go there specifically for their health."

"I confess I should not like to be there much in the summers. It would be much too hot to work more than a few early morning hours, and most people use that time to research and catalog. But they say the new Lady Crosbie seldom returns to England, her health grows more fragile in our damp winters, so I am not sure! But as far as we know, Sir George is quite well. He has written several times that he's eager to reveal a new finding to us , though he hasn't yet indicated what that would be." He glanced around at the cases, the jewelry and scarabs and shabtis. "In fact, Miss Flowerdew, there is to be a special event here at the Museum on Tuesday! Sir George sent us a few more artifacts, including a grand sarcophagus said to contain the mummy of a priest of Nephthys. It will be opened and examined for a select few before it's taken away for greater study. Perhaps you would care to attend? Sir Edward shall speak about the work at the Temple, and I can personally make sure you have a seat with a very fine view."

"Most kind of you, Mr. Ottway! So thoughtful. I did plan on attending, a friend mentioned it recently, and it sounds like a most fascinating evening indeed."

His smile was a veritable ray of sun, and he took her hand as if he would kiss it. "Then I shall see you there! I fear I must return to my work now, but it has been a great pleasure to meet someone so enthusiastic about Egypt, Miss Flowerdew."

As Mr. Ottway hurried on his way, Flora continued through the galleries, taking in statues and carvings, watched by ancient eyes as she tried to take in all the information she'd just learned. She turned a corner, and glimpsed a man in the distance, tall, golden hair alight like the sun. A familiar figure indeed—Benedict, Duke of Everton.

For an instant, Flora thought it was another dream. The last time she saw Benedict they had been in danger together at Windermere Abbey. Now there he was, in all his tall, golden reality. He always looked like he was about to go a-Viking, despite his stylish, well-tailored coats and silk waistcoats.

He glanced up and saw her there, frozen in her tracks like a startled goose. A smile lit up his handsome face, radiating the warmth and confidence that always seemed to glow around him. "Flora!" he called happily, and hurried toward her.

"Dukie," she said, trying to be casual, careless. She met him next to a statue of Osiris, majestic with his shepherd's crook and flail. It was a statue once found by Sir George, and she remembered that he was Benedict's godfather. She longed to touch his hand, to let him know how her heart ached for him. But she felt strangely shy with him. "Haven't seen you in an age! I've read in the Society pages you're always on the run these days. Balls and teas and theaters."

He laughed wryly, and ran his hand through his sun-gold hair, leaving it tousled. It only made him look even more handsome, blast him. "It's a bore, Flora, I feel so cold with it all. Have to make the rounds, though, if I'm to make a good run at being a dukie, and Aunt Imogen would never leave me alone after I didn't marry Marianne Windermere. She's determined to find me another bride."

She smiled to remember chasing around Windermere Abbey for the lost letters. "That was a good time in the end, wasn't it? That crumbling old tower, like something in a play!"

"I'd certainly much rather be chasing ghosties with you and Chou-Chou than standing about like a statue in an overheated ballroom." He smiled down at her, his blue-sky gaze lingering, filled with unspoken affection. Their eyes met and held for a second longer than usual, a subtle shift in the air between them. Or at least so she imagined. He coughed and glanced away. "How have you been, Flora?"

She turned away, too, trying to cover the way her cheeks had grown too warm. "Not many ghosties to chase lately for me, I'm afraid. Chou-Chou is getting plump and rusty. Hopefully, that's about to change, since we got your aunt's message! Did you put her up to writing to us?"

"Not at all, though I'm very glad she did. Aunt Imogen has been hand-wringingly worried about dear Sir George, we both have, ever since that package arrived. I told her that after the Windermere case, you were certainly the one to help decipher whatever is going on."

"I have a hard time picturing your aunt in a hand-wringing state! Nothing seems to ruffle *her* feathers," Flora laughed. Benedict offered her his arm, and she took it as lightly as she could with her gloved hand. They walked slowly on, past those always-watching statues.

"I think it's just the sheer oddness of it all! We haven't heard from Sir George in a long time, and for his journals to suddenly land on the doorstep ..." He frowned, his expression suddenly vanishing behind a cloud. "It's unlike him."

"Oh, yes! I'm so sorry, I forgot he was your godfather. He must have met your father in Egypt?"

"On a dig, yes. Sir George was just starting out, had his first dig at Edfu. My father had left England and my pregnant mother, and was just passing through Egypt on his way to Turkey, I think. But apparently they quite took a liking to one another, and my father stayed for a few months to assist with the new work at the temple of Nephthys, which was just starting. When word arrived I had been born, my father asked Sir George to be one of the godfathers. No doubt he hoped the sense of adventure would somehow rub off on me." He laughed. "I don't think the grandparents were terribly pleased."

Flora laughed to think of the grumpy duke-ghost and the lofty dowager duchess. "I would certainly imagine not! I'm sure they only wanted princes to sponsor their wee dukie."

"Exactly. No scruffy scholars, mucking about in the sand." He glanced around at all the monumental statues around them, silent and watchful with everything they'd seen for so many centuries. "No one knew then how famous he would become with his beautiful and invaluable discoveries. ."

Flora squeezed his arm. "You must be so worried. Are you very close to Sir George?"

Benedict shrugged, but she could still see shadows in his green eyes. "Not much at all, though he was certainly a fine godfather by his own light. As I got older, he wrote to me sometimes about his work in Egypt—he would send me little things like scarabs and papyri, tell me what they meant, how to use them. I could so easily picture the places he described, the pyramids and temples, the river. I longed to see them for myself, to discover such beautiful things and bring them back to life, just as he did." He stopped to examine a stone falcon, his lips downturned in a flash of sadness. Flora took a step back to keep herself from wrapping her arms tightly around him. "Two or three times, when I was at school, he returned to England and stole me away to bring me to places like here."

"That must have been exciting!"

"Indeed. To escape Latin recitations and boiled beef and potatoes to spend the day amid all this beauty. I could see why my father loved it so much. Sir George even took me to the back offices and store rooms to see items being unpacked. His tales of it were all so magical. He also talked of my father, which my grandparents never would. He helped me see the wider world through curious eyes, as my father must have."

Flora slipped her hand into his, her heart aching for the lonely boy he had been. He smiled down at her, and for a moment they seemed all alone in the crowded, cold world.

She'd sometimes dared to let her imagination run a little wild, wishing he could be a lowly law clerk or some such thing, or that she could be a real lady. That they could be on equal footing and find each other there. She knew it was all just a daydream, but it tugged at her when he was so near.

A crowed jostled past them, seeking the Rosetta Stone or the mummies, and Flora was startled back into the gray winter day. She stepped back from him and smiled carelessly.

He looked away. "Shall we get some tea?"

"Good idea. You can tell me more about this mummy in the sarcophagus business." She took his arm again in a very proper manner, ignoring the way it felt under her touch, and they strolled onward. "A mummy-unwrapping sounds like something the magician, the Spectacular Samuel, at the Follies used to do! His mummy was just plaster, but proper gory it was. Blood and entrails, and a screaming open mouth with lots of sharp teeth. They had to station people at the doors to help fainting ladies escape! All his acts were that way, but he wasn't bad at all."

Benedict tilted his head in curiosity. He did always seem to enjoy hearing her old theater tales. "Was this Spectacular Samuel a good magician? Did he astound and awe the crowds with his feats of impossibility every time?"

"Blimey, no. But he was very dishy, so all the girls kept coming back for his show, fainters or not."

He gave her a tiny smile. "And did you wait for this Spectacular Silas at the stage door?"

"Samuel!" She nudged his arm. "And I didn't have to wait about, Dukie dear. He always tried following me home, 'til I could lose him in Tailors Lane." She was quite sure Benedict would never, *ever* follow a girl through the foggy alleys until she had to use her longest hatpin on him. She'd never known a man quite like him before. His every action, no matter how small, such as holding the door for a stranger, or lovingly supporting his aunt and friends, made his kindness radiate from him, just enhancing his astounding good looks. He had a rare ability to make people feel that they mattered, they were heard.

It was very bad for her heart, which she'd thought long hardened.

They left the museum and found a quiet teashop across the way, warm and welcoming behind floral curtains, complete with little nooks where two people could talk without being interrupted. As they settled in with their Darjeeling and cakes, Flora asked him about his estate at Thornhill. ("Still crumbling away, I'm afraid, but at least the staff is starting to think I might not be as hopeless as they first feared!"). He inquired after Mary and Chou-Chou. They sighed wistfully about their days of adventure in Cornwall caves and French casinos. The Cote d'Azur was not Egypt, certainly, and not India and Russia as Benedict's rebellious father once explored, but miles better than the frosty day beyond the condensation on the teashop window.

"I think all this talk of Egypt must be giving me the willies," Flora said, pouring another cup. "I had the oddest dream last night."

Benedict tilted his head in inquiry. "What was it, then?"

She told him about her vision, describing the temple and the silent man, the voice that told her she shouldn't be there "yet." She didn't say how the man made her feel, so filled with electric excitement, so eager to run to him.

"It does sound rather like Sir George's Temple of Nephthys, with its reflecting pool and columns," Benedict said. As usual, he didn't sound doubtful or dismissive of the strange things she had to say, but eager to hear more, to decipher it all.

"Does it? I did rather think so when I saw the sketches in the Museum."

"The reflecting pool in the courtyard ..."

"And Mr. Ottway said it was devoted to the worship of Nephthys, goddess of night and mourning."

He scowled. "Mr. Ottway? Another admirer, like Spectacular Simon?"

"I just met him at the Museum. A very interesting young man. He says he's soon to join the dig at the temple. He gave me a little tour of the artifacts."

"Maybe he'll follow you through the streets like Spectacular Steven and tell you more about the pharaoh's passion," he grumbled, and looked so adorably grumpy that Flora laughed.

"Why, Dukie! If I didn't know better, I'd say you must be jealous of the nice Mr. Ottway. Just for being an archaeologist and not stuck duke-ing."

"I might be. Just a little." He graced his fingers over the back of Flora's hand, and a wistful sadness flickered over his face. "Not just for his job digging in the sand."

Flustered, her face growing ridiculously warm, she reached for the cakes. "Well. Mr. Ottway says that as far as he knows, Sir George is alive and well, working at his temple; no one has heard anything different. He has been hinting he has something new to reveal, but won't say what yet."

Benedict sat back in his chair and crossed his arms. "What else did this talkative Mr. Ottway have to say?"

"He did seem rather sweet, concerned about my delicate sensibilities until I assured him I love a bit of gossip. He told me Sir George has some scandals in his past. What do you know of the first two Lady Crosbies? And his son? James Crosbie. I think I read of him in Evie's archives."

"Not much. The first wife was an archaeologist's daughter, the second is quite a great deal younger and runs a shop or something. Though her father was a viscount and sponsored many digs."

"You are hopeless at useful gossip, Benedict!" Flora poured out the last of the tea, wishing it would last all week so they could just go on and on sitting there. "We'll have to find out what Lady Imogen thinks. But I should be getting home soon. Mary will want to know what I've heard today."

"Shall I go with you?"

Flora was greatly tempted; she loved it when he sat by her fireside, Chou-Chou curled up with him as they chattered on about nothing over a bottle of brandy. But she shook her head. "I do have some shopping to do first, and that would bore you to tears. But your aunt says you'll both call for me for this sarcophagus-opening business?"

A sunny smile spread over his lips, and the day seemed brighter, sparkly. "Of course! Does it seem too terrible to say I'm greatly looking forward to such a gruesome-sounding evening? Though Aunt Imogen was sure to say they will not be *unwrapping* anything, unlike other, more vulgar events, merely looking."

Flora laughed. "Oh, I am looking forward to it all myself, Dukie. Vastly so."

Four

If Flora was directing a play set around an old parchment-brown, crumbling, pharaoh-priest-ish mummy that probably had a curse on it (all mummies surely carried curses), she wouldn't have set it *here*. Eerie scenes where ancient ghosts were released—no doubt very cranky about it all—into the modern world deserved dank, windowless cellars or creaking garrets. Maybe a castle turret, or a medieval crypt lined with shadowy effigies draped with cobwebs.

This was no such thing. In fact, this was a grand reception in a gallery beyond the Mummy Room, and seemed more like a Society reception than a scholarly lecture. Just through a doorway, the mummies contorted in their long slumbers in glass cases. Here, crowds swirled around in bright satin and taffeta gowns, finely tailored black coats and ivory brocade waistcoats, gleaming pearls and sparkling diamonds. They drifted in to titter over the mummies, then back to fetch champagne, nibble on caviar and salmon mousse, and listen to the string quartet, so crowded together one could hardly see the artifacts displayed on white-draped tables. Beautiful little statues of Anubis and Isis, alabaster jars that once held precious oils, a golden collar, a beaded headdress.

The sarcophagus, the star of the show, sat at the front of the room on a low dais. It was a large, reddish stone edifice, elaborately carved, traces of paint and gilt clinging to it. It seemed to glow malevolently.

"Shocking," Lady Imogen sniffed. She took a glass of champagne for herself from a passing footman, watching the crowd with narrowed, jewel-like lavender eyes, famous for their beauty in her storied youth and still magical. She was tall, slim, glowing in green satin and emeralds, majestic in a way that caused everyone around them to stare in awe. No matter she'd had men throwing themselves at her feet all her life. "Dear Georgie would not have approved of this at all. He was very serious indeed about his work. No such fuss and nonsense!"

Benedict found champagne for himself and Flora, giving her a conspiratorial little smile as he handed it to her. It made her feel like the bubbles in the glass, giggly and light. "Oh, come now, Aunt Imogen, you know as well as I do that sometimes even serious people must bow to fuss and nonsense for the sake of their bread and butter. Or, in Sir George's case, the sake of his temples and sphinxes. Someone must fund the excavations, yes?"

Flora realized she hadn't thought of that. It must take a lot of pounds and pence to keep an archaeological dig running so long. Money always did seem the start of most trouble. Maybe Sir George was involved in shady practices to keep up his work, or relied on unscrupulous backers? Maybe he was in debt?

Imogen sighed, and snapped open her green lace fan with her free hand, wafting around the stuffy air. "I suppose it is true that even George needed help from this museum if he wanted to continue his work. The French concession would eat alive any archaeologist braving it alone, with no powerful patron to secure their permits and pay their crews. Heaven knows he had no vast fortune of his own, as Lord Vyse does." She studied a turquoise scarab in its case. "Do you think maybe he is in trouble because of money? That may be some sort of shenanigans have been happening at the temple?"

"You always say he is a scholar of the most impeccable standards," Benedict said. "What sort of shenanigans could he possibly allow?"

"And so he is. It's why he has worked at the temple of Nephthys for so long—he is scrupulous about every bit of information he uncovers. Yet he could have decided that something about his precious work, something he was protecting, was worth a risk. Oh, poor Georgie! I always thought he was too noble for such work. Too much like a white knight, protecting the truth at all costs." A worried frown creased her brow under the fringe of silver curls, and she gulped down her wine.

Benedict gently touched her arm. "Aunt Imogen. We can't get upset now, we don't know anything at all yet. The letter could have been a mere joke of sorts, and he will stroll in here as hale and hearty as ever at any moment."

Lady Imogen shot him an irate glance. "George was never the joking sort, Benedict. Certainly not for such a lowly, prankish sort. Adventurous, dashing, and daring, but I fear humor was never among his sterling qualities."

"Was he perhaps of a rather dramatic bent, Lady Imogen?" Flora asked. It certainly wasn't the first time earnest scholarship and over-reacting drama came together. "After such long years amid grand temples and tombs, I know I would be. Perhaps it's some plan to gain attention for his latest finds. I've heard of such ploys before. I worked for a theater owner once who thought he could persuade audiences that monkeys were demons, set them to pop out at people from closets and such. Until a panicked bunch of rioters tore

up all her nice new velvet seats." She laughed to remember it.

Lady Imogen frowned thoughtfully. "I would not
have thought it. Shocking that such amateur theatrics
would be deemed necessary by any scholar! But it has
indeed been a long time since I met with him, and he
would do anything for his work. Perhaps some such sad
and desperate situation has befallen him as to require
such attention."

Flora glanced around the room and saw lots of famous faces. A duke, an archbishop, a writer whose tales
of dramatic woe flew out of bookstores. Any of them
could have secrets with Sir George, could want to protect themselves or their investments in his work. "Who
here might know something about Sir George, Lady
Imogen? I heard his wife and son were not in England,
but maybe they arrived here in secret?"

"I suppose you heard that from your new admirer
here at the Museum," Benedict said. He looked about
them as if Mr. Ottway would leap out at any moment.

Lady Imogen's head swiveled toward Flora in curiosity. "An admirer, my dear?"

Flora felt herself blushing in a most ridiculous manner, and snapped open her own fan. "A Mr. Theodore
Ottway, and he is not an admirer. In fact, I only recently
met him, here at the Museum. He is young, but an archaeologist of a most enthusiastic nature, soon to join
Sir George's work at the Temple of Nephthys. He was
eager to tell me about the finds there."

"It rather sounds like he could be an admirer," Lady
Imogen said thoughtfully. "And so useful, if he could
help us decipher the hieroglyphs in the journal! But you
are right about Sir George's family, I highly doubt Lady
Crosbie would be here ... they say she is of a sickly nature and never travels. Strange that Georgie, who is so
very energetic, would marry such a lady, but there is no
accounting for male taste. Why, I once knew a gen-

tleman who built his whole Parliamentary career on churchgoing rectitude, and behind the scenes he had quite a collection of Inquisition-style, er, tools ..."

"Aunt Imogen," Benedict muttered, a blush staining his own high cheekbones.

"Oh, pish, Benedict, you have traveled! You are a man of the world—you know I am not wrong. They do say Lady Crosbie, for all her ill health, is quite beautiful and well-to-do, the daughter of a viscount who often invested heavily in archaeological digs. You'd do well to find such a match for yourself." Lady Imogen studied the crowd over the scalloped edge of her fan. "Oh, look, there is Lord Pennington. He was recently traveling in the East—perhaps he heard something of Georgie. *And* he has a lovely daughter, so accomplished, they say. We must speak to him." She took Benedict's arm in an unbreakable grip and steered him across the room. Benedict cast an imploring glance back over his shoulder, and Flora waggled her fingers at him. They all had burdens to bear, even dukes.

Flora moved through the party, taking in the soft hum of conversation and the delicate strains of music. The room gleamed awash in the warm glow of gaslight, and the scent of hothouse roses lingered in the air adding a sweet fragrance to the atmosphere, quite unlike the dust one would expect. She wandered through the crowd, taking a bit of caviar here, a glass of champagne there, studying the Worth gowns and diamond hair ornaments, the array of artifacts in their cases, the flowing notes of music in the air along with whiffs of expensive perfume and hothouse flowers. She was quite glad she'd worn one of her favorite new gowns, a garnet-striped creation in the newest "princess" lines from Paris, with a deceptively loose Psyche knot Mary insisted on trying after she saw it in an issue of *The Lady*. It made her blend in among the colorful crowd, helped her glide seamlessly past the groups and knots of people and pick

41

up bits of their conversation unnoticed, as Florrie Gubbin could never have done.

"How astonishing!" she heard a woman say with a musical laugh, as she and her black-coated companion examined a mummy in a glass case. "Look at the nose. I would never have expected such a thing on a *king*."

"And the teeth! Shocking. I should fire my dentist straight away. Look at that bit there, mildewing away ..."

It astonished and saddened Flora that these mummies, these people, had once been just as the crowd was now, the aristocracy of their society, drinking, laughing, listening to music. She half-closed her eyes and imagined a very different party. The courtyard and reflecting pool of her dream, this time with a burnt-blue sky stretching overhead. Wall paintings and statues whole and gleaming, people in white linen and golden sandals drifting through all the beauty. Whole and real.

Now those were reduced to a morbid curiosity to giggle over at a party, before people flitted off for more champagne. Something warm and soft brushed against her hand, and her eyes flew open. But nothing was there at all, no one nearby. She hurried on her way, stopping to examine a beautiful turquoise jar with a lid that formed the head of a woman, her long hair perfectly rippled and curled, pierced with tiny metal slots.

"A kyphi," a musically-accented voice said from behind her. "Used for incense. You are interested in the XVIII Period, mademoiselle? You have the look of a scholar."

Flora glanced back to find an older gentleman studying her, his bright blue eyes under bushy white brows focused intently on the curls of her red hair before they flickered down again and he smiled widely. He was tall and stoutish, his skin heavily lined and almost mahogany, as if he'd spent a great deal of time in the sun. His evening suit was impeccable, his cravat fastened with a beautiful carved agate scarab, but his white hair was long and thistle-wild. A dark stone cat, tiny but perfectly carved in every feature, hung around his neck on a ribbon.

"Just someone fascinated by Egypt, I'm afraid, and quite amateur. As so many here are." But not him, she suspected. He had the look of a very scholarly scholar indeed. "This is indeed very beautiful."

"It tells the tale of Nephthys, and her son Anubis whom you see etched on the back here." He stepped up beside, and pointed out the dog-headed Anubis, a bird perched on his shoulder. "You see this falcon? It is a symbol of the goddess. It must have been used in her worship rites." He studied Flora again, especially her hair, until she nearly fidgeted and tugged at curls. "Just like you, she has hair of flame. But surely you have at least been to Egypt yourself, mademoiselle? You do seem to belong there. You have secrets behind your eyes ... you have seen much, I think."

Flora laughed, somewhat discomfited. "I haven't been to Egypt, I'm afraid, though I would love it. I have been studying much of goddess magic lately." She took a glass of wine from a passing footman to give her an excuse to look away from his too-penetrating attention. "But you, monsieur, have been there many times, I think."

He beamed at her. "Ah, yes, *vraiment*. I am Jacques d'Etrages, of the Department of Egyptian Antiquities of the Louvre. Or rather, I was—I have mostly retired from my work, I only travel for my own amusement now. I confess, Egypt has always held my heart and soul. There is such magic there, just as you say. Magic in its very language and scent and sounds. In its people." He peered at her closely, until she was sure he could see deep into her heart. It was most disconcerting. "You feel it, too, I am sure, this magic."

Flustered, Flora glanced down at the cat amulet, which seemed to shimmer in the candlelight. "Is that where you found that beautiful cat? Your work in Egypt?"

He held it up, his expression tender as he studied it. "The goddess Bastet. She is the protector, who every morning rides with her father, the sun god Ra, on his chariot through the sky to bring light, protecting all that is good in the world. I discovered her at Amarna. She has been my guardian for many years, has seen me through many dangers." He took it off and held it out to her. "You must take it now, mademoiselle."

She was so surprised, she fell back a step. Yet the cat seemed to sparkle, beckon for her hand. "Oh, no, monsieur, I couldn't! She is your special spirit."

"Bastet guards those who need her most. Thus, she seeks you now. I can see it. She has been waiting for you."

Flora slowly held out her hand, and he placed the cat gently on her palm. She turned it over, studying it. It was small, but perfectly carved, a black stone that gleamed as smooth as glass, but hard as a diamond. The delicate, pointed ears, the tail curled elegantly around its little paws, the half-closed eyes formed of green agate. She felt a warm brush against her other hand, the sway of her skirts as if in a breeze. She knew she couldn't hand it back.

"But you don't even know my name, monsieur," she whispered.

He smiled at her. "Is it not Merysekhmet?"

"Merysekhmet?" Flora liked the sound of that. It would have been perfect as a Follies stage name.

"It means Beloved of Sekhmet, mother of Bastet. A warrior goddess with the hair of a lioness. She is drawn to the glow of your own hair." He took it back and looped it around Flora's neck, where it lay against her garnet bead necklace. "Yes, I am sure you have need of her now. She will bring you to your true home very soon."

He stepped back, and she was suddenly aware again of the music, the laughter, the clink of crystal. She noticed Benedict watching her from across the room, and he looked strangely concerned.

Monsieur d'Etrages bowed, smiled once more, and melted into the crowd. She turned to hurry toward Benedict, reaching up to feel the smoothness of her new cat guardian. It was warm under her touch.

She'd only taken a few steps when she was distracted by a shrill cry, a commotion near the doorway to the gallery. Some of the curators and guards hurried past, as if to quell whatever wave waited to crest there.

"No! No, you must let me fly to his side! These are my people in these horrid glass cases, I must be with them. I must fly to his side, he summoned me!" a woman cried. Her voice, high and fluting, breaking on sobs, put Flora in mind of an actress she'd once known named Moll Eversby, and her signature work of Cleopatra. Moll had been very impressive at wailing and flinging herself on Marc Antony's body, making the crowds sob and actors refuse to work with her, she bruised and deafened them so. This promised to be an impressive sort of performance, too.

"Madam! This is a private gathering," one of the curators insisted. "You must leave at once!"

"Leave? No, no, I cannot! He has *called* me." Something bright fluttered in the air, like a scarf or shawl. "I cannot refuse him."

Fascinated, Flora drifted closer to get a better look, as did several others. She felt Imogen take her arm, heard the warm music of her laugh. "All this, and a floor show, too! Aren't we lucky, Flora dear?"

"Quite," Flora answered. She stretched up on her toes to see a tall woman dressed in flowing, silken robes of green and blue and amethyst, her head wrapped with a high turban fasted with a large carnelian brooch. She waved her hands above her head to

45

evade her captors, ancient gold snake bracelets flashing. Flora wondered if Monsieur d'Etrages mistook her for this lady, she so obviously thought her "home" was Egypt.

"The wheel of fate is turning! He needs me now," she wailed, and finally broke free of the frantic guards.

"Let her through, messieurs, she is a friend of Sir George," Jacques said. He emerged from the crowd, taking the lady's arm. She smoothed her robes, and with Jacques sailed onward, despite the guards' unhappy mutterings.

"Do you know her?" Flora asked Imogen.

"Not at all, but I wish I did! So entertaining. She does *look* like someone Georgie would befriend. He does like to collect oddities and eccentrics."

"She is Elspeth Rosse," someone said next to them.

Flora turned to find Theodore Ottway. A wide smile spread across his face when he saw her there. "Mr. Ottway! How nice to see you again."

He beamed at her. "And you, Miss Flowerdew. I did hope you would indeed attend this evening. I knew it would be most interesting, but not quite so ..." He glanced at Elspeth Rosse, who was wafting through the crowd on a cloud of blue and green silk. "Dramatic. Mrs. Rosse often likes to visit the Museum. She believes she is the reincarnated lover of a famous pharaoh."

"My dear chap, I have the distinct sense this is not half as dramatic as Miss Rosse can produce," Lady Imogen said. She held out her hand to him. "I am Lady Hastings, also a friend of Sir George. And of Miss Flowerdew."

He bowed over her kid glove, looking quite awestruck. "Theodore Ottway, my lady, an archaeologist. What an honor to meet you."

"Ah, yes, I have heard of you, Mr. Ottway. You are leaving soon for Egypt, are you not?"

"I am, yes, to join Sir George at the temple of Nephthys. It's something I have worked toward for so long, I can barely believe it is happening at last."

"And you are acquainted with the colorful Miss Rosse, then? I would love to know who her milliner is." Imogen gestured at Elspeth Rosse's turban as it wafted through the crowds toward the front row of seats.

"She is often found here at the Museum, yes," Theodore said. "She once lived in Egypt herself. I believe she likes to perform healing "spells" and such, though she's also a very useful draughtswoman and translator. She likes to say she was once a lover to the pharaoh who built the temple, and was a priestess at the temple herself, dedicated to the service of the night. I've even heard funny tales that she thinks Sir George himself is the reincarnation of the amorous pharaoh! So strange."

"Amazing thought indeed," Imogen murmured. "And is the Temple truly dedicated to Nephthys as goddess of the night?"

"Very probably," Theodore said. "Everything there seems to be dedicated to the worship of Nephthys. Mummified falcons, Anubis statues. Though strangely there has also been a great deal of Bastet images found there, which Sir George couldn't decipher yet." He noticed Flora's new pendant, and his eyes widened. "Much like your necklace, Miss Flowerdew. Bastet's spirit guides and protects those whom she loves. What a beautiful specimen."

"That is very pretty, Flora," Imogen said, examining the cat closely. "Have you been wearing it all evening?"

Flora held up the little cat amulet, whose green agate eyes seemed to flash in the candlelight. "Oh, no. I met a kind older gentleman, a Monsieur d'Etrages, who insisted I should have it. He said she calls to me now. I could hardly say no to destiny."

"Of course not. How generous of him," Imogen murmured.

"What an honor, Miss Flowerdew," Mr. Ottway

said. "Though no less than what you deserve, I am sure! Jacques d'Etrages is so well-known in our profession, he has discovered so many important sites, mentored so many scientists."

"Dear ladies and gentlemen," a curator announced from the dais. "If you would kindly take your seats, our presentation shall soon begin."

"Please, Lady Hastings, Miss Flowerdew, let me assist you in finding some seats with a fine vantage point," Mr. Ottway said. He shyly offered his arm to Flora.

Benedict frowned at him. "Very good of you, Mr. Ottway, but I have just procured seats for my aunt and Miss Flowerdew," he said, uncharacteristically curt. Imogen smacked his shoulder with her folded fan.

Mr. Ottway's back stiffened, and he scowled in return. "And you, sir, are ..."

"I am His Grace, the Duke of Everton. And you?" Benedict said haughtily.

Flora almost laughed aloud at all the silly preening. Benedict almost never "duked about," and Mr. Ottway seemed the sweetest of gentlemen. "This is Mr. Theodore Ottway, an archaeologist who works here at the Museum. He is soon to join Sir George's work in Egypt. Which is *very important*."

"And he has been very kind," Imogen added. "My dear man, do ignore my nephew. I promise he was not actually raised in a mannerless barn." The curator repeated his statement about the commencement of proceedings, and Imogen gathered her lace shawl closer about her shoulders. "Well, come along, my dears, we must sit down somewhere, or we'll miss the show we came here for. Two for the price of one, thanks to Mrs. Rosse!"

She sailed majestically ahead, the crowd automatically parting for her, and Flora and Benedict hurried after her. She glanced back at Mr. Ottway over her shoulder and gave him an apologetic smile. He really was very sweet, and she was sure his information and expertise could be quite useful later.

"Really, Dukie," she whispered. "You didn't have to snap the poor lad's head off! He is very kind. And you aren't usually so duke-ish and stuffy."

Benedict hung his head, looking charmingly abashed, but his jaw was stubbornly set. In that instant, he looked terrifyingly like his dowager grandmama. "I didn't like the way he looked at you. So—smarmy."

"Smarmy?" Flora laughed. "I think he is sweet. And I hope I am not quite such an old crone yet. I do sometimes still have an admirer or two." And maybe she'd found *two* tonight, she thought, remembering Monsieur d'Etrages and his comments on her "lioness" hair. It made her feel rather grand, she had to admit.

His expression softened. "Of course you do," he said quietly. "How could they ever help it?"

There was no time to say more, though Flora thought that was a pity. She'd love to think maybe Benedict himself admired her, just a teensy bit. That was the most she could hope for. They found some seats very near the front, on the end of the aisle of gilded chairs. As Flora settled onto the velvet cushion, she noticed Evie at one of the long, damask-draped refreshment tables along the wall, nibbling at caviar, watching Mrs. Rosse with great interest.

Monsieur d'Etrages walked past toward his own seat, and paused to bow and smile at Flora. Imogen's fan waved a bit faster.

"Who is *that* pulchritudinous gentleman?" she murmured.

"That is Monsieur Jacques d'Etrages, the archaeologist I told you about," Flora answered. "He is retired from the Louvre, and is most interesting."

"I say, my dear Flora, you have been gathering

49

suitors tonight!" Imogen trilled happily. "Young Mr. Ottway looks positively smitten, and now that ever so renowned Frenchman gifts you an amulet. That glorious hair of his!" She waved her fan a bit faster.

"It sounds as if you are the one with her eye on Monsieur d'Etrages, Aunt Imogen," Benedict said.

Imogen sighed, and smoothed the lace of her shawl over her elegant shoulders. "It is true it's been some time since I indulged in a bit of *amour*, but I doubt I could divert his attention from our dear Flora. What were you talking of with him, darling, that inspired the gift of that lovely little cat?"

"Archaeology, of course, what else could there be here? He was telling me about the temple of Nephthys." She examined the cat pendant again, and decided not to mention his slightly more personal remarks about her hair.

"Perhaps he could help us decipher some of dear Georgie's journals," Imogen said. I have asked Mr. Dymocks, a friend of mine from Oxford, about some of the images, but have sadly discovered little so far. It all seems to be copies of wall paintings and carvings at the temple. All anyone really seems to know is that Georgie must be at his Temple, or perhaps even at another, more distant site, and has not actually been heard of for some time. But that is not at all unusual, he likes to go off exploring on his own."

"Yet he sent this sarcophagus to the Museum," Benedict said, gesturing to the star of the evening, the hulk of the gilded sarcophagus, lying there as if waiting to come alive and pounce. "When was that?"

"It was sent from Egypt some time ago, naturally. He wrote to Sir Edward that it was found near the temple, and he wished to keep it safe here at the Museum until it could be properly and extensively examined," Imogen said. "I had a little chat with him over luncheon yesterday ... such an eccentric but helpful little man. Sir Edward said Georgie's message sounded rather worried about the artifact's security at his site, as perhaps there had been some thefts. But that is sadly not uncommon as well, and no other details were given. The curators decided to show it this evening, get a bit of publicity for it, before conducting more studies. To raise more interest in the Temple, as it were."

"Does it need more interest?" Flora asked. "Sir George and his work have seemed like a great object of fascination for some time."

"Indeed," said Imogen. "Who would not be intrigued by a handsome, daring archaeologist and a beautiful jewel of an ancient temple dedicated to love? It should be a novel! But you know how such things are an endless maw, devouring the next bit of gossip, the next object of furor. It has to be kept fresh."

"Would Sir George object to it being on display in such a way?" Benedict asked. "In his letters to me he sometimes mentioned how much he deplores the way serious scholarship becomes an object of more prurient interest."

"I am sure he would hate it, yes. He abhors such cheap spectacles as mummy-unwrappings and things of that ilk. I know they are putting a fig leaf on tonight's event by calling it a "display" or some such, but Georgie would still have protested. He is a veritable tiger in defense of the people of history, of their objects which should be there to teach us so much and not be exploited and destroyed." She sighed in admiration. After rummaging in her beaded reticule, she found a pair of opera glasses she used to examine the sarcophagus. "We shall have to report to him about what happens tonight, when he finally appears and explains himself. In the meantime, we should ask your admirable Mr. Ottway to assist us with the journal, Flora, if the handsome monsieur is unavailable. I am sure he would be very eager to help *you* in any way."

"Ladies and gentlemen, our most esteemed guests," the curator announced from the dais. "We shall begin this evening's event with many thanks to Sir George Crosbie. Without him, we would be bereft of so many unique and precious objects, so many invaluable insights into the world of ancient Egypt. Tonight we look at his latest offering, this most extraordinary sarcophagus found in the adjacent tomb chamber of the Temple of Nephthys. For thousands of years, no one has ever seen inside, as we shall right now."

An excited murmured whipped around the room before an anxious silence fell. Flora found herself holding her breath as she stared at the stone monument. Imogen handed her the pair of opera glasses for a closer look. Made of a reddish granite, the sarcophagus was carved with strange symbols and scenes that seemed to be the deceased making their way to the afterlife. Traces of bright colors could still be seen in spots, and the heavy lid was in the shape of a much-chipped and hard to see person, with an elaborate headdress and a serene gaze. It was astonishing.

"I should like to introduce Mr. Richard North before we begin," the curator continued, ushering forth a young man who bowed to audience. He was tall, reedy, his skin burned and creased beyond his youthful years with the Egyptian sun, awkward in his evening suit, but with intense, intelligent brown eyes, an eager smile. Altogether a handsome man. "He has worked with Sir George very closely at the Temple of Nephthys, as well as at a new site at the nearby village of Al-Fashn, and has escorted the sarcophagus to our keeping here. I am sure he will have many insights to share here in Great Russell Street before he returns to his duties."

"I am greatly honored to be here this evening, amid such very distinguished company, to share the genius of

Sir George and his vital work. To open this sarcophagus for the first time," Mr. North said, his voice deep and gravelly, solemn and authoritative despite his youth. It was quite believable that he would be the *protégé* of an important archaeologist. "It has certainly been my great privilege to be of some small assistance in uncovering the heretofore unknown site of Al-Fashn, which will surely add much to the knowledge of the Temple and the people who lived near and served there." He went on to the describe the carved symbols in the stone, the ways it would help the deceased find their way to the afterlife. "Now, if you would all care to gather as closely as possible ..."

The crowd eagerly rose to their feet and surged forward as the guards stepped forward to lift the heavy lid. Flora held onto Imogen's arm so they wouldn't be parted in the crush, and they found a spot as close as possible where they could see the proceedings clearly.

Flora felt the breathless, lurching excitement of the moment deep inside, and she leaned forward along with everyone else. She knew what they longed to see, what that delicious thrill meant. She'd read about such events many times in Evie's newspaper. Browned bandages slowly peeled away to reveal flaking skin the color of old, curling parchment. Leather-like lips, yellowed, broken teeth. Hollow eye sockets, which had once looked onto the blazing blue sky above the Nile. Maybe, if they were lucky, curses were released into the air.

Despite reading of such things, Flora had never really wanted to see the real thing, or even imagine them lurking out there. She took a deep breath, and dared one tiny step forward as everyone else eagerly surged around her, nearly lifting her from her satin evening slippers.

Benedict seemed to sense her sudden queasiness. He took her hand tightly in his, and gave her a reassuring smile she couldn't help but return.

She dared a quick peek into the shadowy, stony

depths of the sarcophagus, and was surprised to find the bandages were not nearly as brown and stained as she expected. In fact, they seemed only the palest of yellows. Mr. North also looked rather startled, but he quickly smoothed his sun-touched features into a small smile.

"The wrappings of a mummy contain various objects placed for protection, spiritual significance, or practical use in the afterlife. These items reflect the ancient Egyptians' beliefs in the afterlife and the desire to safeguard the deceased on their journey. We should find scarabs over the heart, representing rebirth, and shabtis, small statues to serve the soul in the afterlife," he said. "We shall not do such a full reveal this evening, for reasons of important research. Sir George has theories this could be an official of the pharaoh himself, perhaps even the man responsible for beginning to build the temple, as there was only the one burial in the temple, and we must make absolutely certain. The procedure, however, would begin thus ..."

He cut away a portion of the bandages, and soon revealed something truly beautiful, a golden ankh pendant. It gleamed as if it was new, and made many in the audience gasp.

"And then if we cut this way ..." Mr. North said, tracing the scissors along the line of the throat. Suddenly, he gasped, his sun-browned skin turning quite gray, and the scissors fell from his hands to clatter to the dais floor. Mr. Ottway and two senior curators stepped forward, and one of them let out a piercing scream.

The crowd swirled in panic, some back, some forward. Flora was shoved hard and nearly tumbled to a fall, but Benedict grabbed her arm and held her close. They were both jostled ahead, and for an instant she found herself staring down into the very sarcophagus itself. There was no ancient brown skull, no broken teeth, no parchment skin. It was a very gray-blue, very dead, but quite *fresh* face. Once it must have been handsome, with angular features crowned by black hair streaked with silver, but distorted now, its mouth open in a silent scream.

"The mummy's curse," a curator moaned.

"Oh, blast it all!" Imogen gasped. "Georgie, no!"

Five

" I confess, I am no smelling-salts sort of lady, but I felt much in need of them at that moment." Lady Imogen reached for a glass of Madeira Mary put within easy reach and tossed it back.

Flora was tempted to do the same. After a turbulent night spent pacing, turning, doing anything but sleeping, she'd invited everyone to her flat to analyze the messy aftermath of their evening at the Museum. Benedict, Imogen, Mary, Evie, and Chou-Chou gathered around the round table in her séance chamber. Its dim silence seemed a sort of soothing serenity after the tumult of the mummy unveiling. Benedict had gotten them out through the screaming pandemonium of the crowd; he'd made sure the police had their information, and seen them back to Flora's flat for restorative brandy and shocked quiet.

In the center of the deep purple tablecloth, next to teapots and wine bottles and the crystal ball, were Sir George's journals and letter to Imogen. Flora still couldn't believe what he wrote there had come true—*If you are reading this, I have surely departed this earthly plane to lay my soul at the mercy of Anubis ...* He really was quite dead, left in the ancient tomb he himself had discovered. How did he get there? He'd obviously not been deceased for long. His face was quite recognizable. What happened? Who put him there? How did he know it would happen?

Exactly what everyone else was thinking, surely, in the tumult that surged just beneath the quiet of the darkened chamber.

"Who would have done such a ghastly thing? To Georgie!" Imogen sniffled. Mary handed her a handkerchief. "How did no one at the Museum even notice?"

"Such a man must have many enemies, in a cutthroat world like archaeology" Evie said. Chou-Chou clambered up onto her lap, staring intently with her amber eyes into the crystal ball as if she could divine an answer. But really, she only seemed to want a sandwich from the plate. "Rival scientists who wanted his concession at the temple? Scholars who didn't agree with his conclusions? People he'd offended? And that's not even getting into his private life!"

Flora sighed. "It is rather a lot." She touched her new amulet, and Chou-Chou growled. She did not care for cats at all.

A knock sounded at the door, and Flora smiled. "Ah, that will be Mr. Ottway, come to take a look at the journals." Mary showed him in, and he beamed as he bowed over Flora's hand.

"Miss Flowerdew! I am so happy I can be of some small service to you, I am happy to do anything at all."

"Well, I hope there is no favor too onerous I ask today!" Flora said with a laugh. "We would just like someone with some expertise to take a look at Sir George's journals."

"Sir George's own journals," he said quietly, an awestruck look coming over his face. He sat down at the table where the book was open, and studied the words and symbols written there for a moment. "Ah, yes, this is a ghost story you see." He pointed at a row of signs, roughly sketched, smudged. "They are common in this period ... spirits could be set to guard tombs and temples. This row is a warning to thieves of what will happen to their souls if they enter the temple with a lack of reverence." He told them more about the warnings, the tales written there.

Imogen frowned as she examined the tiny sketches. "So a ghost killed Georgie and stuffed him in the sarcophagus? After following him to England?"

Chou-Chou tilted her little fuzzy head in interest. Unlike Flora, she actually usually enjoyed ghostly visits.

"Surely a ghost wouldn't be strong enough to do that," Evie scoffed. "Or a vengeful pharaoh, as I heard someone scream last night."

"Oh, surely vengeful pharaohs can do all sorts of things," Flora offered. "Why, in *The Haunting of the Red Tomb*, a book I read just last month, the pharaoh Aken-Rah came back to avenge himself against those who removed his mummy from the side of his true love, Entremet! It was all quite fearsome, despite the silly names. He crushed a few villains under statues, poisoned one with bad cheese, hacked a few with his old sword. Did ancient pharaohs even have swords? I was up all night reading it." She noticed people gaping at her enthusiasm, and sat back, adding softly, "Not that I think that's what happened here, of course."

Ottway gently patted her hand, his smile rather awestruck, as if the Red Tomb was some stroke of brilliance. "There are many such stories around all sorts of archaeological sites, of course. Curses are often carved above doorways, warning everyone sternly against entering, and several have indeed died soon after entering such places. People who work there can be terribly superstitious, too. Maybe someone who worked with Sir George felt he was breaking some taboo, releasing a curse, and did away with him to stop it? Those who are caught in the fear of such curses would go far to stop them."

Imogen examined him with a new gleam of respect in her eyes. She nodded. "What an interesting idea, Mr. Ottway! I daresay you are right—people who put faith in such things could be driven mad by fear and apprehension if they saw something they thought released a vengeful spirit before them. Were there rumors of a curse on the Temple of Nephthys?"

Theodore tapped his chin thoughtfully. "I have not heard of anything in particular; no warnings were found carved on the doorways and portals, but rumors of such things can spread like wildfire. I wouldn't be surprised if no one will work on the site once they hear of what happened in the Museum." He looked suddenly startled, fearful. "Oh! I only hope I can still travel there myself! The work is so vital in our understanding of this period of the XVIII dynasty. Sir George would have been furious if all his efforts came to naught because of such a villainous act!"

"It is true his work was his great love," Imogen said. "I wonder what Lady Crosbie felt about that! Poor lady. Who will tell her of this awful business? They do say she's of a most fragile nature."

"Well, obviously he wasn't killed in Egypt," Evie said, shifting Chou-Chou in order to jot a few notes into her ever-present notebook. "So a pharaoh would have to come a long way to do the job, vengeful or not. What about human hatred and envy? A man in his position would surely make some enemies along his career pathway, people who would desire such a prime site for their own, or who disagree with his methods or conclusions. Remember when that Oxford don was beaten quite bloody by one of his colleagues when they disagreed about a point in a line of Aeschylus?"

"Oh, yes," Benedict said. "And a line in a play is much less than an intact temple in Luxor. It's a prize any Egyptologist would spend a whole career and life seeking, longing for."

"There's Paul Lewis-Clunes," Theodore said. "He worked with Sir George when he was first starting in the field, at Edfu. They quarreled most bitterly, though no one is sure about what precisely, and Mr. Lewis-Clunes now works at the Egyptian Museum in Cairo, doing restoration. He has often declared that it was *his* study, *his* conclusions, that led to where the Temple would be found, and Sir George stole his work."

"I heard some chatter last night by the refreshment tables that a man of that name has been angling to take over the Temple site," Benedict mentioned. "He has complained that Sir George did steal his work, and declares to any who will listen that *he* would bring order and respectability to the dig. Not everyone agrees with Sir George's more unorthodox methods. There have also been some rumors of theft. If Sir George had been lax about security ..."

Flora glanced at Theodore. "Have you heard of any thefts, Mr. Ottway?"

"Not of any particular object, though of course theft is unfortunately very common in this line of work. And the Temple site has yielded many objects lots of people would greatly covet. Jewelry, for instance, and beautiful statues of the goddess."

Flora gently touched her cat amulet, and felt it warm under her fingertips. Had her pendant been one looted from the temple?

"And what about love?" Mary said.

Everyone turned to stare at her. "Love?" Mr. Ottway said, as if confused by the concept.

"Yes. Miss Flora mentioned the pharaoh in the book was angry they moved him away from his true love. You always say, Miss Evie, that most murders are over money or love."

"Very true, indeed," Evie said. She popped a bit of cake into her mouth and chewed thoughtfully. "Usually both! Or respectability. Someone wants the money or love, but also wants to be seen as an upstanding member of the community. Amazing, really."

"There was that rather odd lady last night," Flora said, as she remembered the woman who burst into the event, silken draperies swirling as she screamed that she had to "fly to his side." Whose side had she meant? "Oh, what was her name? Something Scottish. Yes—Rosse. Mr. Ottway, you said she thought Sir George *was* her ancient lover, or his reincarnation, and he rejected her? Sent her away?"

"She does seem tall enough, and determined enough, to fight back against her fantasies being quashed," Evie mused.

"And what about his wives? His real wives, not his ancient harem or whatever," Mary said. "You said he had two. Is number one dead, then, or was there some scandalous divorce?" She rubbed her hands together in avid interest. Mary was devoted to the scandal columns, to tales of forbidden romance.

"What a fine motive that would make," Imogen said. "But one *is* dead. The first was a Patterson—they are quite a well-known archaeological family—she did many of the early watercolor images you see of the temple. Everyone thought they were devoted, and she is the mother of their only child, James. There are terrible rumors she killed herself in despair over something in her marriage, but I'm sure that cannot be. James Crosbie works in archaeology now, as well, though not at all distinguished, from what I've heard. I suppose one of their families might bear a grudge against Georgie—he was never known to be an attentive husband, but that does seem like a great deal of trouble. Still, love is always a possible motive."

"Did he have lovers in Egypt?" Flora asked. "Not Mrs. Rosse, but something quite serious? Maybe the wife of another archaeologist? Or the daughter of one of his workers? A husband or father could certainly take violent objections."

"I've heard no rumors," Theodore stammered out, his cheeks a bit pink at the mention of romantic scandal. Flora thought him so terribly cute. "Archaeologists are much more likely to fall out over the dating of an artifact, or become burningly jealous over who has concessions. Personal matters always seem rather—secondary."

"Oh, they can become terribly important, even among you ivory-tower sorts," Evie declared. "You just need the right bit of circumstance. Like the author of some very dull histories of the Crusades, who killed his mistress last year because she wouldn't lick his ... erm, well, yes, you see. Could be any sort of person at all."

Theodore's eyes widened in astonishment. "Well—I suppose Sir George's foreman would know best. Assim. He worked with Sir George for many years, is said to be very highly skilled and entirely trustworthy. He would have known everything that happened at the Temple site. And there are many who would love to lure him away from Sir George to work with them—he has a reputation for the greatest competence and reliability."

"And he's in Egypt, as are so many others who could be involved," Flora said with a sigh. "So how did Sir George end up dead here in England? He was surely killed here; from what I could see, he looked rather—fresh."

"Who brought the sarcophagus in, and when?" Evie said, jotting down questions in her notebook. "Where was it stored? Who had access to it? I shall just trot back to the Museum when we're done here, see if I can find some of these answers. That might give us a glimmer to start on." Her lips were set in that stubborn line Flora was quite familiar with. She knew if anyone could bash out answers from secretive curators, it was Evie.

"I can examine the journal more closely, as well,"

Theodore said. "These hieroglyphs will take a bit of time."

"That is so very kind of you, Mr. Ottway," Flora said. "I'm not sure Lady Hastings would like it to leave the flat ..."

"Oh, I can come back to read it," he said quickly, eagerly, smiling at Flora. Benedict crossed his arms and sat back in his chair. "At any time that is convenient for you."

Imogen glanced over them all, and clapped her hands in satisfaction. "Well, my dears. This is all very fine. But I think the one thing we can do to really help Georgie is to travel to Egypt and examine the scenes of his life. All of us."

A great clamor of excitement rose in the somber séance room. Flora felt a flutter of hope that maybe her days of adventure with Imogen and Benedict were not quite over after all.

"I am already scheduled to leave Southampton on the *Empress of India*. I'm sure you could all travel aboard her, as well, and I could decipher the journal on our journey," Theodore said. He smiled shyly at Flora. "With your assistance, of course, Miss Flowerdew."

"Excellent idea, Mr. Ottway," Imogen said briskly. "Now, Evangeline my dear, can you arrange leave from your newspaper? We shall need someone to chronicle this tale so the world will know the truth. Once we discover it."

"Certainly!" Evie declared most robustly. "This could be my biggest story yet. They'd have to promote me if they want it."

Mary glanced at Flora. "Maybe we should consult the cards first, Miss Flora? See what they have to say about a journey."

"By all means," Imogen said. "We need every bit of wisdom we can find!"

Flora took her cards from their velvet case and laid them out on the table. She studied them closely, but they said nothing out of the ordinary. Nothing to fear.

Except for one card, the Tower. From the cards that surrounded it, she saw upheaval, change. Danger.

She frowned as she looked at it. Surely every journal was a potential danger? If she feared the world every time she walked out the door, she could only bar herself inside and never experience anything at all. Not excitement, or panic, or yes, change. But when she looked at her friends' eager faces, she couldn't out that fear into them, as well.

"Well?" Evie said.

"Just a journey. Change. Nothing more," Flora said, and swept the cards off the table.

They stayed a little longer, making plans, before getting ready to depart to prepare for the voyage. Flora walked to the door with Benedict. "Remember our time in France?" he said softly, his fingers brushing the back of her hand. "And Cornwall?"

Flora glanced up, and fell headlong into the swirling emotions of his green jewel-eyes. She thought of their days walking the beaches, sitting in pubs, talking and laughing together so intimately. So full of understanding. "Of course. How could I forget? It's been so dismal here in London, the sunshine of France is all I cling to sometimes, Dukie."

"Me, too." He glanced out the door at everyone leaving, at his aunt giving Mr. Ottway a ride to the British Museum, and stepped a teensy bit closer to Flora. "Egypt surely holds even more beauty, more adventure. Something to remember when days are so gray." He smiled at her, a small, intimate smile that seemed to say so much. Or maybe she was a victim of wishful thinking. "I'm glad we'll do this together. I know you will never stop until we find out who did this to my godfather, my determined Flora." He gave her hand one last warm squeeze and stepped out into the night. As Flora shut the door behind him, she curled her fingers into her palm tightly. *One last adventure.*

Six

Flora moved through the hushed galleries of the British Museum. It was amazing how quiet, how calm it all was after the wild drama of the sarcophagus opening. Mary had stayed with Imogen, who was still a bit tearful at the discovery of her old friend's body, and Flora thought returning to the scene of the crime could be useful.

She would never have known during the light of day that such a terrible thing could have occurred in that dignified spot. The doors to the room where the event was held were closed and guarded, but the galleries were open. Most of the crowds were in the mummy rooms, children running and shrieking in delicious horror, and the dim corridors beyond were empty.

Flora examined the statue of a seated scribe, his stylus in hand, his lapis eyes gazing dispassionately into the present day, and remembered a few precious times when she was a wild kid, running from the orphanage and hiding wherever she could. She'd managed to slip into the British Museum, just wanting to be quiet and warm, and she'd found such things to marvel at. Ancient goddesses and warriors, glittering gold jewels. It gave her the first inkling of history, the past, other lives lived. It seemed to set her on the path she followed now, looking into the lives of others. Searching for ghosts.

She came to a case filled with artifacts from Sir George's temple. Alabaster jars, turquoise bracelets, fragments of wall paintings. She wished she could read the carvings there, could take a glimpse into Sir George's world. What had led him to such an end? Who could have done such a thing to him? And why was he in England now?

She thought she heard a soft click, like footsteps, but there was no one there behind her. She couldn't quite shake off the taut sense of not being alone, though, and hurried into the next gallery.

There she heard the murmur of voices, no one trying to be sneaky, and glanced to the end of the corridor. She saw the curator from the party, along with a few other men, all of them with black bands on their sleeves, talking in low, intense tones. One of them was Richard North, who worked with Sir George, the tall, handsome one. He shook hands with the others, and walked in her direction. "Miss Flowerdew, isn't it?"

"Yes, indeed, Mr. North. I'm surprised you remember," she said, studying him carefully. He looked only sad, solemn. "It was quite the crush at the gathering."

"Such a tragedy it has been. I hardly know where to turn next. But a name like yours would be hard to forget! Or such a charming lady. Your hair would be much renowned at the Temple of Nephthys, you know."

Flora found herself wanting to giggle girlishly, which didn't seem at all appropriate to the circumstance. Many ladies in Cairo must be quite enamored with Mr. North. "How kind you are. It was indeed most overwhelming! Someone I know was an old friend of Sir George, and says he was one of the most highly respected of men in his work. It must be a great blow indeed."

He nodded, a sorrowful glint in his eyes. If he was

acting, he was very good. "Very. British archaeology will be much diminished, his finds have been legendary. I was most fortunate to work with him."

Flora wondered about that "work." Had he agreed with Sir George's methods, been content to be an assistant? Had the two men been friends? "Were you with him for very long?"

"Not as long as I would have liked. I had much to learn from him. I fear I am rather a newcomer to the work of archaeology. After university, I served as a private secretary to the current Lady Crosbie's father, who sponsored many excavations, and I found I also had a great passion for such work. Uncovering the lives of people long gone, bringing them into the light again. I worked at the Egyptian Museum for a time, until I had the great fortune to be taken on by Sir George at the Temple of Nephthys."

"Just from seeing these artifacts, and the glorious sarcophagus, I can see what an extraordinary place it must be."

"Yes. Wonderfully well-preserved, with a few chambers even undisturbed, it's a marvelous glimpse into a period of time."

"And such a romantic tale! A pharaoh's true love."

Mr. North laughed. "If one believes such penny-dreadful business! It sells newspapers."

"Then I confess to being a romantic soul!" Flora admitted. "And you accompanied Sir George here to England. You must have been very important to his work."

"I do hope my work has been valuable to him," he said, ducking his head in a modest little nod. Flora didn't quite buy that gesture. "But also, most of the team couldn't be spared for the journey; there is still much work to be done at the Temple. Sir George didn't want to let the sarcophagus travel without him. It is an astounding find, one of many to come, I am sure. The dig must continue uninterrupted."

And Flora would wager Richard North wanted to be the one to continue it. "You said you once worked with Lady Crosbie's father. She will surely be devastated when she hears what has happened, I do feel so terribly for her."

His expression softened. "You are a kind lady, Miss Flowerdew, with such a feeling heart. They were certainly a most devoted couple. Lady Crosbie has fragile health, and I fear for her. We will all find it most difficult to move forward."

They walked on, past the stone gaze of statues, watching yet another drama unfold in their long lives. Flora wondered what Richard really thought of Sir George, what their lives were like in Cairo. "Were you with him all the time since arriving at the Museum?" she murmured, studying a jet falcon in a case.

"No, not all the time. He wanted to be alone to examine the sarcophagus a final time, and sent me on an errand at a gallery in Bond Street he suspected had an artifact from the Temple. It was a copy, of course, and by the time I returned it was time to prepare for the party. I thought he had finished with the sarcophagus and gone to make final preparations, that he would show up when needed." He shook his head. "I should have stayed with him! I shall always regret it. If I had been there, whoever did that dastardly deed could not have come near to him. The guards here said no one unauthorized was nearby, but I would surely have sensed any danger."

Flora laid a comforting hand on his sleeve. "It could not have been your fault at all. I am sure Sir George could have no notion an enemy lurked here, of all places."

"I know you are right, but I cannot help but blame myself. Anyone could have followed him, really. He has been arguing most vehemently with his foreman of late."

"Did Sir George have many enemies?" Flora asked.

A strange expression spasmed across Richard's face, only to be quickly covered in that sad little smile. "Any man with the fame of Sir George attracts enemies, people who are jealous. But I would not have imagined any could kill him! Most of them do not have his strength. Like his old assistant, a Mr. Lewis-Clunes. He never did receive what he thought was his due in the work. And serpents' hearts do often lurk behind innocuous facades."

"I have never heard truer words, Mr. North," Flora murmured.

"Ah, but I should not speak so with a tender-hearted lady. Most men in our work are dedicated to their studies—they would never have time for such villainy. Come, let me show you this fragment of an inscription, it was found above one of the temple doors ..."

Flora studied the inscribed symbols, the bird, the lady on the throne, and remembered such sketches in Sir George's journal and wished she could read it. If only studying the human heart was as easy as ancient symbols ...

Seven

The evening was clear and cold, the light starting to fade. Flora leaned over the rail of the *Empress of India* as the vessel prepared to carry her away from England and into an unknown future.

She touched her cat amulet as she studied the docks far below, the rush and hum of activity, luggage being wheeled up gangplanks, sailors cursing, ropes flying, people tearfully parting from loved ones. She'd had no dreams lately, even though she'd been reading books about Egypt every night. She'd seen no moonlit temples, heard no "meows," but somehow, she still felt something nearby. Something seen out of the corner of her eye, but when she turned it was always blank.

She wondered who out there, or possibly even someone on that very ship, was a murderer. And not just an ordinary murderer, oh no. Someone who would painstakingly wrap a man in bandages and stuff him into a sarcophagus. Did they think it would be a long time before Sir George was found? Or was it set up to cause maximum sensation at the British Museum?

Flora shivered, and touched her amulet again. It seemed to warm against her gloved hand in the cold evening wind.

"It's horrid cold up here," Mary said, as she came to

Flora's side, fresh from tucking Chou-Chou away in their cabin. "Colder 'an a witch's—well, witch's *nose*, eh? But we'll soon be in the sunshine. Just imagine it, miss! I never thought to see such a place as Egypt."

"Me neither, Mary." Flora thought of her childhood bed at the orphanage, the broken glass in the window, the bugs swarming over the floor, always cold and damp. She'd never even dared think of pyramids and temples and palm trees. Even if ghosties came with it all. She sniffled a bit at the thought of that sad, cold little Florrie, of all the dreams that seemed so futile.

"Here now, miss, what's wrong?" Mary cried. "You do look pale. Is it the seasick already?"

"Not at all. I just didn't sleep well last night ... too excited about all this." She glanced around at the bustling crowds, the gray clouds sliding overhead, and wondered exactly what lay before them. "I've been having rather peculiar dreams before we left England."

Mary frowned. "Ghosties bothering you, then, are they?"

"No, no. You'd think they might, if they knew I was off to Egypt. Sending messages to their descendants and such. They say the veil is very thin there. The dreams are more like—I am *there*. In Egypt, long ago. I feel the warm breeze, see the palm trees and the stars overhead." She didn't mention the man. Something held her back from acknowledging him, from trying to decipher how his presence made her feel.

But something must have shown on her face, for Mary looked quite worried. She leaned closer, her mouth opened to ask questions, when a whistle blew shrilly over their heads. The crowd surged to the railing, eager to watch the departure, and Benedict and Imogen joined them. Flora was glad to know that whatever happened, she'd be with such glorious friends.

"Just think, my darlings," Imogen said, as she gathered the fur collar of her cloak closer. "Soon we shall leave all this gloom far behind! We'll see Malta, Brindisi, Alexandria, Port Said, then Cairo. Then up the Nile, to find dear Georgie's Temple. He will have his justice then. I do trust ..."

She was interrupted by a sharp scream, carrying even above the creaking of the gangplank starting to move away from the ship.

"You shall not leave without me! Wait, wait, oh, *do* wait," a woman cried.

Flora leaned over the railing for a closer look, Benedict next to her. She gave a startled laugh to see a figure in fluttering, draped, bright green-and-blue garments racing up the dock, waving her hands wildly. The crewmen froze in their tracks, as if entirely unsure as to what to do next.

"Good heavens," Flora gasped. "It's Elspeth Rosse! From the Museum."

"Seeking her immortal love aboard the *Empress of India*?" Imogen said, her head tilted as if in mild curiosity. Surely racing along after one's dead pharaoh romance was something she'd seen a hundred times in her adventures.

"It'll liven things up right quick, I'm sure," Mary said with a laugh.

Flora thought again about her dream, how real it all seemed, how sharp the emotions around that distant man. Was that the sort of thing Elspeth felt? How she knew she'd once been there? Flora knew she needed to talk to the woman further about these matters. "Maybe she can tell us tales of ancient life beside the Nile. Since she was there and all."

"Do you think she might *really* be the reincarnation of a pharaoh's lover, then?" Imogen asked. "Most extraordinary if so."

Flora thought of all she'd seen since the old duke came to her insisting she find his lost diamonds, opening a sort of floodgate into the next world. "Who knows? If nothing else, she should have some fascinating fashion advice. I rather do fancy a turban like that one she's wearing."

～

"Flora! Yoo-hoo! Are you in there?" Evie called from the corridor outside Flora's cabin.

"Come in," Flora answered. She patted at her up-swept red-gold curls as she glanced in the mirror. She noticed a new light in her eyes, a new sense of lightness. Ghosts and mummies' curses aside, the further they sailed, the more free she felt. The worries of London were left behind, and she had an important job to do!

Evie pushed the door open and tumbled inside, as usual in too much of a hurry to walk carefully. She always plunged ahead. Tonight, she'd left off her tweeds for a dark-blue chiffon evening gown, rather elegant despite the fact that her hair was still haphazardly pinned atop her head, with spectacles and a pencil caught in the curls.

"I bring goodies to share," she said, and plopped down on the bed beside Chou-Chou's cushion. The Pom eagerly greeted her friend, who could usually be relied on for a treat, and Evie did not disappoint, slipping a biscuit from her large tapestry bag.

"Whatever it is, we can't wait to hear all about it," Flora declared. Much like Chou-Chou, she knew that where Evie went, juicy information followed. Mary drew up a chair, and they both leaned in close.

"I was able to find this just before I left London to meet you in Southampton, no time to share." She pulled a folder from that capacious bag and waved it in the air. "*Et voila*! A treasure. Notes on Sir George's autopsy. Isn't it glorious?"

Flora laughed. Only Evie would call an autopsy report "glorious." But they certainly were intriguing. "You always pull off the greatest coups, Evie darling. How do you do it? Oh, no, don't tell me—secrets of the trade."

"The greatest journalists' secrets of all. Friends in all the most useful places. Including the Milsom Street morgue, where Dr. Johnson, esteemed physician to royal dukes, did the honors."

"Any surprises?" Mary asked. "Like maybe he really was felled by a mummy's curse?"

"I'm not even sure how such a thing would show up in an autopsy," Flora mused. "A curse carved on the heart, revealed with a puff of smoke?"

"Well, I've no doubt whoever really was the original occupant of that sarcophagus wouldn't be best pleased, so curse away," Evie said. "But really, the details are a lot more boring. He was hit on the back of the head, probably dead instantly, thank heavens for small mercies, before being put in the sarcophagus. There was also some bruising on his arms and chest, maybe he was pushed? And it would have taken more than one person to put the lid on and off that sarcophagus. The coroner thought maybe a fight, hence the bruising, but not sure what hit him on the head. Our old friend the blunt instrument, probably."

"At least it seems he was dead *before* being shut in there." Flora shivered. She really hated being shut in tight dark, spaces! Left over from childhood punishments, she was sure. "How long do they think he was deceased?"

"Estimated at a day or two. The sarcophagus and bandages acted as a small preservative, though, so it could be as early as a week or so ago. Definitely not killed in Egypt and shipped on to the Museum, then. What did you find out at the Museum? I suppose you weren't lucky enough to have an eye-witness who saw a mummy being hauled in the back door of the place?"

"Sadly no." She told them what Mr. North told her —he had gone on an errand while Sir George examined

77

the sarcophagus one last time, and no one had seen anyone unusual at the Museum.

A knock sounded at the door. "Madame Flowerdew, this is your steward. The bell for dinner will ring soon, I merely wanted to see if you require anything."

Flora hurried to open the door, letting in a dark-haired, dignified man in a white coat. He bowed to her briskly. "Good evening, Mr. ..." she greeted, as Chou-Chou sat up in interest. Surely stewards would be fine sources of biscuits!

"Assad, madame." He bowed low, his sharp eye sweeping the cabin as if in search of any speck of dust or crease in linen to be corrected. "I am steward for this corridor. Anything you require, you must only let me know. I have brought extra towels, and more hot water will be waiting after dinner." He carefully placed the snowy stack on the wash-stand, along with wrapped bars of rose-scented soap. As he turned back, he seemed to notice Flora's cat amulet, and his eyes widened. He made a small gesture with his hand, and she instinctively covered the stone with her fingers as if to protect it. But he said nothing about it.

"Where is your home, Mr. Assad? When you are not aboard the *Empress of India*?" Evie asked, always curious about everyone she met.

"Not many ask me that, madame," he answered with a small smile. "I am from Al-Fashn, a tiny village near the Temple of Nephthys. Most of my family is in Cairo now. Shall this be your first visit to Egypt, mesdames?"

"Oh, yes! I'm sure we'll have ever so many questions, if you don't mind us peppering you with them," Flora said.

"I would be honored to answer anything you wish. Will you visit the pyramids, and the Egyptian Museum? Most guests find them very educational."

"Of course. I've longed to see the pyramids for ever

78

so long." Flora remembered a cheap little book she'd found in a gutter as a child, its stained pages illustrated with sketches of pyramids and drifting sands and camels. Maybe that was why she was so excited now, so haunted by dreams. "Mostly, though, we're planning to be near your hometown, visiting the Temple of Nephthys, so this is most fortunate indeed. A member of our party who was friends with Sir George Crosbie longs to see his work close-up."

Assad's expression shifted, his smile flickering then widening. Was he happy they were going there—or the opposite? "My brother, Assim, has long worked with Sir George. He is foreman at the Temple site. He does love to speak of it, I am certain he'll be most gratified by such interest."

Flora clapped her hands in delight. More help on the way!

"Oh, I say, what luck," Evie declared. "We heard of your brother—they say he is a man of great value and efficiency."

"Some might indeed say fate has brought us here," Assad said. "But yes, luck is more likely. Everyone has been quite shocked by the news of Sir George's demise. He is a very important man in Al-Fashn, and my brother has always had the strongest respect for him. They worked together so perfectly in service to the Temple."

"What do you think will happen now with the work?" Flora asked.

"Who can say, madame?" Assad glanced away, straightening the towels as if he considered his words. "I have heard there are some who declare they would manage the site better, or so Assim has told me. Other archaeologists, who envy the findings there, argue with Sir George's methods. There is even one such aboard right now. A Mr. Lewis-Clunes."

Flora, Evie, and Mary glanced at each other. They'd heard of his quarrel with Sir George while at the British

79

Museum, but had been told he worked at the Egyptian Museum in Cairo. "Mr. Lewis-Clunes is aboard this ship?" Flora asked.

"Perhaps racing back to Cairo to claim the site as his prize," Mary said.

Flora looked to Assad. "Perhaps we might meet this gentleman, have a chance to converse with him in some depth?"

He gave her a conspiratorial wink. "I am sure madame could be seated rather conveniently close to this party at dinner, if she so wishes. Very conducive to conversation."

"Assad, you are an utter mind reader," Flora said. "I think we'll work rather well together."

"Maybe you met with another passenger, as well, Mr. Assad," Evie said. "She is most—distinctive. Flowing robes, turbans, things such as that. Named Elspeth Rosse."

Assad's lips made a little moue. Of disapproval? "Oh. Yes. She told everyone on her corridor she will soon be reunited with her ancient lost love at the Temple, though no one wants to hear about such things. The site is one of serious study, not curses and souls. But I fear my homeland often attracts those with—unique ideas, along with scholars and lovers of art. Most regrettable, but yes, sometimes amusing. But I am not the steward for Madame Rosse's cabin. Can I get you anything else, madame? Shall I have tea waiting for you after dinner?"

"Yes, thank you." As he bowed and departed, Flora wrapped a cashmere shawl over her evening gown, and patted her amulet to make sure it was still there. "I'll be back soon, CC. Don't get into too much trouble." Chou-Chou just sighed, and rolled over on her cushion, as if she couldn't care less Flora and her stone cat were leaving.

In the dining room, Benedict, Evie, and Imogen

waited at the table, but no Elspeth Rosse yet. A string quartet played soft waltzes, and everything was golden-lit and quiet. Half the chairs seemed empty.

"Well, my darlings, this is no such terrible place to spend a few days," Lady Imogen declared. She waved at one of the footmen for wine. "If the seas stay calm and we stave off *mal de mer*, unlike so many of our fellow passengers, we should have much time to study poor Georgie's case! What have we discovered so far?"

Evie told them about the autopsy, and the little they had learned of the people around Sir George, like his foreman Assim, the rivals for the Temple site. As she was finishing, a gentleman, tall and very thin, with a thin mustache that obviously aspired to higher things, arrived with a lady in a very fashionable gown of pale pink ruffles and lace bows, pearls in her brown hair, arrived at the table. They were introduced as Mr. and Mrs. Lewis-Clunes.

So *this* was the covetous Mr. Lewis-Clunes! Flora gaped at him, hardly believing this man could be anyone's archrival. She'd pictured him as old, white-bearded, positively Zeus-ish, he and Sir George clashing with lightning bolts over the prize of the Temple. But this man was early middle-aged, if that, slight, much too pale to have worked much under the Egyptian sun, his fair hair thinning. But his blue eyes, very light and piercing, scanned everything around him as if he memorized it all and found it wanting.

"Your Grace, an honor. Lady Hastings," he said, with a graceful little bow before he helped his wife into her seat. She, too, was pale and slender, her blonde hair escaping its combs, her smile shy. "An honor to meet you in person at last, I have heard much of your family. Your father was a most renowned explorer and cartographer."

Benedict blinked. "You have heard of him?"

"Indeed. His work is most helpful in my field. And

your grandparents, of course ... their diplomatic brilliance is always highly spoken of."

Lady Imogen flashed him a flirtatious smile. "But you cannot possibly have known my sister and her husband, or my nephew, in person, Mr. Lewis-Clunes! You would have been a mere toddler when Benedict's father was on his travels."

He smiled back at her, as his wife studiously folded her napkin on the lap of her *eau-de-nil* gown. "Merely by reputation, I fear, though I wish I could have talked with him of what he saw in India."

"We shall certainly look forward to hearing more about your own work. We are all most intrigued by Egyptology." Imogen waved at Evie and Flora. "There are our dear friends, Miss Flowerdew and Miss Finnegan. Another of our party is soon to join us, a Mr. Theodore Ottway. He is also an archaeologist, on his way to join the dig at the Temple of Nephthys. Perhaps you know him?"

Flora watched Mr. Lewis-Clunes for any sign of his feelings about the Temple, but he seemed good at diplomacy, just as Benedict's grandparents were. His smile didn't waver, though his wife glanced at him rather anxiously. "I have not had the pleasure. Our work is a wide world, though it can seem very insular at times. And the temple is not under my care."

Lady Imogen's smile turned teasing. "Not yet, perhaps? It sounds like a place anyone would want to survey, so full of mystery and beauty."

"So it is, Lady Hastings. A most extraordinary find, practically undisturbed, which is such a great rarity in our world. But my position is at the Egyptian Museum now, and I have long been devoted to that work."

"You must have known Sir George, though," Benedict said. "Perhaps worked with him?"

"When I was young, barely more than a student, I did assist him at Edfu. I learned a vast deal; he was a great man of formidable scholarship. His methods were quite revolutionary. Yet I have now developed my own methods of excavation, which I have found works to everyone's great satisfaction. Sir George was a great man, yes, but also rather—set in his ways, to his own detriment at times."

"Paul would never allow any breaches of security at his own sites," Mrs. Lewis-Clunes said, letting her voice be heard at last. She sounded like a delicate bird fluting from a tree-top, but there was a thread of steel beneath.

"Indeed I would not," 'Paul' agreed.

Evie leaned forward in interest, her fingers twitching as if she longed to reach for her pencil. "Have there been such breaches at the Temple, then? That would be alarming indeed!"

"And with the great shock of what just happened to Sir George ..." Flora said.

The Lewis-Clunes couple exchanged long glances, and Paul nodded most solemnly. "Very sad indeed. A great tragedy for our work. Do you know if the foul murderer has been apprehended? We have been in Brighton rather than London, far from the latest news of the atrocity."

"No one has been arrested as of yet," Imogen said.

As Imogen and Mr. Lewis-Clunes talked of Sir George's past work, Flora studied the wife. She was dressed rather dowdily, in gray velvet cut in loose lines around her wispy figure, but she wore a gorgeous collar of turquoise and lapis. "What a very beautiful necklace, Mrs. Lewis-Clunes. I am quite envious."

She touched it with trembling fingertips, almost as if she had forgotten what she wore. "Oh—thank you, Miss Flowerdew. It was a gift from Paul. I do tend to prefer more modern designs, but when one is in Egypt ..."

"The colors are most striking." Flora studied it

closer. She noticed a pendant of a cat, rather like her own but in gold. "It is an antique, then?"

"I believe so, yes," Clara Lewis-Clunes began, and her husband interrupted.

"My dear! I have tried so many times to explain antiquities to my wife, but the information just will not linger," he said with a humorless laugh. "I procured the necklace from a small shop in Cairo, it is one of a kind. If only it was appreciated."

"That is too bad. I should love to have one for myself," Flora said.

"Oh, but your pendant is very pretty, too," Clara said. "I do love sweet little kitties! I wish I could have one of my own."

"My dear, you know we travel about too much for pets," her husband scolded. "And the dander would be unbearable! But indeed, that is a very pretty artifact, Miss Flowerdew. The goddess Bastet, or one of her acolytes, if I'm not mistaken." He studied it closer, his eyes narrowed. "XVIII dynasty. Yes, very finely done. You must have purchased it in one of the more discerning shops. Too many places will insist on dealing in shocking counterfeits."

"It was a gift," Flora said. "I am very glad to hear it's authentic, though."

"Undoubtedly. See how the eyes are set? Very hard to copy. You must be very cautious if you wish to find more such pieces in Egypt, though. Sadly, almost everything people buy there is faked; it's the largest industry in the country."

"*This* must certainly be my seat! I sense it is for *me* alone," a woman cried.

Everyone at Flora's table, indeed everyone seated in the dining room, fell quiet and stared as Elspeth Rosse sailed across the green and gold carpet in a sunset-colored gown of flowing lines. Like Clara, she wore Egyptian jewels, ropes of carnelian beads, lapis amulets, a pin of golden rays of sun in her turban. Flora wondered if they, too, were real.

Benedict glanced at the empty chair beside his. "Surely she can't mean ..." he whispered.

But of course she did. The waiter drew out the chair and ushered Mrs. Rosse onto the gold-striped cushion. One of her fringed shawls trailed in the water goblet, and her sandalwood perfume wafted over the table. Mrs. Lewis-Clunes coughed into her handkerchief, and Flora's eyes watered.

"Yes," Mrs. Rosse said, almost preening with satisfaction as she glanced around the table. "This is my place. I feel I must know *all* of you, that we have been *together* before." She turned large, kohl-edged blue eyes onto Benedict, and laid her jeweled fingers on his sleeve. He glanced at Flora, terrified. "Especially *you*. Oh, yes. You were a great prince of Egypt in your previous life, weren't you? A brave warrior. A courtier to my own darling pharaoh. Were we secret lovers, then? I feel sure we must have been, with this *longing*."

Benedict mouthed *help me*, to Flora, and she held her napkin to her mouth to stifle a laugh. Everyone was quickly introduced, and Flora noticed Theodore Ottway wasn't there yet.

"Not *the* Madame Flowerdew of Kensington?" Elspeth gasped. Her hand flew to her heart, the emerald and turquoise rings sparkling. "The renowned spirit medium?"

The Lewis-Clunes looked at her as if seeing her for the first time, Clara fascinated, Paul suspicious.

Flora was glad the waiters appeared to serve the soup course, giving her a moment to organize her words. "Not renowned," she murmured. "I may have some small gift ..."

A "small gift" called Chou-Chou, who seemed to have learned to summon spirits with her little paw. Flora

85

thought she should sneak the Pom into the dining room and see what she made of Elspeth.

"But you found the Everton diamonds! You are too modest, I am sure," Elspeth said, and drained her wineglass. "Do you not also sense that this beautiful man sitting right here was once a prince, a warrior? A guardian of the Nile?"

Flora looked at Benedict. He *was* undoubtedly handsome, but a guardian warrior? "Er—um. Yes, perhaps."

The soup was cleared and lemon sole laid before them, with asparagus in a lovely, piquant sauce. The food on the ship promised to be as luxurious as the accommodations. If only the company was as rich a mine.

"I am going to Egypt to reunite with my own pharaoh. We have an appointment to meet at the Temple of Nephthys," Elspeth said, clutching at her heart again. "Poor Sir George, he was to assist me. We could find our lost, wandering souls together. Now, it is too late for him."

"Too late for his wanderings, indeed," Paul snickered.

Elspeth ignored him. "He was a kind friend, much in tune with our previous lives and how they deeply affect our present. I fear it may have had something to do with his sad fate, the dear man. Miss Flowerdew, perhaps *you* can help me? I am sure you plan to visit the Temple—anyone with such sensitivity absolutely must."

"Oh, yes, it is one of our foremost goals," Flora murmured, not sure how she could help this woman find her pharaoh at all. The ghosts who visited her were not predictable.

"We are to hire a dahabiya to take us up the Nile all the way from Cairo," Imogen said. She stared fascinated at Elspeth's headdress, a wrap of red and gold taffeta fastened with that massive brooch. It was set in a golden snake, hissing at the observers.

Evie leaned close to Flora and whispered, "If only her pharaoh *would* appear! What a story that would make for the *Star*. Maybe I could even write a whole book. People quite eat up tragic love."

"It's not enough to find a murderer now?" Flora whispered back. "We also need an un-dead pharaoh?"

Evie shrugged, and dug into her veal blanquette. "Never think small, Flora. Every story is miles better with a ghost or two, you know that."

Flora thought of some ghosts she'd met, especially the late Duke of Everton, and how the story would have been infinitely more simple without them. "I'm not so sure about that."

"By the way, where is your admirer, Mr. Ottway? He doesn't strike me as the sort to miss out on such luxurious meals."

Flora glanced around, but couldn't see Theodore anywhere among the silk-clad diners. "I'm not sure."

"Where are you staying in Cairo, Lady Hastings?" Mrs. Lewis-Clunes asked, her voice a bit desperate, as if she sought to change the topic from pharaoh lover/ghosts to anything else.

"Shepheard's, of course," Imogen said. "I stayed there once as a young lady, before I married Hastings. I'm quite looking forward to seeing it again.

"I'm sure it must have changed, and not for the better at all," Paul grumbled, poking at his potatoes dapuhinois.

They talked more of Cairo, of tours to the pyramids and shops to visit, and Flora thought of what she'd learned. Mr. North had said Mr. Lewis-Clunes had fallen out with Sir George in some way, and that was why he worked now at the Egyptian Museum. But what was the real nature of their quarrel?

"What are you doing here?" someone cried, and Flora glanced up to see Theo Ottway had arrived. Strangely, it was Paul he stared at, red-faced, irritated.

Most unlike the affable, awkward young man Flora had come to know.

Paul just smiled nervously, and Clara said, "Oh, dear Mr. Ottway! What a surprise you are on this ship. Do sit down, tell us all about your work lately."

Theo did sit, but still looked angry. Flora would have loved to know what was between the two men, what quarrel lurked, but when she asked Theo is he was all right, he just said, "Fine, Miss Flowerdew, fine indeed," and the talk turned to much more dull matters.

Eight

"And you see this seated figure here? And here? This is the deity, and the bird with the extended foreleg is strength or wisdom." Theodore said, pointing out a line of hieroglyphs to Flora as they sat in the ship's library the next morning, Sir George's journal open before them. He hadn't mentioned why he was tardy for dinner last night; in fact, he seemed positively cheerful as they read over the journals.

"Yes!" Flora cried eagerly. She definitely saw why this would make him so happy. It was astonishing how the lines and squiggles seemed to form before her now. "And this? It's not in the same style." In fact, it looked rather like the carvings she'd seen on the moonlit walls in her dream. It had a more wave-like movement about it.

Theodore leaned closer to examine one small drawing, his hand brushing Flora's. Then he brushed it one more time, for no good reason of getting close to the journal. "It seems to be just a sketch of a place. It resembles an oval, which could stand for *mer*. Or—love. I've seen others like it in the files of the Temple dig, sketches of the naos."

"The naos?"

"The sanctuary of the Temple, the most sacred area,

89

where offerings to the gods occurred. See here?" He reached for a blank sheet of paper and a pencil and quickly sketched a few lines. "It's laid out in just such a way. You enter through the forecourt, to a hypostyle hall lined with sculptures, into the treasury room, where objects and amulets were stored for rituals. Then you would enter the sanctuary, but only if you were very important indeed. Much like the grand temple at Karnak, but on a more intimate scale. A—a more *romantic* scale."

He glanced up at her from beneath his eyelashes, and Flora recognized infatuation when she saw it. "Romantic?"

"Yes. You've heard it was built to honor the patron goddess of the pharaoh's love? The goddess Nephthys and her moon can be seen everywhere, here and here, see? And this statue, much more life-like than one usually sees of royalty, probably placed to be always close to a loved one.

Flora brushed her fingertips over her cat amulet as she studied another drawing, a man in a chariot running down smaller, fleeing figures. "And what of this wall painting here? It doesn't look very lovey-dovey to me."

Theodore's cheeks turned pink, and he coughed into his hand. "Er—no. The usual sort of smiting things one sees in such places, whether it be temple or tomb. Victory in battle, feats of strength. If this beautiful place was built to impress a lady, surely a man would wish to prove his strength to her. His worthiness."

Flora examined the sketch, and despite herself, she couldn't help picturing Benedict in nothing but a pleated loincloth, driving his chariot into battle. "If a man built such a glorious place for me, he wouldn't have to prove anything else. She must have been a wondrous person, an angel, really."

Theodore eagerly shuffled through the papers, searching for something. "See this one? It's thought to be the pharaoh's love, offering flowers to Nephthys. Look at the delicacy of her face, the expression of her sweet smile. And it's an image that retained some of its original colors. It's thought she had red hair." He reached up and almost, just barely, brushed a loose curl that twined beside Flora's ear. "Like yours."

Flora remembered Monsieur d'Etrages mentioning her hair in just the same way. "Maybe I am like Mrs. Rosse, then!" she said, trying to laugh. "Seeking for lost souls from my distant past."

His hand fluttered over hers on the table. "Surely, we are all searching for that. Egypt is such a special place, Miss Flowerdew, as if the wall between worlds is very thin there. As if we were all there before."

Flora nodded. Just like her own work, looking into past lives. But it amazed her that someone like Mr. Ottway would feel that way. "Is that what drew you to this career?"

He shuffled the papers, flustered. "Oh, yes. Perhaps. My father was a vicar, but he didn't mind so much when I decided not to study theology. He, too, loved history. At the British Museum, I found people who understand me, whom I understand in turn. I seem to —to belong there."

Flora nodded. Had she not found her own sort of family, in Mary and Chou-Chou and Evie, even in Benedict? A duke and a chorus girl! Family wasn't always bound by where you were born, but what your heart said. But she didn't know how to say that, how even to express her deep gratitude and joy at what she'd found in life. Instead, she reached for the journal.

"Sir George does seem quite pre-occupied by some wrongdoing he senses at the Temple, enough that he feared for his life. Thefts, maybe? A feud? Has anything specific been taken from the site?"

"There are always such troubles in Egypt, I'm afraid," Theodore said solemnly. "It's impossible to fully guard against it. But I haven't heard anything specific about the Temple. Most of its greatest treasures are sent elsewhere to be guarded."

"And you can think of nothing else, no rivals at the site itself?"

"I've only been able to progress though about half the hieroglyphs, trying to make a code's pattern. I'm sorry to admit I can't make sense at all of most of it. I'm not much a code-breaker. Sir Francis Walsingham would have found me quite useless!"

"Neither am I, I fear. You think it is a code, then?"

"It must be, or much of it doesn't make much sense. But these images, this scarab beetle and this lotus, repeat quite often. It's rebirth, creation. But here is a warning that all is in danger, that we must call on the goddess to restore order." More people came into the salon, chattering and laughing loudly, and Theo soon took the book away to study more in quiet.

Flora wandered onto the deck, where it was rather chilly, but she loved sitting alone in a deck chair, watching the waves and going over things she'd heard. How she wished she could weigh and measure human hearts, as the Egyptian deities did! Could understand all. But it seemed to sink beneath those very waves the more she tried to grasp it.

She was not alone for long. "Oh, Miss Flowerdew, how lovely to meet with you in a quiet moment," Elspeth said, settling back into the chair bundled in her fur-collared cloak. "Isn't the eternal peace of the sea so *soothing*? I feel a person can be themselves in its midst, in a way we can in no place else."

Flora tilted her head as she studied the white-tipped water, washing up against the ship then away again, never changing. "I think so, too. The waves don't care who we are or what we've done. They are indifferent to everything. They just *are*."

"I just knew we were sisters of the soul, Miss Flowerdew. That we both can see beyond these mundane, daily doings." Her chin settled into the softness of the fur in a most satisfied way. "Shall we have tea? Or—no! Champagne." She waved for a porter.

Flora laughed. "Sisters of the soul, Mrs. Rosse?" Maybe Elspeth was quite right. After all, what were the Madame Flowerdew's black gowns and veils but a costume, just like Elspeth's vivid robes and turbans?

"Of course. We can both see that existence is not merely on this visible plane. We've seen and done so much. Lived and loved many times."

Flora didn't always want to think of "all she'd seen and done." She'd scraped and schemed to keep her head above water, and she couldn't help but wonder if Elspeth meant they were sisters in shenanigans as well as costumes. "I do believe there is more to life than the physical matters we can see, true."

The champagne arrived, and they watched as the porter uncorked it and poured the effervescent golden liquid into glasses. "Cheers, Miss Flowerdew!" Elspeth toasted, and took a long sip. "Tell me, have you visited Egypt before?"

Flora took her own sip, letting the wine flow over her tongue in a most delightful manner. Lolling about in deck chair, drinking champagne and chatting with a reincarnated pharaoh's lover wasn't such a bad way to pass the time of day. "No, never. I do love to read about it, though. Petrie's *The Pyramids and Temples of Egypt*, things of that sort."

"Those books are just *surface*, my dear. You will only find the real essence when you are on the banks of the Nile yourself. It will open your eyes to so much that is hidden. To the truth of the earth, of people's souls."

Flora wasn't sure she wanted to know much more about people's souls. "You have spent much time there, I'm sure? In Egypt?"

Elspeth sipped at the champagne, studying the crash

93

of the waves as if she saw deep into them, beyond them. "Oh, yes. Dozens of times, since the first voyage I made when I was seventeen. But even before I saw it with my eyes, I knew it in my heart. It was all there, just waiting for me."

"What do you mean?"

She closed her eyes. "I was in a terrible accident as a child, a fall from a carriage. I was entirely unconscious for hours, my mother quite despaired. When I awoke, I cried and begged to return to my true home. I saw a great building with vast columns, covered with brightly colored images of people and chariots and strange birds and animals. There was a garden filled with fruit trees, rich with the scent of flowers. Tall palms, a reflecting pool lined with stone sphinxes. When I woke, I thought I saw a cat at the foot of my bed, a sleek, midnight-black creature with a lapis collar. The only thing to follow me out of my dreams. I wept to lose it when it vanished."

Flora shifted on her cushion, thinking of her own catly vision, her own reflecting pool. Could it be she was not alone in her images? That they had some meaning, some reality? "When did you realize it was Egypt you visited while you were injured?"

"My dear grandfather gifted me with a book of Champollion's engravings. I was overjoyed to see my own columns in those illustrations! It was a true place, just as I knew it to be in my heart. After that, I went to the British Museum whenever I could. I found my greatest love there."

Flora found herself quite intrigued. It was like a novel! "Mr. Rosse?"

Elspeth gave a silvery peal of laughter. "Certainly not! Though he did take me to Egypt on our honeymoon, the old dear. No, I found my pharaoh. The one I saw in the statue. I knew we were lovers at once, in the temple of Nephthys. And then we were reunited at last, in these current fleshly iterations, at the same temple, by

our reflecting pool. Oh, the ecstasy! The perfection."
She clasped her hands at her breast, the grayish sea-light
catching on the rings stacked on her long fingers. "And
then—then he was lost to me again. At our greatest moment of discovery."

"You mean—that Sir George was your pharaoh?"
Flora felt like such a fool not to realize it all before, not
after Elspeth's performance at the Museum when poor
Sir George was found.

Elspeth sniffled and wiped at her eyes, leaving a
smudge of kohl. "His reincarnated soul, yes. I had once
been his most-beloved wife, the one who dwelled in the
Temple. He worked through this courtier to build the
halls in my memory, when we lost each other in our first
lives. It was why the place called to me so strongly."

"Er—what did the current Lady Crosbie think of
that?" And numbers one and two. Not to mention
Imogen.

Elspeth's ecstasy faded into a scowl. "That foolish
woman! She could never begin to understand the depth
of such a love. The way it transcends all time. She is too
busy with her shop, her fashion, her parties and her
health."

"Then why did he marry her?"

"As all great men do, he longed for more children
and was sure she would give him some."

"But she didn't?"

"No, of course not. There is only that disappointing
James." She smiled smugly. "But we shall find each other
once I have avenged him. Then all will be perfect."

Flora wondered if somehow Elspeth knew what
would happen at the British Museum, that she would
find her dead love there. Maybe she even arranged it all,
so they could reunite once again. It sounded barmy, but
Flora'd seen worse. "That's why you're going to Egypt
now?"

"Certainly. Surely whoever committed this foul

deed still lurks there, a serpent poisoning our fair Temple." She leaned closer to Flora and whispered, "I have great hopes that *you* can help me, Miss Flowerdew."

"Me?" Flora laughed.

"You found the Everton diamonds, did you not? You are said to have great powers of divination. Egypt will surely only strengthen them." Her hand flashed out and clutched at Flora's arm, surprisingly strong. Maybe strong enough to shove her lover into a sarcophagus. "And your soul recognized its own past life there, its destiny, as mine did! You will see your fated love there for what it is."

Flora wanted to laugh in a pure rush of fun. It really *was* like being in a novel, meeting outlandish characters! "My fated love?"

Elspeth winked, and sat back in her chair again. "Your own golden prince! You shall certainly come to see the truth of each other's hearts in Egypt, there is no doubt of it."

Flora thought of Benedict, of his smile that made the whole world burn with happiness, of that lock of golden hair that always fell over his brow. His curiosity, his kindness. But he was a duke and she was an ex-Follies girl. Worse than a pharaoh and a temple maid, surely.

It was entirely absurd, yet Flora thought she saw such a gleam of sincerity in Elspeth's brown eyes. She loved her pharaoh—er, Sir George, apparently. Loved her dream of him. Could such love turn to hate?

Flora wondered if she should ask Elspeth about her own dreams of the temple and reflecting pool, the cat, when she heard Mary calling her name. She turned and saw Mary hurrying along the deck, Chou-Chou cradled in her arms.

"Madame Chou-Chou Bossy Boots here insisted on a walk, then wouldn't let her precious paws touch the ground," Mary grumbled, trying to hold onto her hat with her other hand against a gust of wind.

"I'm sure she's having no fun cooped up in the cabin, cozy as it is," Flora said. She reached up for Chou-Chou, but as she drew the pup down onto the deck-chair, Elspeth cooed and clasped her hands.

"Oh, the sweet darling!" she cried, as Chou-Chou preened and posed, sensing a new fan. "*She* is an old soul, too, just look at her precious eyes. Oh, I just know you two will be of the greatest help to me in seeking justice! Do say you will."

And Flora found her old downfall, curiosity, got the best of her. Of course she agreed to help. Heaven help them all.

back her head, letting the sun dance over her face. As the brilliant light played over her powdered cheeks, she seemed both older than usual and younger, more free. "I must soon reunite with my pharaoh, and you must find the path you were always meant to travel. A path where such folderol as English titles mean nothing, convention means nothing."

She was not at all convinced there *was* such a path. No one could entirely leave themselves behind, and titles were not just empty words in their world. She would always be Florrie Gubbin deep down inside, and Benedict would always be a duke, with all that meant. But faced with the magical, blinding sparkle of the light and the washed-blue of the sky, she could maybe see a glimpse of something else.

Elspeth straightened her layers of robes. "I shall be journeying up the Nile very soon, but I hope we may join forces first? Call on me in Cairo as soon as you arrive, my dear, do. Where will you be staying?"

"Shepheard's."

Elspeth laughed. "Of course you are! You will *adore* the deep bathtubs, and tea in the lovely gardens is not to be missed. But you shall want to venture far beyond its walls, to see the real Cairo."

"What will I find *within* the walls?"

"Oh, lots of Anglo-Indians who are bound for home. English residents in Cairo, certainly. They are constantly homesick, you see, and make wherever they are a patch of England. People waiting to head up the Nile. It is not a *dull* world, to be sure. You'll find artists and invalids. Collectors—not all quite above suspicion, naturally. Sir George *loathed* the thieves and forgers! Yet it is not the real world. The real Egypt."

"And where should I seek that?"

Elspeth smiled gently, and drifted a light touch across Flora's cheek. "Within yourself, my dear. It's where I've always had the most luck." She took a pair of

101

pale silver gloves from her tapestry bag and tugged them on. "*Au revoir*, my dear! I shall see you very soon. We have a villain to catch."

She had no time to answer, as Theodore hurried to join her at the rail. He positively vibrated with excitement. "Miss Flowerdew! How exciting to be in Egypt at last. Are you preparing to disembark, then?"

Chou-Chou narrowed her eyes at him. She was not quite convinced to be friends with Mr. Ottway for some reason. "Yes, indeed. I'm just waiting for the others. Our train to Cairo leaves this afternoon."

"I am to be met by someone from the Egyptian Museum." He frowned in disappointment to be parted. "But we will meet very soon in Cairo. There is still a great deal to be discovered in Sir George's journal, and I know the resources of the Museum will be of much use. In the journals." He smiled shyly, and brushed her hand with the back of his fingers. "And there is the possibility of seeing the Temple itself together. It would be my greatest honor to escort you through its glorious chambers."

"You are much too kind, Mr. Ottway. I do fear we've taken up so much of your time already," she said gently. He did seem nice, just not really her type. Not a golden-haired dukie.

He beamed at her. "It has been my grandest work to undertake, assisting poor Sir George in such a fashion! We shall meet again soon." He raised her hand to his lips for a lingering kiss, and left for the gangplank. Flora laughed, and turned to find Benedict scowling at her.

"I see Mr. Ottway continues to be attentive," he grumped, as she came to her side.

Flora smiled at him sweetly. Was he jealous? It was really quite adorable. "He's been very kind, sharing his knowledge with us."

"Maybe too kind?" he huffed.

"Is it too extraordinary to imagine I might have an

admirer of sorts?" she said lightly, bouncing Chou-Chou in her arms. "I may not be as young as I once was, but I had a suitor or two back in the day."

Benedict smiled down at her, bad mood forgotten, his blue eyes crinkling at the corners, making her breath catch just a tiny amount. "You are a vision of Titian perfection, Flora Flowerdew, and you know it. Mr. Ottway would be a fool not to admire you. I only meant he seems close to Sir George. Maybe he was holding Mr. Ottway back in his career in some way? Maybe he had disappointed him? Heroes do have feet of clay, too."

Flora hadn't considered that before. "You really think Mr. Ottway could be a suspect?"

"Surely almost anyone could be, at this point. Someone who wanted his concession at the temple. Romantic jealousy. Past grudges. If anyone knew you were asking too many questions ..."

"I will be cautious, Dukie, I promise. I don't trust anyone at all, to be honest, except for Mary and Evie. And maybe Chou-Chou."

He tilted his head and gave her the most winsome little smile. "What about me? Do you trust me?"

Flora laughed. Oh, she did trust him, far too much! "You, sometimes. But Mr. O's knowledge is very useful right now, if we're to find out who did this to Sir George." She walked away, and suddenly she felt more than the warm sun on the back of her neck. She felt a sharp tingle, as if someone watched her intently. Chou-Chou shivered in her arms. But Flora refused to give in to fear, to let anything ruin this moment. "I should go find Mary—we'll be leaving soon. Cairo, here we come!"

~

Flora tried not to actually press her nose against the train window; that would be just too schoolgirlish gawky, tourist-like. But she couldn't quite help herself.

She'd never seen or even imagined a place quite like that before.

As the train swayed and clacked around a bend, swinging and jarring until Mary vowed her very hair curled with it all, her cheeks gone pale. Chou-Chou clambered up in her lap as if to comfort her, but mostly stared out of the window with Flora. There wasn't much room in their compartment, crammed in with Benedict, Mary, Evie, Imogen, and Monsieur d'Etrages, who seemed rather taken by Imogen. Mr. Lewis-Clunes and his pale, quiet wife also shared their compartment, along with Mr. Ottway, making it very cozy indeed as he told them of the scenery they passed, what to expect when they reached the city.

Luckily Elspeth Rosse was ushered to a different car when they boarded the train. She was frightfully amusing, but Flora feared her voice would be rather piercing combined with Mr. Lewis-Clunes, and Imogen and Jacques flirting.

"Her compartment is closer to the drinks car, one fears," Mrs. Lewis-Clunes had whispered. "Poor Mrs. Rosse."

"Does she—imbibe freely, then?" Flora had whispered back. She didn't remember a scent of gin hanging about Elspeth, but one never knew. Especially when someone believed Sir George was the reincarnation of her dead pharaoh lover.

"Enjoys a wee dram, as she puts it," Mrs. Lewis-Clunes clucked.

"*Certainment*, I'm afraid," Jacques added. "What else would give rise to such Pharaonic fantasies? Yet her knowledge of the XVIII Dynasty is extensive, so useful."

"And one should not gossip so, Clara," Paul chided his wife.

As the Lewis-Clunes bickered quietly together now, and Jacques and Imogen laughed, Flora studied the land beyond the window with a wave of excitement she could barely contain. She glimpsed bright green fields along the fertile valley, a patchwork of them with squares of rich, black soil, not like a desert at all. The shimmering violet shadows of the distant sand dunes beckoned to her. The pale amber light of the sky—blasting it almost white—burned down on it all even through the thick, wavy glass.

"See the egrets," Mr. Ottway said, leaning so close to Flora she could smell the scent of his hair oil. "Just over there. You can always see where the river lies."

Flora, who knew nothing about birds except the city pigeons and the plumes on hats, was enthralled when she glimpsed the snowy plumage soaring and dipping in the distance, like messengers from a different world.

"They tend to follow the crops, when it's sowed or reaped, 'clearing' up after it," Jacques said. "Egrets symbolize harmony and balance, life and regeneration. I am sure your friend Mrs. Rosse would agree with the new beginnings of old things."

Regeneration. Flora liked the sound of that. The past never had to be the present, or the future, all was changeable. She watched an ox-drawn plough in a field by the tracks, drawn by a swarm of men in blue dahabeyas. There were water buffaloes, cows, donkeys, horses, goats. An exhilarating glimpse of a shadowed pyramid in the distance, a row of run-down mud huts surrounding a stone tower. Tall palm groves, women with water jugs balanced on their heads. It was like a painting. She couldn't help but wonder what secrets lurked out there.

The train slowed to a crawl, and someone muttered about animals on the tracks again.

"So typical of this place," Mrs. Lewis-Clunes snapped, waving her fan vigorously. "So unorganized, nothing is ever on time or efficient! Someone should *do* something." She glanced at Flora. "Miss Flowerdew, I must say, it's so brave of you to leave the comforts of

London and venture here. If I had a settled home there, I should never leave."

"Not at all," Flora said. "London is so cold and dark right now, I'm happy for the chance to see some sunshine."

Clara frowned. "It's all so ruinous to the complexion. If I did not take great care, I should be so terribly freckled!" She studied Flora's cheeks closely, until she wanted to fidget for fear a freckle was popping out on Flora's fair cheek what with her red hair. "You should be even more cautious, I daresay. They say red hair is a magnet for sunburn."

"The Egyptians say red hair is the luckiest, the most sacred of all," Jacques said.

Flora made herself laugh. She'd always wished for raven hair, or golden waves. "It's quite unfashionable, I know. I always longed for beautiful brunette curls like your own, Mrs. Lewis-Clunes. But I shall certainly always keep a parasol at my side." She studied Clara's milk-pale skin. "Have you been coming here to Egypt for very long with Mr. Lewis-Clunes?"

Clara glanced out the window. "Ever since we were married, so many years ago. It is expected that a wife will help in her husband's career if she can, of course, but I did hope he would soon take a position at the British Museum and we could make a proper home. Instead, it has been one dusty tomb after the other." Her lips pursed. "I do stay in Cairo whenever I can—I don't venture out into the wilderness."

Flora looked at Benedict, thinking of his parents, his father running about the world, his delicate mother at home until she faded away. He seemed to think of them, too, his gaze very far away. "Is it the same with most of the Egyptologists' wives? Such as Lady Crosbie?"

"Usually, yes, though some do have their own health troubles that confine them to England. I don't know Lady Crosbie very well, I confess. I think they've not been long married, and she tends to rather keep to herself." Clara leaned closer and whispered, "She owns a *shop*. Can you imagine? How very shocking. A woman in trade, and in Egypt, too." She didn't look terribly shocked, though, rather more envious. "Though she is very beautiful."

"What sort of shop?" Flora asked. That sounded terribly enticing. Shopping was her great weakness.

"Oh, I certainly have not visited the premises! I never venture to that area of the city. If I must live there, I stay close to Shepheard's. I hear she sells fashion items of some sort. Hats, maybe, or jewelry?"

"Do she and Sir George have any children? I have only heard of an older son." One who was also an archaeologist, though not of his father's renown.

Clara's expression softened, saddened. Maybe she'd once longed for children herself. "No, I doubt she has much time for maternal matters. Of course, it is much easier to live such an unsettled life without the worries of children. The heat is so bad for them. It is probably for the best Paul and I have never been so blessed, but as a lady it is a grief to me." She glanced down at her gloved hands twisting in her lap. "But really, you must not believe all they say of poor James Crosbie! He is a true gentleman, always courteous, and they do speak well of his work at the Egyptian Museum. Sir George has always been most unfair to him, never giving him any responsibilities at the temple. Yet if Sir George had listened to his son's quite understandable concerns before he married Lady Crosbie, much trouble might have been avoided. And look what has happened!"

"Did he have concerns for his father, then?"

"What son would not? Sir George's first wife, she was a Patterson, used to the life of the archaeological dig, but she was of a fragile nature. She had not been long deceased, and everyone knew Melanie was looking for someone to give her a home in Egypt before she had to return to England. Everyone says she needed financial help for that shop, and her father—a viscount!—refused to give it."

Her voice dropped to a whisper again, muffled by the flap of her fan. "I am not one for idle gossip, Miss Flowerdew, but I heard Lady Crosbie was greatly infatuated with Richard North before she married Sir George. And they are still often seen together at parties and such." Clara's lips pursed in disapproval.

Flora widened her eyes and hoped she looked suitably shocked. Richard North had indeed been a handsome man, and as Sir George's assistant, he must have been around a great deal. "Are you saying Lady Crosbie is having a—a liaison?"

Clara's lips pursed prissily again. "I would not know of such matters, I'm sure. I do know Mr. North is many years younger than Lady Crosbie, and very handsome. Many of the English community's daughters would love to be courted by him, as would their fathers—he is quite the promising archaeologist. Yet he is always dancing attendance on Lady Crosbie. Most odd."

"Are you whispering about Lady Crosbie and Mr. North again, Clara?" Paul interjected sternly.

Clara sat back with a guilty little smile on her un-sunbrowned face. "Miss Flowerdew merely asked about our local society. I was telling her of Lady Crosbie's shop."

"Lady Crosbie and Mr. North knew each other from their families being neighbors in England years ago, that is all," Paul said. "I'm sure she will be prostrated with grief when we meet her in Cairo, and we must seek to console her, not gossip about her."

"Of course," his wife said sullenly. "I shouldn't dream of doing otherwise."

"And her shop is most respectable. I bought that necklace for you there, and you seem to like it very much indeed."

Flora remembered the beautiful necklace Clara wore at dinner on the ship, and how she'd envied it. Lady Crosbie must have very good taste indeed.

"So Lady Crosbie really has a shop?" Imogen said. "How amusing. I should like to have one myself. I've often thought my organization skills could surely be put to better use than charity committees and garden parties. I would have hats, I think, or chairs and blue-and-white china. Perhaps a tea shop with the loveliest strawberries cakes?"

"You would be superlative at anything you chose to do," Jacques said gallantly.

Chou-Chou barked in enthusiastic agreement, and Flora could just imagine her supervising a shop from a cushion behind the till. Or devouring all the products, if it was indeed a tea shop.

"You would be the most charming shopkeeper imaginable, *chere* Lady Hastings," Jacques declared. "You could surely sell anything to anyone. I would happily buy the most expensive hat from you."

Clara sniffed. "Well, Lady Crosbie also went to far too many parties for someone meant to be in such fragile health. So unseemly."

Before Flora could ask who frequented those parties, Paul said, "Look, we're coming into the city now. I'm quite sure no one wants to hear more tittle-tattle, Clara."

"Oh, we always adore tittle-tattle," Imogen said cheerfully. "It's quite our life-blood!"

~

Flora was sure she'd never seen—or heard, or smelled—anything like the scene before her in her life. And she'd grown up near Whitechapel, filled with teeming crowds!

Holding onto Chou-Chou, she leaned out the window of the hansom-style carriage, gawking at everything around her. Chou-Chou, her paws perched on the edge of the door, seemed just as enthralled, but Mary held tight to the hem of Flora's jackets, as she feared they would go tumbling out.

"Oh, Miss Flora, do have a care," Mary cried. "If you fall out in this muck ..."

"There's hardly any room to fall out, Mary," Flora declared. "I would just tumble into the next carriage." The lane was so packed with vehicles, horses, and people, there was barely an inch to spare. "It's all so marvelous!"

Benedict leaned out beside her, holding onto his hat. He looked just as eager to take it all in as she did. "Just look at it all, Dukie! No wonder your father was addicted to seeing new places."

"Indeed," he agreed, and let out a whoop that made her laugh.

All around, everywhere she turned her head, there were bicycles, carriages of all sizes, wagons heaped with vegetables. Flocks of sheep trotted down the edges of the lane, sometimes stopping the flow of traffic. The hot breeze smelled of fried fish, sheep dung, smoky incense, spices, flowers. All so rich and organic, like the essence of life itself.

"Look at that," she said, pointing, and she and Benedict and Chou-Chou all turned to take in an organ grinder and his monkeys, the flash and dazzle of their little red-and-gold jackets, the lively hop-skip of the music.

Every corner seemed to hold some conjuror doing magic tricks, flower sellers, and food carts. Flora wondered if she should drape herself in spangled veils and add such conjuring tricks to her séance repertoire. Sidewalk vendors offered oranges, alluringly unheard-of in wintertime London, along with sweet dates, lamb kebobs, and fruit water. Men in blue robes shooed away ragged children, women in dark robes hurried past carrying market baskets, European couples in suits and walking dresses, their parasols held aloft.

The buildings, stained white, all loomed above with their upper balconies latticed, casting shade and sun. Chanting music rang out from minarets.

"It's wonderful," Flora breathed. "And we haven't even seen the Nile yet!"

She looked at Benedict, and they grinned at each other in delight.

The carriage turned down a quieter street, lined with palm trees and gleaming white villas, along with enticing shops, and jolted to a halt in front of their destination, the famous Shepheard's Hotel. Lacy-pale, like a wedding cake, rising above them with balconies and green-striped awnings.

It felt like stepping past an invisible wall into a different land, one that was hushed and slow after the roar of the streets. A warm wind bent the palm trees, wafting the scent of white flowers. A few people took tea at the wicker tables in the garden, cast in glimmering shade. Elspeth was right about the crowd to be found here. All English. They whispered and laughed to the strains of a string quartet. Across the street was the grand opera house, its facade square and dignified and almost Georgian, framed by those palm trees.

A uniformed doorman in the hotel's green-and-gold helped them alight from the carriage. Flora stepped down behind Imogen, clutching Chou-Chou against her as she gawked up at the hotel. A shady canopy covered the front steps, and the glowing glass of the doors opened like magic. It was a storybook place, white stone embossed with ornamental swirls around the doors and windows. Carved pediments around the roof crowned it with lacy ironwork, and there were shaded windows and fanciful cupolas. Palms lined the walkways where ladies in pastel gowns and fashionable hats strolled beneath their parasols.

Flora followed Imogen through the doors and into the cool dimness of the lobby. It was also unlike any hotel lobby she'd ever seen. More like a seraglio in an operetta than a staid hotel! She craned her neck to take in the domed skylight above, which bathed the space in buttery-yellow light, casting a glow over the green-and-gold carpets, the burbling fountain, and more palms in brass pots. Delicate wicker chairs alternated with deep, pale-gold velvet armchairs and tufted footstools.

Magazines and books in English, French, German, and Arabic were displayed on elaborate, alabaster-topped tables. The pale walls were inlaid with mosaics of pastel pink, green, and blue, wrapping an air of serenity over the vast space. Even though it was crowded with people reading and talking, and porters with luggage, it felt like an oasis of calm.

They hurried past tall pillars tipped with gilded palm fronds, carved with hieroglyphs like an ancient temple. Her boots sank into the sable-soft green-and-gold carpet, and she felt distinctly grubby and frumpy after the train journey, especially when a lady in a pale lavender silk gown, scented with attar of roses, wafted past. Benedict watched her ruffled train pass, and Flora nudged him.

The reception desk rested under a crystal and gilt chandelier, twinkling like the stars in a night sky. The glass doors behind it were open to a terrace. The concierge, an older, distinguished gentleman in a green-and-gold suit, smiled widely at their approach.

"Ah, Your Grace, Lady Hastings," he said with a small bow. "What an honor for our hotel! Your father did stay with us rather often—he was a favorite guest."

"I'm very happy to be here in his footsteps," Benedict answered, looking boyishly, charmingly eager. "You knew my father, then? I should so enjoy hearing what you remember of him. Seeing the things he loved so much."

"We have set aside his favorite suite for you," the concierge said. "With fine rooms nearby for the rest of your party. They are on a quiet corridor, with windows looking onto the courtyard. Most peaceful. But if they are in any way unsuitable, you must inform us immediately. Shall you join us for tea in the garden?"

"That sounds exactly like what is required, " Imogen said. A bellman led Mary toward the staircase, telling her the luggage would be waiting in the room, and Evie wandered away to examine some newspapers. "And hot baths right away?"

"Certainly, my lady." He rang a little brass bell on the desk. "Hamad will show you to your suites, and your luggage will be delivered right away. There is a dining room and a garden cafe on the rooftop, along with the American Bar. We hope you'll join us for our weekly dances."

Holding onto a squirming, fascinated Chou-Chou, Flora brought up the end of their little procession toward the lifts. She didn't want to miss a thing. There was so much opulence to be seen at every turn, so much quiet luxury. Velvet and gilt, marble and brocade, ancient Egyptian statues interspersed between romantic oil paintings, carpet muffling every footstep, the whisper of elevators whooshing guests to their rooms.

Yet, something nagged at the back of Flora's mind, that familiar tingling sensation that usually indicated someone was watching, someone was paying attention. She glanced behind her, but saw nothing at all.

Ten

Flora blinked her eyes slowly open from her afternoon nap, sleep and dreams clinging to the edges of her mind like tattered shreds of tulle until she could brush it away. For a moment, she had no idea where she was at all. The wall she blinked at wasn't her own pale-blue watered silk paper, dotted with flowered still-lifes and portraits of Chou-Chou. This wall was a light straw-gold, with a subtle sheen to it, hung with framed papyrus scenes of women in filmy white robes making offerings, of pharaohs on their thrones, and cat-headed Bastet.

She rolled over, and found herself not wrapped up like a silk-worm against cold drafts, but under a light, soft-as-silk linen sheet, lavender-scented pillows heaped around her. Chou-Chou snored softly atop one of them. Pale gold-and-green striped curtains fluttered in the breeze at half-open, floor-to-ceiling windows.

Then she remembered—she was in *Egypt*. Eons from the cold London fog, and it was no dream at all. Could hear the call of the muezzin in the distance, and a band playing waltzes in the garden below.

Flora slowly sat up, careful not to wake Chou-Chou. A coffee service sat on an octagonal mosaic table, left there silently while she slept. A gold-edged porcelain pot and cups, a plate of tiny honey cakes and fruit, beckoned enticingly with heady scents of sugar.

She slid her feet into a pair of satin slippers and reached for a floral silk wrapper to cover her chemise. Her trunks had also been unpacked by mysterious hands, her gowns tucked away in the mahogany wardrobe, her hat boxes lined up on a shelf. Walls papered in pale-green silk, chaises and armchairs in green-and-white stripes, glass doors opening to a balcony with the vista of the distant pyramids whenever she wanted to take a peek. Crystal vases filled with white flowers were placed everywhere, and there was a white brass bed, spread with more green silk and heaped with tasseled cushions. It was all a delightful oasis, a place far from her troubles, at least for a time.

A small ormolu clock on the dressing table rang out the hour, and she realized it was almost time for dinner. She hurried to the windows and pushed back the filmy curtains to peer out into the light, a light unlike any she'd ever imagined before. Nothing she'd read in books could begin to describe it.

Evening sunlight washed all around her, over her, absorbing her in pink and gold and coral, edged with turquoise, just like Clara Lewis-Clunes's beautiful necklace. She stepped out onto a small balcony, and held up her arms as if she would let that jewel-light lift her up and carry her away. The white walls of the hotel were pink now, like the inside of a rose. The sky high above was deepest indigo, sprinkled with the last of the tiny, diamond-like stars just blinking on.

Flora glanced over the lacy balustrade of her balcony to the courtyard below. White iron tables were scattered about under the trees, between the tumbling flowerbeds, circling a bubbling marble fountain. Wicker chairs upholstered in turquoise stripes held pairs and quartets of people, laughing, sipping champagne, and listening to the music that blended with birdsong and distant, oh so distant, car wheels and vendors' cries.

And—oh, heavenly dream! Could it be possible? She turned her head and glimpsed the pyramids, stained orange and outlined with gray shadows in the sunset. She'd seen images of them so often, she couldn't quite believe they were a real thing.

At last, she felt warm again.

"I swear this is Nefertiti I glimpse," she heard a man call.

She leaned over the balustrade to see Benedict standing below her. He wore his evening suit and white tie for dinner, but his golden hair was tousled, and his smile carefree.

Flora knew he teased, but truly, with the pyramids seeming so close she could touch them, and the wondering expression on Benedict's face as he looked at her —well, she was no Nefertiti, but neither was she now Florrie Gubbin. She never could be again. Maybe Elspeth was right about Egypt.

"Our table is ready in the dining room," Benedict said. "I know your ardent admirer Mr. Ottway will be jostling to sit near you, but I hope I can claim the seat beside you tonight."

When Benedict smiled at her that way, he could claim anything he liked when it came to her.. If only he wasn't a duke! It was a curse. But she'd jump from the tip of the pyramid before she'd ever admit that she wished he could be someone else and they could be together. Not to him, or even to herself.

"If you're quick enough, Dukie," she called to him. "I'll just get dressed. See you soon."

An arc of color flashed through the air, and she realized he'd tossed up a jasmine flower. She caught it, inhaling its sweet, intoxicating scent before she tucked it into her upswept hair. At least she could hold onto that small part of him.

~

The dining room at Shepheard's was just as glorious as the rest of the hotel. A vast space made to look like an ancient temple, it was bisected with rows of carved pillars that made it feel more intimate, cozy even. Niches for groups of two or four surrounded larger tables, all bathed in golden, glowing light from acanthus-shaped chandeliers and papyrus sconces. The thick carpet was Nile green, as were the satin cushions of the gilded chairs. Towering potted palms gently waved in every corner, and arrangements of lilies on each snowy linen-draped table cast an intoxicating scent into the cool air.

Imogen and Evie were already at their table, which Flora could see was one of the best in the room, a large, round space under a dome painted with a scene of ancient Egyptian gods and goddesses, and crowned with a skylight that let in a peek of the night sky.

"Are we having a party already, Lady Imogen? Is our mystery solved?" Flora teased, as she took her seat, next to Benedict as promised. She was glad she'd worn her new azure-blue and white lace gown when she saw Imogen's cream and crimson Worth creation. Evie wore her dark-blue chiffon, of course. Even in Egypt, she wouldn't change.

"Keep one's enemies close, my dear, and never let them know your plans," Imogen said. "Especially if you're not entirely sure yet who they are! Mr. Ottway will be joining us, of course, and I asked that charming Monsieur d'Etrages. He is so amusing." Was that actually a *blush* on Imogen's powdered cheeks as she indicated the empty chair beside hers with a bejeweled hand. Maybe love was in the Cairo air! "The Lewis-Clunes have also accepted my invitation. So tiresome, of course,

118

but I am sure he has more information that we have yet to winkle out. Best of all, I discovered that Lady Crosbie is in residence, and will join our little party! Along with her stepson, James Crosbie, and the, er, secretary, is he? Mr. North, whom we met in London."

As Benedict held out her chair for her to be seated, she hoped he couldn't see the little sentimental touch of the flower in her hair. "Oh, goodie! So many questionable motives all in one place."

As a waiter poured out the excellent wine, Theodore Ottway rushed in. His face quite fell when he realized he wasn't seated beside Flora, but he took his place across the table. "Do excuse my tardiness—I was at the museum, receiving updates on my work."

"Not at all, my dear Mr. Ottway," Imogen said. Ah, here are the Lewis-Clunes!"

"A pleasure to see you again, Lady Hastings," Paul said, snapping out his starched linen napkin. "And you, Ottway. Didn't I see you at the museum today? Such chaos it's all been without me!"

Clara Lewis-Clunes sat at Benedict's other side and reached for her champagne glass, gulping it down. It was immediately refilled by one of the attentive waiters. A platter of gorgeous, gleaming fruit was laid out in the middle of the table, but she ignored it for the wine. Maybe Elspeth wasn't the only one who liked the drinks car on the train. Clara fanned herself vigorously with her scrap of lace, stirring her necklace. It wasn't the collar from Lady Crosbie's shop, but a carnelian scarab set in elaborate gold filigree. "So much *dust*! I had quite forgotten. And the insects. I forgot how dreadful it all is while I was lucky to be away." She shot a glance at her husband, who ignored her. "Paul simply adores it all. You can see how happy he is to have returned."

Paul scowled at her. "It is my work, Clara, and it's vital to me. You knew that very well before we married." He turned to Imogen with a strained smile. "You will give our new friends, especially the *Duke*, the wrong impression of us. We are devoted to Egypt, to preserving it for the ages to come."

"Devoted," Clara muttered.

Monsieur d'Etrages came into the dining room, with Elspeth Rosse on his arm. It seemed she had overcome any aversion to Shepheard's to venture to its dining room. Their heads were bent together as they whispered intently. It seemed he didn't just enjoy a bit of flirtation with Imogen and Flora's red hair. He seated her at a single table nearby, and Elspeth waggled her fingers at Flora.

Jacques hurried to their table, greeting Imogen with a gallant kiss to her hand that had even her blushing a bit, before he took his seat between her and Flora. "*Pardonez-moi* for my tardiness. I encountered our old friend in the lobby, as you see. How exquisite you all look tonight, *mesdames*! The air of Egypt agrees with you, just as I was sure it would." A waiter poured him a glass of wine, and he smiled at Imogen who definitely smiled back.

"I did not know you were friends with Mrs. Rosse, monsieur," Flora said.

"The world of Egypt is a small one, Mademoiselle Flowerdew; it is rare when one of us never encounters another, especially when one is as vivid and outgoing as Madame Rosse. A fascinating lady, one with a great deal of useful ideas and notions."

"I am sure she would be, as she has seen the past," Flora murmured. Elspeth also said Flora could see the past, but she wasn't sure that was true. Maybe it was all Chou-Chou, just like the ghosts.

As they watched, a man joined Elspeth at her table. He was outrageously handsome, like a statue of a pharaoh, with a sharply sculpted face, bright green eyes, set off by a bronzed complexion. His white robe shimmered, as if touched with silver, his gray-flecked black hair glossy. He bowed over Elspeth's hand before sitting across from her.

"Who is *that*?" Evie whispered in admiration. Evie usually preferred female beauty, but Flora certainly agreed with her now. Anyone would surely think this man glorious.

"Why, that is Monsieur Assim, Sir George's foreman!" Paul Lewis-Clunes cried. "What on earth is he doing here in Cairo, not at the Temple?"

Flora studied him with curiosity, as she remembered the steward Assad said his brother had been Sir George's faithful steward at the temple. He looked nothing like she would have imagined a long-time, grizzled foreman should! This man was tall and handsome indeed, and watched the dining room with a serenity that seemed to conceal every thought.

"And eating at Shepheard's! Most shocking," Clara hissed. "Standards are certainly slipping here."

"You are quite right, my dear," her husband said. "He will soon realize his place."

The fish course, a marvelous garfish in a tarragon sauce, had been served and most of the tables were occupied when a couple appeared in the doorway. Flora was sure that could only be Lady Crosbie with Richard North. She was indeed a great beauty, like a Gainsborough painting, tall and slim, all pink-and-white, with dark-gold hair twisted atop her head and crowned with a turquoise-and-gold headdress that contrasted with her gown of black taffeta and lace. On her arm was Richard North, whispering in her ear most attentively as they crossed the dining room. Everyone stopped for a moment to stare at them.

"My dear Lady Crosbie," Paul said, leaping to his feet to go and greet her, all appropriate solemnity and solicitude. "How very, very sorry we all are for your great loss. For the loss to all of us."

Lady Crosbie smiled at him, a smile of such sweetness and sadness she seemed like a heroine in a romantic novel. "How very kind you are, Mr. Lewis-Clunes. How kind everyone has been. I am comforted that George's important work will not be forgotten. He has been sadly unappreciated lately. Quite ill-treated, I fear. Now this tragedy!" Her voice sounded a bit rough, as if she'd been crying.

Richard quickly took her arm, before she could work up a full operatic aria, and seated her between him and Evie.

"How truly shocking that a man of Sir George's great reputation would be treated thus!" Evie clucked kindly. Evie, as well as being tough when she needed to be in her job, also knew when to use kindness and softness. And Flora could tell her friend was not entirely immune to Lady Crosbie's great beauty. "In what way could anyone dare to denigrate him?"

Lady Crosbie tilted her golden head to study Evie, with eyes that matched her turquoise headpiece. Even Evie blushed a bit. "I confess it is so tragic, no wonder something truly dreadful happened." She dabbed at her eyes with a lace-edged handkerchief. "And you are Miss ...?"

"Evangeline Finnegan," Evie offered, in her low, sympathetic, *you can tell me anything* voice. "What an appalling thing that a great man's peers would add to such a horrific situation for you, Lady Crosbie."

Lady Crosbie sniffled. "Indeed, you are right! I could never have imagined anything like this happening. I live in an atmosphere of beauty and harmony at all times, any ugliness is such a shock." She buried her face in her embroidered handkerchief, and everyone, especially Richard and Paul, leaped to her assistance. But not, Flora noticed, Benedict.

Richard North gently touched the jet-beaded lace of her black satin sleeve, frowning in concern "Melanie, my dear, do not upset yourself. You are among friends here, quite safe. Is that not so, Lady Hastings?"

"Indeed," Imogen said. "We should never in a hundred years wish to add an iota to your sorrow, Lady Crosbie. Your husband was a man of great scholarship ... we admired him so much."

"How kind you are. All of you." She tossed a watery smile around the table, and reached for her wineglass. "Richard said you would be, and urged me to join this dinner."

"It will take you out of yourself, Melanie," he said.

"Richard and I have known each other since our very infancy," Lady Crosbie said. "I could not do without him now ... he is assisting me in the running of my darling shop, and in making sure my George's legacy is honored. If I did not have my work to distract me now ..."

"I think it is so fascinating that you have a shop of your very own," Flora said.

Lady Crosbie beamed. "Yes, my great pride and joy! I had it before I met my George, though my parents disapproved." She turned those jewel-blue eyes onto Flora, and Flora found that even she wanted to giggle and flutter, it was so captivating. "I do feel I know you, Miss ..."

"Miss Flora Flowerdew. I don't see how it could be ... I am new to Cairo."

"Ah, yes, you are the gifted medium! In such a place as this, you will have more spirits clamoring about you than you will know how to manage, and of course everyone here has high respect for such powers. Have you perhaps visited my shop yet? It is in a very old part of town."

"I fear not, Lady Crosbie. I've only just arrived, though I have heard good reports of it." Flora glanced at Clara's necklace. "I quite envy Mrs. Lewis-Clunes' gorgeous necklaces, which she says she acquired there."

"It is a veritable Aladdin's cave, Miss Flowerdew,

you really must go," Clara said, sounding far more enthusiastic about shopping than she had about anything else. "There are so many beauties to be found in the souks here, Miss Flowerdew. Perhaps we could have an excursion to the merchants one day before we leave the city."

Flora, a champion shopper herself, agreed. It would be a great chance to learn more about Sir George and his life and enemies. A curried lobster was served, and Flora could clearly see that Shepheard's certainly did not stint in their dining room. She heartily approved.

"Do forgive me for the lateness of my arrival," a man said, led to their tableside by one of the waiters. His voice was low, rough, uncertain, catching a few words on a stammer. Silence fell, and everyone turned to study the new arrival.

He was tall, lean, handsome in a sun-burned way, though his haircut and uneven beard were rather atrocious. He looked a bit like Imogen's photograph of a young Sir George.

"James," Lady Crosbie cried, for of course it must be Sir George's own son. "Here you are at last." She rose in a graceful swirl of black taffeta, and went to take what must be her stepson by the arm. She nudged Richard to slide his chair over a bit so James could sit beside her, ignoring Richard's scowl. Though James was clearly older than her, she was kind and gentle with him, smiling and reassuring. "No worries at all, my dear. I know how much work you are facing right now—you must be quite exhausted. And famished! Here, have some wine, it's quite nice, and you must eat something."

"Don't fuss so, Mel, I am quite well," he said impatiently, shaking off her arm. Her smile trembled. Flora remembered hearing stepmother and son did not quite get along as well as they might. She wondered why that was.

After an awkward moment, conversation and wine

flowed again, swirling around the silent gray rock of James Crosbie. It was rather too loud to hear much conversation, so Flora studied everyone around the table and mulled over what she'd learned so far, which was not nearly as much as she wished.

After platters of fruit and cheese and goblets of spiced wine were finished, Flora strolled out to the gorgeous gardens with Benedict and Evie, leaving Imogen to chatter in the lobby with her new admirer Monsieur d'Etrages, and Lady Crosbie coaxing James to talk with the Lewis-Clunes.

It was truly a magical night. The moon hung low in the dusty-purple sky, a perfect crescent surrounded by the twinkle of dotted stars with the puff of smoky clouds skittering past. Flagstone walkways wound around fragrant mimosa trees and Shepheard's famous roses of yellow, pink, and white. People gathered for post-dinner tiny cups of strong coffee and brandies at small round tables, whispering and laughing softly in the warm night air. The music of the string quartet blended with the cries from the city's minarets.

The world Flora had glimpsed beyond the hotel walls, the conjurers and magicians and wagons laden with vegetables, the monkeys and organ grinders, seemed so distant. The only reminders of where they really were remained an obelisk or two, an unblinking stone sphinx, there in the garden.

Flora touched her cat amulet, and took a deep breath of the heady, sweet-scented breeze.

"It's hard to imagine murders can percolate just beneath the surface in such a place," she murmured. Yet truly she could not be too surprised; she'd seen the worst side of human nature in beautiful places before, like the South of France, the beaches of Cornwall.

Lady Crosbie emerged from the hotel, Richard on one arm and James on the other, with Imogen and Jacques trailing behind them as he explained the origins of one of the obelisks to her. Flora was pulled out of her reverie, and smiled at Lady Crosbie as the lady floated over to her, leaving her escorts at loose ends.

"Oh, Miss Flowerdew," she said, with a flutter of her lacy sleeve, her eyes glittering with unshed tears in the moonlight. "I am afraid you will all think me so cruel-hearted to be out so soon after—after the horrible thing that happened to my Georgie."

"Not at all. As Mr. Lewis-Clunes said, it's good to be among sympathetic friends at such a time," Flora answered. "Life is brief, and we must carry on as best we can. Our loved ones would wish it for us."

Lady Crosbie flashed her a radiant smile. "And you would know! Oh, it is so true. My husband was all about *life*, whether in the here and now or in ancient days. The Egyptians have always been great lovers of life. It is why their tombs are so filled with lovely things, they want to have them in the life to come, to keep enjoying themselves." A sob escaped her lips, and Mr. North quickly came to her side to take her hand. "I cannot fathom it all. What was George even doing in England? I thought he was far up the Nile, at Al-Fashn."

"The village?" Benedict asked. "Is that near the Temple?"

"Yes, not far. They have just started some excavations near there. It was indeed associated in some way with the Temple, perhaps as a place for the builders to live. He often traveled there lately; it was a new find he hoped would shed much light on the workings of the Temple. It's very remote. When he traveled there, he wouldn't return for months sometimes. He said he had found something amazing, something he couldn't yet speak of. I didn't become concerned until—until ..." She broke down into raw sobs, and Mr. North tightened his clasp on her hand.

"You were not much involved in your husband's work, Lady Crosbie?" Flora asked gently.

She shook her head, the blonde waves not even mussed in their turquoise headdress. "My health is rather fragile, I fear. It is all I can do to manage my dear little shop. Archaeology is so very *demanding*." Her eyes narrowed. "And George thought my brain could never fathom hieroglyphs and dynastic lineages. I wish I could have helped him! Oh, why was I so foolish!" She began to cry in earnest, and Mr. North wrapped his arm around him.

"Do excuse us, Miss Flowerdew, Your Grace," he said. "I fear Melanie has overtired herself, she must be sure and rest."

"Of course," Flora said, and watched as the pair moved away through the shadows. "What do you think ails her? Just grief?" she asked Benedict.

"Opium, perhaps," Jacques said from behind them, his tone absolutely neutral, speculative.

Flora glanced back at him in surprise. Had she been so taken with Melanie Crosbie's fragile beauty she hadn't noticed signs? She'd certainly known people in her younger days in London who frequented the dens, losing their troubles in a haze of sweet smoke.

"The dilated eyes, the changeable mood, the bright cheeks," Benedict said calmly, as if indifferent to Lady C's charms. It rather warmed Flora's heart. "Yes, I see what you mean."

Jacques shrugged, and reached for a fresh cigarillo to light. "I'm afraid it is rife here. It comes from India and crosses through Cairo frequently, hidden to evade taxation. Almost as big an industry as smuggling antiquities and art. In fact, the two are often intertwined."

Flora wondered if Lady Crosbie could have quarreled with her husband while under the influence of opium or something like that. Or maybe she got it from her husband in the first place. "Could it have something to do with what happened to Sir George?"

"Maybe the reason the Temple might be taken from

him?" Benedict asked. "Someone did mention there had been some problems with thefts."

Jacques shook his head. "Who can say? The dealers in stolen art can be secretive—they have to be. Sir George was an outspoken opponent of the trade in illegal art. He loved history. He valued the objects for what they can teach us, not just for their beauty. The lessons are lost when they are removed from their original places. He has certainly made some powerful enemies in the course of his career. I never heard him speak of the drug trade, but I would not be surprised if he held it in abhorrence."

"And who would gain the most if Sir George lost the concession?" Flora asked. Or lost his life.

"Lewis-Clunes, of course, has been longing for the job for a long time. He often speaks of how he finds Sir George's methods old-fashioned and slow. But really, any archaeologist would pluck out their right eye for the chance to take over such a place as the Temple. It's a beautiful place, relatively unlooted. You'd have to scour the ranks of the French, the Germans, and all the English. There would be no lack of motive." He frowned in thought. "What I do not understand is the method. So dramatic, so attention-seeking! Why not just a shove down a shaft?"

Flora sighed. "We hardly have the kind of time to question *everyone*! I wouldn't even know where to start."

Jacques gestured with the glowing end of his cigarillo across the garden, toward Assim and Elspeth where they examined a statue of Anubis. "You could do much worse than to begin by having a chat with Monsieur Assim. He has been Sir George's foreman for years ... he knows as much about the Temple as anyone. Might be a bit of a challenge, though—I've never heard the man say more than four words together, keeps his own counsel. He is friends with Madame Rosse, though."

Flora remembered their steward on the ship, Assim's brother. Surely he, as foreman of Sir George's dig, could tell her a great deal! "Thank you, monsieur, I shall certainly talk to him soon." They chatted for a few more minutes before Jacques excused himself, and Flora headed to her own chamber. She certainly had many things to mull over.

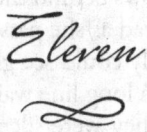

Eleven

I t was early when Flora ventured out of the hotel,
before the day grew too hot and anyone could urge
her to stay in or take someone with her. She even
left Chou-Chou behind, as the Pom was happily
snoozing in her little bed. She wanted to explore, to ob-
serve, and to take in some of the wondrous new world
she'd found herself tossed into. The concierge told her
where to find Lady Crosbie's shop, which was popular
with visitors, in the Khalil Building of the souk.

Clutching her parasol, she made her way out of
Shepheard's, past the grand opera house and into the
square, beyond the large villas quiet behind their lush
gardens. She didn't see very many people at that hour;
they were surely lingering over breakfast or still in bed
after dancing all night. Flora loved the whisper of the
warm breeze, swirling around her with the scent of iris
and daffodils, the brilliant splashes of color as blossoms
tumbled over gates and climbed up walls. Especially
after the swirling, secret currents of her dining compan-
ions, the real world was invigorating.

Someone was certainly hiding their true thoughts,
their real intentions behind fluttering opaque veils. It
was like trying to read the hieroglyphics in Sir George's
journal. Sir George himself seemed like a genius of ar-

chaeology, renowned by everyone. But what did his assistants, like Mr. North, his wife, his son, his foreman, *really* think about him? And who, or what, was lurking in the constant shadows behind the vivid Egyptian sun?

She shook her head as she passed a carved courtyard gate. If only she really could see ghosts at will! She was sure there would be a long line waiting to tell her all the scandal-broth. But they were silent behind their bland masks.

As she hurried nearer to the souk, the streets grew more narrow, more crowded. Children shrieked and dashed past, called after by women in flowing robes, and the smell of spices clung enticingly to the breeze. She could hear the strains of music, mizmars, and neys, the rise and clash of voices. The tall, dingy white houses to either side, roofed in faded red tiles, were so close they nearly touched overhead with their latticed balconies. Just past those were stalls pressing close, overflowing with alluring goods. Silks of every rainbow hue, delicate muslins, red shawls, copper-colored slippers. Pottery jars of olive oils, baskets spilling out with fruit, pineapples, dates, figs. Sugared almonds, white, sticky squares of Turkish delight. Songbirds in cages that warbled above the chatter and clamor, the cries of merchants trying to lure patrons into their shops. She smelled the spices: cinnamon, ginger, cardamom, amber and floral perfumes, and it was hard to resist it all, to remind herself of her errand.

She sadly shook her head at the offer of carpets woven in brilliant blues and reds, which would look so splendid in her séance chamber at home, and followed the hotel concierge's directions up a set of wooden stairs at a three-story warren of shops. She looked for Lady Crosbie's establishment and saw elegant shops laden with colorful silks, delicate muslins, jewelry, and silverwork, all most tempting.

At the second-story landing, she peeked through a

shadowed open doorway and saw something rather familiar—a fortune teller's parlor. It was beautifully set up, she had to admit; she should take some ideas home to spruce up her own space. It was small but evocative, the walls lined with tapestries of ancient Egyptian scenes and gods that gave it a rich, cave-like feeling. Most of the light came from small, pierced-tin lamps in the corners, which shone passing beams on silver threads in the cloth. A statue lurked in a niche, the jackal-headed Anubis, god of death.

The only furniture was a round table in the center of the room, circled by carved chairs and draped with a dark crimson cloth edged with gold embroidery in mysterious hieroglyphs. Tall golden candlesticks, unlit, sat atop it, along with a crystal ball on a filigreed stand. The air smelled of incense.

It all seemed to be empty, but something drew Flora inside. She tiptoed carefully to the table, and found a set of cards laid out on the red cloth. The symbols painted there were like none she'd ever seen, stars and whirls, but she could decipher some of their meaning. The snake for the circle of life and death; the Amenta for the land of the dead. They appeared a lot in Sir George's journal.

"You have come, then," a low, rough voice said. A woman emerged from a door half-hidden behind one of the tapestries. She was dressed somewhat like Elspeth Rosse, in flowing silk robes of emerald-green and flashing silver, but her face was as heavily lined as a dried apple beneath her green, plumed turban, her eyes burning-dark. She sat down on one of the chairs, and gazed up at Flora with an air of calm expectancy.

Confused, Flora slowly sat across from her. "Where have I come, madame?"

"I am called Asenanth. And you are the Daughter of Nephthys."

Flora was impressed by the woman's deep, all-knowing tone, her serene demeanor, her air of certainty about whatever strange thing she was talking about. It would be a valuable lesson to learn in her own business. This woman must be a friend of Elspeth's. "Daughter of Nephthys?" She remembered what she'd heard of the goddess who inspired Sir George's temple, the mother of Anubis, goddess of rebirth and darkness.

"Your hair." Asenath waved her hand, long, gnarled fingers adorned with turquoise and lapis rings, at Flora's whorls of red hair pinned beneath her straw boater hat. "I knew you would be here one day. We need you." She fanned the cards out over the table, tapping at her chin as she studied them.

"What is it?" Flora asked, her hand closing reflexively over her amulet. It somehow helped her feel more steady.

"The Tower," Asenath said, tapping at an image of a winged goddess casting a beam of light down on an altar presided over by the dog-headed Anubis.

Flora nodded. The same card she'd drawn at her own table, signifying change, upheaval. Coming to Egypt had certainly been a change!

"And the Reversed Magician," Asenath said. "Deception, the misuse of power. You must be careful." She gasped as she studied the next one.

"What is it?"

"The Reversed Sword. A high number."

"The potential for violence," Flora whispered.

"But you must seek the surrounding cards; look for a more nuanced horizon. You know that, my dear Nephthys." She tapped at a card, a woman in a pleated robe and crown, holding onto a wild beast. "The Strength card. This is you. You have courage, and you shall need it very soon." She frowned, and closed her eyes as if suddenly weary. "Beware! Always be careful."

The silence that fell between them was heavy, thick. Confused, Flora rose to leave.

"You must stop suppressing your true gift. You

must fulfill your destiny," Asenath said in a low, rough voice. "Be very careful." She waved Flora away.

For a moment, emerging into the sun after the close darkness, the feeling of being out of real time and space, was disorienting. Flora blinked, letting the distant noise of the souk and the heat of the advancing morning, wash over her. She was in the spirit business herself, she knew all its little tricks and illusions—trap doors and sliding panels, painted balloons, wires, cheesecloth as ectoplasm. Yet this woman had her rather flummoxed. She glanced back, half-expecting the shop to have vanished altogether. The door was shut tight, no sign of what lay behind it.

"It's just this place, the light here," she whispered to herself. It was disorienting to someone used to the fog and gloom of London. She turned and hurried along the wooden walkway to her original errand.

Lady Crosbie's shop was very different from the cramped booths of the souk below. Large, bright, with tall windows draped in sheer organza, lined with glittering glass cases overflowing with carefully arranged treasures. The whitewashed walls were hung with paintings and mosaics, while gowns and shawls fluttered from racks. It was elegant, quiet, beckoning shoppers in for a closer look. Flora leaned closer to one of the cases, examining an array of beaded cuff bracelets.

"May I assist you?" she heard someone ask, and glanced up to find a clerk watching her. A slim, neat young man in a well-cut blue suit, his dark hair pomaded to a patent shine, pince-nez balanced on his nose. He looked like someone who would keep any shop in utmost tidy, customer-ready shape. He watched her with a little frown.

"How do you do?" Flora answered with a bright smile. "I am Miss Flora Flowerdew. I met Lady Crosbie at Shepheard's and heard all about her lovely shop. I just had to see it." She moved around the cases, examining a

135

tumble of bright silk scarves setting off gold collars. "It is certainly very beautiful."

The young man's suspicious expression shifted a bit at the little compliment. "We do pride ourselves very much on our unique items, Mademoiselle Flowerdew, and on our discerning clientele. I am Thomas Baynton, the manager."

"You do a lovely job here, Mr. Baynton, I'm sure Lady Crosbie finds you an absolute treasure. Have you worked here very long?"

"A year or so. Let me find Lady Crosbie for you, I am sure she will want to greet you herself."

He bustled out of the room, leaving Flora to examine more of the enticing wares. Behind one of the counters was a stack of small crates, labeled "Turquoise headdress" and "Slippers, gold embroidery," in a beautiful, curling penmanship that somehow seemed a part of the whole lovely shop.

"Miss Flowerdew! How kind you are to visit my little place," Melanie Crosbie trilled as she floated into the room on a cloud of black silk and white ruffled lace. In the daylight, she looked even more beautiful than at dinner, her pale cheeks pinkened, her dark hair glossy and piled high, fastened with gold and turquoise combs shaped like pharaohs' feathered fans.

"It is a lovely place indeed," Flora said. "You must have a keen eye to maintain such a fine inventory."

"Oh, it is just my little hobby, to keep me busy while Georgie was away from me so often. I fear I have no head for business, though I daresay I know true style, true taste, when I see it." Her dark pink lips suddenly turned down at the corners, and she dabbed at her eyes with a lacy handkerchief. "But now I suppose this shop is all I have, having lost my dearest love. I shall have to work at it even harder! What are your favorites in these cases, then, Miss Flowerdew?"

Flora swept a glance over the shop. "These bracelets

are very beautiful." She gestured to the case of gold and silver cuff bracelets, etched with images of gods in profile and inlaid with lapis and carnelian and garnets.

Melanie leaned closer, her summer-rose perfume wafting around her. "Oh, yes, these do sell well. Just copies, of course, but so very pretty, and ladies can show them off to their friends back in London with no one knowing they aren't ancient." She removed one of the bracelets from the case, an image of Anubis surrounded by chunks of amber and turquoise. She handed it to Flora and urged her to try it on. "It does suit you. But your pendant is also beautiful. Very distinctive. Cat items do sell very well. I daresay it must be a genuine antiquity!"

Flora touched the cat, fighting the strange urge to close her fingers protectively over it. "I'm not sure, though I suppose it might be. It was a gift from Monsieur d'Etrages."

A frown flickered over Melanie's alabaster brow, quickly banished. "From Jacques? Oh, you lucky ducky! He never parts with any of his findings. He must really like you."

Did she sound—jealous? How strange. Jacques was decades older than both her and Flora, and Melanie seemed to have any man she glanced at wrapped around her dainty finger. Or maybe she very much wanted the cat for her shop. "Your husband must have gifted you with some gorgeous pieces, Lady Crosbie. Like those earrings here, maybe? I'm sure I saw some rather like them at the British Museum." She gestured to the red-and-blue beaded triangles Melanie wore.

Melanie touched the tip of the earring flashing below her curls. "Yes, they were from Georgie. I do have some of similar design in that case, as well." As she showed Flora a tray of earrings, Thomas Baynton appeared in a doorway, watching silently.

"They are very beautiful," Flora murmured.

Melanie flicked at one carnelian bead with a rueful smile. "I confess I much prefer something more modern in style. But things such as these were Georgie's delight, and I always wanted to make him happy. And they do sell so well!" An ormolu clock on a gilded table chimed, and Thomas tapped at his pocket watch. "Oh, my, it does grow late! Time has no meaning for me since the tragedy. Do let me offer you some mint tea, Miss Flowerdew, I always take some at this hour. A local specialty. It is most refreshing in this heat."

Flora could see why. The shop suddenly felt claustrophobic in all that light, the cases crowding closer, and things seemed a bit hazy. It was rather strange. "Thank you, that does sound delightful."

As Thomas left, Melanie led Flora to a table near one of the tall windows, looking down on the canopies of the souk. She chatted lightly about life in Cairo, parties she had attended, her friends, nothing about Sir George.

"And you must try these," Melanie said, holding out a plate of glistening, pastel-colored sweets. "Thomas finds them at the souk, I do love them."

"How delectable," Flora exclaimed as she took a nibble—honey and almonds, like a burst of sunshine.

"They are one of my favorite things about living here, the wonderful sweets."

Flora remembered that Melanie was the daughter of a viscount who had supported archaeology, that she was the third wife of Sir George. "Have you lived in Cairo very long?"

Melanie glanced away, her gaze hazy, as if she remembered—or tried to forget. "Oh, on and off for as long as I can remember. I had delicate health as a child, and my father, Lord Edgemont, had an interest in Egyptology, so it all seemed to come together perfectly. We lived here in the winter, my father sponsoring digs and my mother and I visiting health resorts where I could breathe more freely."

"And did you like it here then?"

Melanie's eyes widened, startled. "Like it?"

"Or maybe you missed England terribly."

"I—I never really thought about it, never could have thought to like or dislike. It was just our life." She took a careful sip of tea. "I suppose I was rather envious about the girls I read about in books, going to stay at school, making friends, playing in snow and ice-skating. And I think my mother missed it, though she was completely devoted to my health, and doted on me as I was her only child. As I grew up, I wanted parties and music, and that can be found here. Society in Cairo can be very merry indeed!"

"Your parents must have been delighted when you married Sir George! With your father's interests and everything."

Melanie turned away to pour more tea. "Oh, sadly they had both departed this plane by then, though Georgie did know my father from years before. I'm sure they both expected me to marry a scholar of some sort, but ..." She broke off, shaking her head until those earrings shimmered.

Flora leaned closer. "But?"

"Well—my Georgie was a darling, but rather *older* than me. And so preoccupied with his work! I seldom saw him, and we were quite disappointed never to be blessed with a little family. James was such a disappointment to Georgie, I'm afraid to say. Not as intelligent and energetic as he should have been. Georgie was always at his temple, while I was here in the city. I didn't even know he had gone to London! That was why I'm glad I have this shop, to distract me, and I do love it! But— oh." Thomas appeared to hand her handkerchief, like magic, and she sniffled into its snowy folds. "How I miss my darling-warling man! How ever shall I go on?"

Flora reached out to squeeze Melanie's hand. "I am so very sorry."

Melanie gave a wavering, brave smile. "How kind you are, Miss Flowerdew! How kind everyone has been. I'm so happy you came here today to keep me company. And so happy you are joining us on our little excursion up the river to see Georgie's beloved temple! It should be a great pilgrimage."

"And it will give us a chance to find a bit more inventory, to talk to Mrs. Herbert, who helps us find supplies," Thomas murmured, as he poured more tea for them. "We are shockingly low, dear Lady Crosbie."

Melanie sighed, and glanced around her shop. To Flora's eyes, the place was a veritable Aladdin's cave, stuffed with alluring beauties. Where would more fit? Though, strangely, no customers had appeared.

"Yes, indeed. I do find many artisans at Al-Kehem, the village near the temple. Mrs. Herbert lives there and helps us with sources, and sometimes I can persuade Assim to help." Melanie's eyes narrowed as she looked at Flora's pendant again. "But maybe you would consider selling me your darling cat, Miss Flowerdew?"

"Selling?" Flora held up the cat on her silver chain, studying it in the light. It looked a little different, a little shinier, and seemed warm under her fingers. "No, I don't think so. It was a gift, after all, and I have become quite attached to her. I daresay something like this, probably a copy, can't be worth much."

Melanie and Thomas exchanged a long glance. "My patrons do enjoy cat items! They had such resonance and meaning for the ancients. I myself prefer a nice Pekingese. You have a dog yourself, do you not, Miss Flowerdew?"

"Yes. Chou-Chou. A Pomeranian, quite my darling." And she would be quite a *furious* darling, if Flora didn't return soon to take her for a walk and a treat from Shepheard's kitchen. She didn't like it when Flora went on errands without her, but needs must. "I'm very excited to see the temple, though! It must have such magic about it."

Melanie frowned. "It has a great deal of dust, and lots of bits of pottery. But it is a pretty site indeed, near the river, set on a rise where there are lovely views. We should have a jolly time!" She reached one polished fingertip toward the pendant, not quite touching it. "And really, Miss Flowerdew—may I call you Flora? I do think we will be such friends. If you ever decided to sell your pretty little necklace, do let me know."

Flora closed her hand tight around her little Bastet. "I will remember that, thank you, Melanie. But I think I'll keep it for now."

"Just don't forget!" She led Flora out of the shop, showing off the glittering wares. Among the fluttering scarves and glittering glass cases, Flora thought she noticed a door hidden behind a rack. When she discreetly tried to open it, as Melanie pointed out a statue of Isis in the other direction, she found it quite stuck. What could be behind it? Just storage, or something more?

Lady Crosbie did not seem the sort to be a criminal mastermind, engineering her husband's death in London while she stayed safe in Cairo, but really one could never tell. It was often the wide-eyed lambikins who were the meanest underneath.

"You must keep this," Lady Crosbie said, gently touching the beaded cuff bracelet she'd given Flora, making sure it was fastened on her gloved wrist. "I shall see you very soon, I'm sure! I have the feeling we will be good friends."

The light outside was turning mellow, like the slow slide of warm caramel, and the souk was not quite as crowded. Flora thought she remembered the way back to the hotel, but once down in the close-packed lanes of booths and tall houses everything appeared quite different. She couldn't quite recall if this was the way she came; everything blurred together.

She took a deep breath and turned one way she thought she remembered, next to a spice shop. After that, she was utterly baffled. The warm, mercilessly clear sun beating down on her didn't help. She put up her parasol and kept walking. Surely she'd have to find *something* she knew?

She made her way down a narrow alley, where sound was echoing and distant, the warm air smelling of rotting vegetables and damp laundry, and emerged into a small square with a cracked old fountain at its center. Weeds sprouted between the flagstones, and the houses were a peeling, dingy, pale yellow with faded red shutters. Laundry flapped on lines between the buildings, a few children playing a kickball game around the fountain, and some ancient old men paused their gossiping in a doorway to stare at her. But at least she wasn't alone there, as she'd felt in the alley.

She tried to ask directions with the few words of Arabic she'd picked up, but they stared and shrugged. She had the strangest, coldest feeling she really should not be there.

She started to walk away, and glanced back to find a figure cast half in darkness at the edge of the buildings. He was not tall, not short, neither thin nor fat, draped in a loose, blue-striped cloak that covered everything and a hood drawn low over their brow. She just could just make out the glint of eyes underneath, staring right at her. A man or woman? She couldn't quite tell.

Flora had spent her whole life on an acute knife's edge of caution and alertness—she had to, with the orphanage, the streets, the cheap theaters. And her tingly-sense told her something was amiss here.

She tucked her amulet into the collar of her pale blue walking suit jacket, and held her parasol handle tight as she glanced about for a swift exit. The men and children had vanished, and the shadows seemed even deeper.

The figure took a purposeful step toward her, then another one, and she glimpsed a distinctive red cap beneath the hood, unlike any she'd seen anyone else wearing. It was time for action. She whirled around and hurried as fast as she could without running and using up her strength, exiting the square. She went down one alley, cursing as it looked like a dead end just before it took a sharp turn down another alley. The sky above her was shut out by the close-packed roofs, and she could hear the echo of steady steps behind her. She wasn't sure which direction to go next.

Suddenly, she felt the hem of her skirt stir, and glanced down to see a little black cat with shining, pale-green eyes. It was just like in her dream of the night-time pool, but this cat seemed real, its glossy fur shining.

"Where did you come from?" she demanded. The cat just shook its head as if to say, *Don't be a fool! Just follow me. Hurry!* The cat trotted off, as if confident Flora would follow.

And so she did. The footsteps, steadily clicking, hastened, came closer. She rushed after the cat, faster and faster, along lane after lane, turn after turn.

Just as she tumbled out into another courtyard, she felt a hand clutch at her sleeve, another reach for her Bastet amulet to try and snap its chain. She beat backwards with her parasol, gratified by the pained grunt. The grasp fell away, and she ran for all she was worth. She glimpsed the cat's sinuous black tail vanish around a corner, and she followed.

To her relieved amazement, she glimpsed the gleaming white hotel in the distance, a straight path. There were suddenly crowds of people. The cat was nowhere to be seen.

To cover her red-faced agitation, Flora snapped her

parasol open to shield her and wasted no time heading right for Shepheard's.

"Flora! There you are at last—we've been waiting for you. Whatever is wrong?"

It was Benedict, his golden hair shining in the sun, his face etched with worry. She longed to run to him, to hold onto him tightly.

"I—I'm fine, Dukie," she gasped as she reached his side, and somehow managed to smile. "Just went out for a bit of shopping."

His expression darkened, turned thunderous as he examined her torn sleeve, the red mark on her neck where her chaser tried to snap the amulet's chain. "Where on earth were you shopping?"

"The souk. I wanted to find Lady C's shop."

"I wouldn't have thought Lady C ran a fight club as well as selling trinkets," he growled.

Flora had to laugh. "Not all. I was—I was followed when I left. Someone in a red hat and striped robe. I think they wanted my amulet."

He gave her a stern frown. "You should have taken me with you."

"It was silly of me to venture out alone in a strange city. I promise I won't do it again." Still a little shaky, she gratefully took Benedict's offered arm and leaned on it as he led her back into the hotel. He was always such a warm, reassuring presence, and she felt safe again.

"Did you learn anything at the shop, then?" he asked, urging her to sit down in one of the green satin chairs around the lobby. He waved to a footman for a brandy.

"Not much." She told him about the inventory of the shop, the locked door, Lady Crosbie's loyal clerk, Melanie's offer to buy the cat necklace. She didn't mention the fortune-teller. "I don't get the sense that the Crosbies had a blissful marriage. She said he was often gone, and she was lonely with no family. But she also seems to live her own life, has her own work to occupy her, and he certainly didn't seem to stand in her way. And she was here in Egypt when he came to London, says she didn't even know he had left. I doubt she has a magical potion to be in two places at once."

'Maybe that's why she wants your amulet," he gently teased. He handed her the brandy, urging her to sip at it. "for its magical powers."

Flora touched the necklace, remembering the cat that led her out of the alleys. "Did you see the cat, then?"

"Cat?"

"A black one, it led me out of the maze of lanes and courtyards, ahead of our robed pursuer."

Benedict glanced around the lobby, taking in the potted palms in silver pots, the brocade chairs. "I didn't see it, no. But if we do find it, it deserves a great deal of fish, I think. Come along, Flora, drink that up, and then you should have a little rest before dinner. Are you hungry? Maybe they could bring us a tea tray in the garden."

Flora was very tempted. The hotel garden was so beautiful, a paradise, and she always loved time with Benedict. But ... "There's no time to waste, Dukie. Did you forget we're off on a Nile cruise tomorrow, to the Temple of Nephthys? There's bound to be more clues there. Oodles of packing to do!"

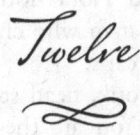

Twelve

lora froze in her footsteps when they came in sight of their dahabiya, the *Falcon*, waiting in its slip. She could barely believe it wasn't a dream, that this would actually be their home for the next few days! It looked absolutely magical, long and narrow with two sails that would carry them down the river, gleaming red-brown in the sun. The decks were shaded with blue-and-white striped awnings, inviting lazy afternoons watching the river float by.

"Like a bleedin' fairy story, it is," Mary gasped, hoisting Chou-Chou's basket higher in her arms. Even the dog was wide-eyed, unable to bark as she took it all in. She held the dog close as they pushed their way through the crowds of shouting vendors on the dock.

"It looks as if we're the first to arrive," Imogen said briskly, and marched up the gangplank, the feathers on her large green-and-white hat waving merrily in the breeze. No one dared get in her way.

Flora wasn't surprised they were the first; some of their party had split off and gone ahead to the temple, including James and Theodore, Assim the foreman, and Evie, who wanted to gather "atmosphere" for her story. But Flora was glad to have a few minutes to explore the boat while it was quieter.

Members of the crew, clad in beige robes and blue knitted hats that matched the paint trim of the *Falcon*, waited on deck to greet them with bows. One of them stepped forward, and Flora noticed he wore striped robes, rather like the man who chased her in the souk, but there were no red caps.

"*Nebty*. I am Farouk, head steward. You are most welcome," he said. "You are the first aboard! Shall I show you the ship? Refreshments have been laid in the salon, and your luggage shall be taken at once to your cabins."

"Thank you very much," Imogen answered. "We are delighted to be here. What a beautiful vessel!"

They were led along the gleaming teakwood deck, shaded with a blue-and-white striped awning and lined with cushioned deck chairs that surely would offer wide, glorious views of the banks of the Nile. Flora could just imagine lounging there with a pile of books, watching temples and villages glide past amid the palms, the snapping of the wind in the sails overhead, birds soaring and swirling in the endless turquoise sky.

Farouk led them through open glass doors into cool shade, the scent of lilies and incense in the air. A narrow corridor led to cabins, sitting rooms, and the large salon at the stern.

"This is where most meals are served, unless it is desired on deck," Farouk said.

Flora gazed around, impressed. It was the most comfortable, cozy space she'd ever seen. Lined with bookcases, it was scattered with deep armchairs and settees, newspapers and magazines fanned atop dressers, with a floral-patterned carpet underfoot. One large table—surely meant to be the dining space—was set up for study now with more books—most of whose titles showed they were about Egyptian history and art—maps, pens, and paper. The light was amber, diffuse, from pierced tin lampshades, and the windows were swagged in blue satin and muslin draperies.

Flora longed to examine the papers more closely, to dive into work, but Farouk led them onward. There was a breakfast room, surprisingly modern with all sorts of chafing dishes and gadgets on the sideboard, and a line of more cabins. Flora's chamber was all pale green and cream, cool against the heat of the day, small but with everything she could possibly need: a tiny desk laid with stationery and an array of pens. A little dressing table holding scent bottles and silver brushes. Cabinets and cupboards. There was even a large cushion for Chou-Chou, and a row of silver-etched water bowls. A stewardess in white robes efficiently unpacked and tucked away the cases, gowns, and toiletries all in their places.

She glanced out the porthole to watch the bustle of the dock as they prepared to depart, and she wondered where Benedict was. He'd sent a note at breakfast at Shepheard's to say he would be arriving a little late, but no explanation. He'd been strangely quiet, watchful since she was followed in the souk.

There was a clatter and commotion on the other side of the deck, and Flora hurried out to see what was happening. With Chou-Chou at her heels and Mary close behind, she made her way outside and up some steps to find Lady Crosbie arriving, along with her clerk Thomas and Richard White, both of them carrying boxes and staying close like attendant knights. She'd left behind her blacks already and wore palest gray trimmed with peach lace and fastened with ancient carved carnelians as buttons. The white feathers and bows of her hat tossed in the river breeze, and blew her lace veil against her delicate face and throat most fetchingly. Flora couldn't help but remember theater scenes, and she'd really never seen one better framed.

As Melanie paused to cast a long glance over the deck, all the men in sight froze and stared at her ethereal, goddess-like figure. The beautiful, tragic widow, bravely marching onward. She didn't appear to notice them at all, until she stretched out a lace-gloved hand to her side without looking. Mr. North took it, watching her intently.

"Oh, Richard," she murmured. "I somehow sense I shall never see my home again in this moment ..."

Amid this strange little scene, there was a crash, a thud, and Chou-Chou yelped. Flora spun around to see some of Lady Crosbie's trunks had tumbled from their cart, cracking, and porters scurried around to straighten them.

Lady Crosbie certainly didn't travel light, Flora noted. Several fine gray leather trunks and cases, stamped MC, formed pyramids of their own, not to mention hatboxes and jewel cases. She wondered what on earth ladies were *meant* to wear in the desert, on dusty archaeological digs, and thought of her own small trunks ruefully.

"Oh, Miss Flowerdew! Flora. I am so glad you're here," Melanie cried when she spied Flora standing there. She rushed to her side and seized her hand, quite as if they were now bosom-beaus. "It's all terribly exciting, isn't it? James has said we are to have a grand tour of the Temple of Horus, which I have never seen before, even though it's quite on the way to the Temple of Nephthys, and Mr. Lewis-Clunes has taken charge of the dig there. It's such a shame my Georgie was not given the concession for both sites—they do say Lord Pebbleston made quite a wreck of the Temple of Horus when it was under his care."

"A wreck?" Flora said. She couldn't help but wonder again if this whole nasty business had arisen from professional jealousy.

"Yes, so sad, so many things going missing from the site," Melanie said, then sighed and pressed her hand to her brow, causing Richard and Thomas to leap to her side. "I am so fatigued after such hurried preparations to depart. I do feel quite faint!"

"Shall I see you to your cabin?" Thomas offered eagerly, reaching for her arm.

She shook him back. "Oh, heavens no! How can I just lie there when there is so much to see? I must do my Georgie proud, and be brave now." She straightened her hat, and took Flora's hand. "Do come with me into the salon, Miss Flowerdew, and I'm sure we can order some champagne to revive us. I am sure we shall be such friends. I felt it when you came to my shop! You do *understand* things. I need such friends now."

She drew Flora onward, leaving Richard and Thomas looking after them forlornly. Melanie waggled her fingers at them, and they rushed to follow.

"I do hope so, Lady Crosbie," Flora murmured.

"Call me Melanie, do!"

"I always need as many friends as I can find." They went into the cool, flower-scented salon, and Flora settled on a silk-cushioned chair at one of the small, round tables, Chou-Chou leaping into her lap. Lady Crosbie sat across from her, like a bird alighting lightly, Richard and Thomas to either side of her. Flora again thought of the theater, and raised a brow at Mary, who sat in the corner to watch it all.

As champagne and platters of fruit, almonds, and honey-cakes were laid before them, Flora noticed a case of jeweled scarabs laid between vases of flowers, glinting green and blue and crimson like living beings.

A steward hurried forward to pour the wine, and she glanced up to find him watching her closely, his eyes wide, face grey-pale. He seemed rather familiar, but his face was partially concealed by the folds of a scarf attached to his turban. "Help us, sahib," he whispered furtively. "We, and you are in danger here." His palpable fear made Flora feel suddenly cold and clammy, her heart pound. Could this be the man who followed her in the souk or something like that? Was it fear, not menace, that drove her pursuer that day?

"What is amiss?' she whispered back, under cover of taking a cake from the platter.

"You're spilling the champagne, man!" Richard snapped, and the steward stumbled back. He was trembling so hard Flora feared he could say no more.

"Look for me on deck later," she whispered to him. He nodded, and rushed from the salon.

Lady Crosbie sighed. "It is nearly impossible here to hire reliable staff. I know I must live here for my health, but how I long for English housekeepers!"

"You have not thought of trying to return to England, then?" Flora asked, still unsettled by the steward. She took a sip of the champagne, letting the fine bubbles settle her nerves. She was still quite unsettled by the steward, so much so she imagined she saw him dashing past the dining room window toward the gangplank. She blinked hard, and there was no one there.

Melanie sighed again, and shook her head. "My health could not bear the damp and chill, no matter how much I long for the civilized fashions and conversation! And I have my shop now, I cannot leave it. It's all I have, now that Georgie is gone."

"It is a beautiful place indeed. You must be proud of it," Flora said. But alongside the memory of the beauty and enticing scents and sights of the souk, she well-remembered the cold sensation of being followed, constantly watched.

"It's my great pride," Melanie said, a wide smile flashing over her face, banishing the weary sadness. Her eyes narrowed as she glanced at Flora, at the pendant at her throat. "But I do wish I could persuade you to sell me your pretty little necklace, Flora! Cats are always such a fine seller."

Flora wondered why she wanted it so much, with all the beauties in her shop case, brighter and flashier than the little cat. It made her feel even more protective of her Bastet, which she'd grown quite attached to. She covered it with one hand, feeling it grow warmer. It seemed to positively purr under her touch, and a low growl started in Chou-Chou.

"It was a gift, I couldn't part with it," she said.

Melanie sat back in her chair with a little pout. Richard poured her more champagne. "Ah, well, as you must! We shall certainly see some fine jewelry at the Temple of Horus, if James can persuade Mr. Lewis-Clunes to show them to us and not be stingy, as he so often is."

"Is the temple under Mr. Lewis-Clunes's concession now? And is he so very protective of it? I understood he worked at the Egyptian Museum."

Melanie glanced at Richard. "He oversees the Temple of Horus right now for Lord Pebbleston. I fear I have no head for such business! I am sure Georgie would not have given him such a task."

"The Temple of Horus was once a center for the rites of Horus, the falcon-headed son of Isis and Osiris. He was said to have lost an eye in the battle with the evil Seth, but it was magically healed by Thoth, and thus he can control both the sun and the moon," Richard said. "And Mr. Lewis-Clunes, like so many of us, is quite obsessed with such tales. Even Sir George avidly studied the myth of Nephthys, her flame-colored hair and domain over the darkness."

"James has long wanted the work there, but Mr. Lewis-Clunes has managed to block him at every turn," Melanie said, reaching for more champagne. Thomas quickly leaped ahead of her and poured it. "He says James's skill will never match Georgie's, and that is true enough. Few could ever match his accomplishments. But I hear that James is quite competent."

"Oh, you know that isn't the reason," Thomas said with a sly smile.

Melanie giggled behind her glass. "Indeed, Thomas, you are quite right."

Flora was most intrigued, as she always was by scholarly gossip. Or any kind of gossip, really, it was her bread and butter in the séance game. She tilted her head in tandem with Chou-Chou as they studied the little group, everyone seeming so ordinary, so at ease. Yet she sensed some tension beneath, something she could not quite grasp yet. "Is there a professional quarrel between them, then? Mr. Lewis-Clunes and Mr. Crosbie?"

"I would say so," Richard muttered.

"Oh, Miss Flowerdew, if we are to be such good friends, you must be warned," Melanie said with a trill of laughter. "We are such a tiny group here in Egypt, and know everything about everyone. I believe—we *all* believe—James is rather infatuated with Clara Lewis-Clunes, and her husband surely realizes it. He treats her so with such shocking neglect, how can he be surprised! It is the green-eyed monster."

Flora was rather surprised by this. James Crosbie didn't seem the sort to harbor an illicit passion, nor did Paul Lewis-Clunes seem the sort to care much. But romance, especially in small, hothouse atmospheres like the one here in Egypt, could bloom in strange spots. Melanie Crosbie was a beautiful woman, with an older husband whose work obsessed him. It would not be strange that she collected admirers eager to rescue her. "How shocking! Are his feelings returned by Mrs. Lewis-Clunes?"

"Who knows for sure?" Thomas said with a smirk. "She is such an odd sort of lady, keeps so many things hidden under all that silly chatter. But I think it's quite clear she doesn't really love her husband, don't you think?"

"How can she?" Melanie laughed. "Just look at his

154

eyes, such a cold fish. And they were *all* so jealous of my Georgie. Of his accomplishments." Richard handed her a lacy handkerchief, and she dabbed at her eyes. "Any of them could have done this dreadful thing! Oh, Miss Flowerdew—Flora. Perhaps you are wise. I should leave this poisonous place. It is too, too dangerous, and I have such fears."

Richard laid his hand on her arm. "You are always among friends here, Melanie. No one can hurt you now."

She covered his hand with her own, making Thomas scowl. "Oh, Richard. My knight in shining armor! What would I do without you all? Yes, I *shall* be brave, I am resolved. I must find out what happened to my husband. I owe it to Georgie." She glanced about for a steward. "More champagne, my dears?"

Richard leaned toward Flora and whispered, "They do say it is not just James Crosbie who is in love with Clara Lewis-Clunes, Miss Flowerdew."

Flora was startled that this man, who seemed so dignified, would be so gossipy. But she wasn't one to turn away information. "Oh?"

"So was Sir George. But Melanie must hear nothing of it."

Now Flora was really shocked. Not that it sounded like Sir George was a saint—he'd been in love with Imogen, lost his first wife, surely he wasn't a monk. But Clara Lewis-Clunes? And if it was true, surely that, combined with professional jealousy, was enough to drive him to murder?

Before she could find words to reply, Imogen hurried into the salon, with Benedict and Jacques on either arm. She had obviously had time while Flora gathered gossip to change her clothes, to fluttering, gossamer pale robes that Flora quite envied. "Oh, my dears! How very cozy you look. Isn't this the most darling little boat you have ever seen? What a grand time we shall all have! Oh, is that champagne?"

Flora almost laughed. Imogen didn't know the half of the "grand times" these people seemed to be having, what with all the newly-discovered affairs to add to the opaque stew of it all. Benedict seemed to notice her flash of wry amusement, and he raised a golden brow at her in question. It was funny how they could communicate without a word now. She shook her head and mouthed, *Later*.

Chou-Chou crept a sneaky paw across the table for a cake, distracting everyone. It was only later, when Flora asked about the steward who had begged for her help, that she found no such man onboard and no one who knew him ...

~

After dinner, their river journey underway, Flora strolled with Benedict on deck. She told him what the strange waiter had told her, and they mulled on who he could be, what he wanted. "I hope you'll be careful, Flora," he said solemnly. "At the souk back in Cairo ..."

"Yes, I know. But you're here with me now, Dukie. I'm sure there's not much that could happen here on the river."

She tilted back her head to take in the vast night sky stretching overhead. She'd really never imagined anything like it, that dusty, purple-blue expanse dotted with twinkling, diamond-like stars that flashed down at her. The moon, a crescent of pale gold, reflected and refracted on the water, washing over the silhouettes of mud-brick buildings on the distant banks. She heard the cry of a bird soaring overhead, smelled flowers and the green, sharp scent of burning herbs covering the ancient smell of the river. It felt as if that place had always been exactly thus, and would be long after they were gone.

Though she heard laughter and chatter from the salon, where the others played cards after a delectable dinner, she felt all alone with Benedict, drifting over the water out of time. She wasn't Flora Flowerdew, or Florrie Gubbin, she was just *herself*. Maybe Elspeth Rosse was right—they were all just souls, moving through lives, worlds, bumping up against the same places, the same people, over and over again.

She studied his profile in the moonlight, as elegant as any Egyptian king. Every glance felt like a stolen treasure, a moment between reality and dreams with him. He was unattainable, a star too far from her grasp, yet close enough to light the whole world.

She turned away from that ache of longing, from him. She reached into her reticule for one of the Turkish cigarettes she'd "borrowed" from Evie, a rare treat, and lit it to let that hint of intoxicating spice add to the strange feelings.

"Got one of those to share?" Benedict asked.

"For you, Dukie, of course." She handed him a cigarette, his fingers brushing hers, lingering just a moment too long. Just like the magic of the Egyptian sky, he took her breath quite away. Made her imagine past lives, new dreams, things that couldn't be.

But he was there with her at that one moment, and it all felt so very *right*. He belonged there, with the stars and the flowered breeze. And for once, she felt she could belong there with him, that she was safe when she was with him. Home. The memory of that dream, the reflecting pool, the man's voice calling to her, and she took a deeper drag on the smoke to try and steady herself.

"This is nice," he said, glancing down at the dark cigarette.

"Thanks to Evie. She didn't even see me filch them back in Cairo. They're ever so much nicer than the gaspers I get in London." She watched how the tiny flame cast his sharply carved Viking face into angles and shadows. He smelled deliciously alluringly of sandal-wood soap. She edged away a bit along the railing, even as she just wanted to move closer and closer.

But he was a duke, and she was a fortune teller, in this life. Bugger it all.

"I can see you wouldn't want to go inside and miss all this," he said, gesturing with the tiny light of his cigarette at the night around them. "Who could ever leave such a sight? No wonder my father's travels just took him ever onward. Thornhill has nothing to compare."

"Would you want to just—keep going? Move ahead, to Africa, maybe, China, Russia, wherever?"

Benedict laughed, rough and dark as a good whiskey on a cold night. "Who wouldn't? To just explore and see and learn—it must be perfection. If a man has someone to see and marvel with him, that is."

Flora didn't dare look at him, didn't dare let her longings show. To wander the world, seeing new places, finding new mysteries, with him, it would be glorious.

"And leave all the London debs bereft?" she said lightly. "That wouldn't be fair of you. But maybe one of them harbors a secret yen to travel, you never know!"

He laughed wryly. "If there is, I haven't found her yet. What are the glories of the Yangtze, the Amazon, next to Royal Ascot and the Glorious Twelfth?"

"But you can't have met *all* of them yet." She glanced back at the laughing group in the salon, brightly lit, so English in this strange place. It didn't seem right. Something was definitely out of place in this puzzle. "And adventures aren't always what they're cracked up to be."

"Are you still afraid, after what happened in the souk, and with that strange steward?" Benedict asked gently. His fingers brushed against her arm, a fleeting touch that shouldn't have meant anything. But it did. It always did with him. "After all this, shall we say, inter-esting gossip?"

"Not interesting in the social sense, I'd say, and that's the thing," Flora said, taking a tiny step back from him, from his tempting warmth. She tried to think only of Sir George, of what she'd learned aboard the *Falcon*. "By all accounts, Sir George was a brilliant archaeologist, a great scientist, renowned. But he surrounded himself with such, shall we say, *mediocrities*! Their devotion to their work here in Egypt seems only to serve their ambition, not the history and culture. James, Richard North, Paul Lewis-Clunes. Why did he work with them? Lady Crosbie is absorbed by her delicate health; she seems like that Sir George, despite her protestations, left her lonely and unfulfilled, with only her shop to comfort her. Maybe he even had affairs! It sounds like he was a dismissive, disappointed father to James. Surely, there are dozens of serious scholars clamoring to work with him, and he chose Richard North. Why this group? Why a wife like Melanie when he could have had someone like Imogen?"

Benedict grew quiet, frowning thoughtfully. "They do seem to have a great amount of ambition to be known, renowned, as Sir George was, in English circles. Ambition with nowhere to put it, thwarted by someone, can be dangerous. Maybe Sir George's death reshuffles the deck for them?"

"At the very least, it will be quite the scramble to find out who takes over the Temple of Nephthys." Flora smoked in silence for a moment, going over all the players. "But why would he, Sir George, choose to keep them near him? There's something, surely many things, here that we can't see yet. They seem like the typical English sorts abroad, but ..."

"But, what?" Benedict asked. "What are you thinking of?"

She laughed. "If I knew that, could see clearly in my own head, we'd have the solution lickety-split. But speaking of secrets, what do you think of the notion that Clara might be having an affair with James Crosbie? Or possibly even one with Sir George himself?"

"Crikey," Benedict sighed, sounding just like Mary. "Mousy Mrs. Lewis-Clunes? You're right, there are hidden depths here. Just like this river." He tossed the end of his cigarette into the dark water, a flashing arc of light.

"Yes, everyone has hidden depths. I wouldn't be so surprised. I've seen the most odd people taken over by passion before. Maybe Melanie had her eyes on another prize, too! So many possibilities ..."

Benedict's expression turned solemn. He touched her arm again, the heat of his skin lingering on hers, binding them together. "And maybe you go too close to one of those, and that's why you were followed, why this chap here wanted to warn you."

Flora waved this away, though truthfully, she felt lingering, chilly disquiet about it all. "I'm sure it was just some ordinary pickpocket in the souk. I shall be more cautious in the future. And as for the steward, he has quite vanished. Maybe he just wanted to scare me."

"If you're sure ..." Benedict said, but he sounded quite doubtful.

"Yes, I think so."

He suddenly closed his fingers over hers, startling her, warming her. "Flora ..." he began, then shook his head. "Promise me you will be very careful. I don't know what I would do if—if for some reason you weren't here. With me."

She told herself to move, to say something, anything, but her thoughts were frozen. Did he feel it too? She tried to laugh. "Oh, Dukie. Things would be much more peaceful for you if I wasn't with you, without me and Chou-Chou dragging you into trouble like this."

"And more boring! I think—I feel ..." His hand slid away from hers, and he ran it through his hair, leaving the golden strands on end. "I'm saying this so badly. I've never known anyone like you, Flora. You are—well, you're like this night. Beautiful and mysterious. You're not just a passing breeze. You're the kind of night that stays. You make life vivid and fascinating. I feel like we understand each other, know each other, without even a word."

Flora was fearful she would start crying at his stumbling words, would sob and sob and never stop. It was just what she thought of him. He was nothing like she would have imagined a duke to be. He was kind and funny, quick-witted, and yes, he understood her. When they were together, everything just *worked*, everything was just where it should be.

But the fact was, he truly was a duke. She was Florrie Gubbin, orphan, chorus girl, a con-artist who summoned ghosts for a living. It couldn't be.

Luckily, before she could sink to the deck in a pile of tearful goo, Imogen opened the glass door to the salon and called out to her nephew. He closed his eyes tightly for a moment, and turned away.

"Just promise you will always be careful, Flora," he whispered. "I beg you."

She nodded jerkily. "I always am, Dukie. But you must promise me the same." Because she wouldn't always be there to watch over him.

He left to go to his aunt, and Flora found herself alone again in the night. The sky seemed to have shifted, grown darker, more ominous, closing in. She couldn't go back inside, smile and laugh like nothing at all had changed. She had to find her cabin, be alone with Chou-Chou. Chou-Chou always understood, never judged.

As she threw her cigarette overboard and gathered up her shawl and reticule, she gasped to see a pale figure in a darkened corner of the deck. She wondered if it was the steward who had begged for her help, then vanished, but she quickly realized it was someone else, taller, in striped robes and—and a red turban with a scarf. Like

161

the steward in the dining room, the man who followed her in the souk.

"What do you want?" she cried, and the man whirled around and ran away on silent feet. She started to run after him, then remembered what Benedict had said. *Be careful*. She shivered and let him go, resolving to firmly lock her cabin door. Even on a boat in the middle of the Nile, there was no safety.

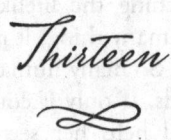
Thirteen

Despite a rather sleepless night, Flora was up early to watch the approach of the Temple of Horus, their first stop on their river adventure. She sat down on deck to watch the sun rise, and just like everything else she'd seen since coming to Egypt, it was like a dream, a wild artistic image that didn't seem real. She longed to pack it up in her valise to take back to gray, drizzly London, the sun rising high in a cloudless, hard-blue sky, its rays strong and commanding, casting a sharp clarity over the landscape. The air shimmered with its warmth, a constant reminder of the life-giving power of light.

Through the open salon doors, the breakfast buffet was being laid out, the click of silverware, the clack of glass, all perfectly set by stewards in their cream-colored robes. But none of her fellow travelers were up yet, and she didn't see the man who had begged to talk to her before he ran away. The man who might have also followed her in the souk. It made her wary of who might have noticed her snooping about, what they had to hide; she would have to be much more careful in the future not to look like such a nosy-parker.

But she knew very well that dark things tended to

lurk behind people's masks. Just like the rot of a mummy behind a golden visage.

She lifted up her little amulet to the gold-and-lavender light, watching the lifelike glint of its little green stone eyes. So many things it must have seen in its long, long existence! So many human foibles, come and gone like dust clouds. If only it could tell her about it all, protect her and help her see things clearly. She thought of the warm brush of fur she'd felt in the souk, or here onboard the *Falcon*, and smiled to think the cat could really come to life for her.

She turned it over to look at the small, flat base, but she could see no seals or stamps that might give her an answer. Except for a few chips and dings, it was smooth.

She let it drop with a sigh, and it lay against the ruffles of her shirtwaist. The sun slid higher now, burning white in the lapis sky, and she could glimpse a temple in the distance, seeming to shine a pale, creamy color. Surely they were near now.

Mary appeared, and flopped down onto the deck chair next to Flora's. She looked just as sleepless as Flora, despite the pretty, comfortable cabin. Her hair was haphazardly pinned, her eyes lined, and she whispered her longing for the lovely strong coffee Shepheard's had served. Flora laughed to think how different Mary was from a proper sort of lady's maid, and how she was lucky to be friends with her.

"Are you sure you're quite well, Mary luv?" Flora asked, as Chou-Chou padded out to join them, jumping up into her lap. "Maybe you should have a nap after breakfast?"

"Oooh, Miss Flora, I don't dare! After the dreams I had last night. I was chased by men with bird's heads, just like on those temple walls! Who knows what might happen if I'm unconscious? Who might sneak into the cabin?"

Flora frowned. She had indeed considered taking a

tincture that night, but maybe she shouldn't. Maybe they really should stay awake, stuck as they were on this boat for the moment, prey to anyone sneaking about. She should never have let her guard down, even in the beauty of the river.

Mary shook her head. "Something's wrong here, make no mistake. I have the funniest queasy feeling."

"I think you are probably right," Flora murmured, reaching down to stroke Chou-Chou's little head. Hadn't she felt it all herself? She found herself wondering what would happen when they reunited with the others.

She squeezed Mary's hand, and found it was cold despite the gathering heat of the morning. "We're all right if we're together. We always have been."

Mary squeezed back. "You should go find breakfast now, Miss Flora. We're going to need our strength."

Still feeling a cold disquiet, Flora nodded and went to find some toast and tea. Mary was right, they were going to need their strength if they were going to find out what was going on. But when she came back to the cabin, Mary was gone and a faint trace of cigarette smoke hung in the air. Flora opened a window, and turned to see her dressing table was somewhat disarranged. Nothing was missing, but she had the terrible sense someone had been there. Someone who did not belong.

~

A small barque carried them from the *Falcon* to the banks of the river, where James Crosbie and the Lewis-Clunes waited for them. Behind them was an array of workers in brown and gray, including Assim, the stern foreman.

The entrance to the complex of the Temple of Horus rose up behind them, a monumental gateway of columns and sphinxes. The weathered stone steps to reach it zig-zagged up to the plateau, sand-swept, lined with tourists in pith helmets and parasols, followed by an array of merchants shouting out their wares of "genuine mummy fingers," beads and brasses, with rising urgency. The sun was creeping higher, burnt gold, sizzling. Flora slid on her new blue-tinted glasses against the glare, and was glad she'd brought a long duster jacket. Chou-Chou fit right into one of the capacious pockets.

"Your Grace," James said, striding eagerly toward Benedict as they disembarked on the busy walkways. "We are so honored you are here today, allowing us to give you a tour! This site is similar in some ways to my father's Temple of Nephthys, so there is much to learn."

"Though it has been rather sadly despoiled over the years," Paul Lewis-Clunes added dourly. "Once it would have been much larger, with more temples leading in that direction, and a procession route lined with votive statues ..."

"Yes, indeed," James cut in. "But we must never forget how much there is still to see! We are most fortunate. Lady Imogen, will you be quite all right? There are many steep stairs, and not a great deal of shade. Would you perhaps prefer to wait in the tents? I am sorry my stepmother did not choose to come today to play hostess, but I am sure Clara here will be happy ..."

Imogen gave him a withering glance. "Nonsense!" she snapped. She waved him back with her stout parasol. "I have walked miles over stormy moors, scaled Welsh mountains, sailed yachts. I can certainly climb a few temple steps. Lead on."

James coughed. "Er-yes. Certainly. If you will all follow me, I know a slightly quieter entrance way."

They all gathered to trail behind James along a narrower side path, lined with cracked and toppled columns etched with unreadable symbols, and up a set of

166

worn steps that was indeed quieter. Quieter, that was, until Clara Lewis-Clunes hurried up beside them, chattering loudly about the "appalling" heat and dust. The workmen fell in behind them, and Chou-Chou craned her neck out of Flora's pocket to watch them.

"Watch for scorpions and snakes," James warned, making Clara shriek and gather up her hem. "They like to warm themselves in these stone crevices."

Flora was glad that, in addition to her duster and dark glasses, she'd worn a shorter skirt and stout boots. She felt quite the intrepid traveler as they made their way up the winding, rough stone steps. At a sharp turning, she paused for a moment to catch her breath.

"You are very agile," a lightly accented voice said. "It is not easy to persuade a sahib to such paths."

Flora glanced back to see the tall, bearded man she'd assumed was Assim, Sir George's longtime foreman, brother of her ship's steward on the crossing to Egypt. He surely knew everything there was to know about these digs, about Sir George.

"I was a champion tree climber as a child," she said. She didn't mention that the tree climbing was mostly to steal fruit at the orphanage. "I'm rather out of practice, I fear, but I feel the knack returning to me. You must be Assim, Sir George's foreman."

"I am indeed. And you are Miss Flowerdew."

Flora glanced at the temple rising above them. "You must be so knowledgeable about this place, and the Temple of Nephthys. I find myself so very curious about it all."

"These temples are made of limestone and granite, usually, as they are the dwellings of the gods, and only human buildings were of mudbrick," he said, gesturing to the walls that rose above them. "The plan, you see, centers on an axis that goes on an incline from the sanctuary down to the temple entrance. This path was for festival processions; on ordinary days, the side doors would be used. This temple aligns with the rising sun."

Assim frowned when he studied the cracked columns. "It has not been maintained as it should, not since Sir George gave this site over to his son and Mr. Lewis-Clunes."

"You do not think James Crosbie his father's equal as an archaeologist?"

Assim shrugged. "How could he be? He works hard, but he does not have the spark of inspiration his father possessed. Yet he had been pestering his father for more responsibility at the Temple of Nephthys. He is not ready for such duties."

"You have worked with the Crosbies a long time, I think."

He slanted an unreadable glance at her. "Indeed. Nearly twenty years. How do you know such, Miss Flowerdew?"

"I met your brother, Assad, on the voyage from England, he was the ship's steward. He told me a bit about your work. And everyone who knows of this work is full of your praises. I hear others want to steal you for their sites."

"I have wanted only to work with Sir George." He led her into one of the larger chambers, a place of mysterious shadows and sudden flashes of sunlight, watched by the eyes of painted gods. "This place holds thousands of years of human emotions, longings, dread, joy. The walls remember everything. Sir George understood how precious such places are."

"It's astonishing," Flora whispered, staring at a soaring column shaped like a palm tree, painted with traces of red paint.

She stopped in front of a dramatic wall painting, still holding vestiges of its bright colors. A seated, winged woman watched a set of scales, a falcon overhead, a feather floating downward.

Assim came to stand beside her. "It is the weighing of a heart against the feather of the winged goddess Ma'at. Osiris, god of the underworld, whom you see there, with his son Anubis. He leads the dead person toward the scales. A moral person, you see, would have nothing to fear—his heart would balance with the feather, and his *ba*, or soul, would then enjoy eternity. If it does not balance, then Ammit, that demon just there, will devour the *ba*. Thoth, you see, the ibis-headed scribe god, records the judgment."

Flora studied it carefully, longing to know how the person's soul fared. "And which is Sir George, do you think? Is his *ba* safe?"

Assim chuckled. "There is one who I am sure Ammit waits for, and it is not Sir George."

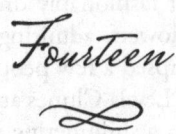

Fourteen

Flora heard the music on the deck, floating from the salon. She'd taken longer to dress for dinner, having laid down to nap after exploring the temple and fallen into fevered-dream-type images: a winged goddess with her scales, a man chasing her through stone corridors, shadows and light. The reflecting pool waiting for her in the distance, safety, sanctuary, but always receding away from her.

Even now, those dreams, the unreality of this place, clung around her like a jasmine perfume. She paused in the doorway to examine the party.

And everyone had decided to be fancy indeed for the evening. She'd read about Court receptions and Society balls in the gossip pages of Evie's newspaper, but they seemed so distant and dull as not to be real. Certainly not anything someone would go to if they had a choice, for laughs. Unless someone had a keen eye for the most absurd theater, then it was all probably a giggle. She would have to ask Benedict, who did go to such things, though she had a hard time picturing her smart, sweet dukie there. But this party before her was different, filled with a sense of effortless elegance Flora always associated with Imogen—and which, to be honest, she longed to possess herself.

The party was most incongruous with the setting, a string quartet playing Mozart behind a screen of potted palms, tall arrangements of red and white flowers on plinths. A crowd of fashionably dressed people moved between banks of flowers, admiring wall paintings and columns. Flora glimpsed a few people she knew among the crowd, like Paul Lewis-Clunes and his bored-looking wife, and Elspeth in a shimmering silver gown holding court with some admirers.

"Flora, my dear," Imogen said, emerging from the crowd to press a glass of champagne into Flora's hand. She took a sip, letting the cool bubbles rise to her nose. It was the best vintage, of course, toasty and golden. "Come in, come in! You must taste some of these nibbles the chef prepared, local specialties. I especially adore this tiny little honey-cake. It goes beautifully with the champagne."

"Of course it does. Everything you put together is always perfect," Flora said.

Imogen laughed, and tilted her head to study the gathering. The plum-colored plumes in her silver hair caught the breeze from the deck, and danced about in (what else?) perfect fashion, fastened with glittering amethysts. Next to her beaded satin and jewels, Flora felt pale and wan in pale-blue muslin. "If your party is impeccable, if every element—food, music, flowers, light—are in harmony, people don't notice it. If it's not right, if the food is sparse and cold, the wine cheap, it's all they talk about."

"Ah, I see," Flora murmured with an admiring nod. "If they are comfortable, happy in their surroundings, they talk about other things. *Interesting* things."

"Yes. And that is our goal here, to find out as much as we can about these people who surrounded poor Georgie." Imogen was called away with a question from a footman, and Flora wandered farther into the salon, taking another glass of champagne, listening to the soft strains of the music. It did indeed all feel very comfortable, quietly luxurious, with the scent of flowers, the murmur of laughter. She saw Mary serving rounds of caviar from her silver tray, smiling blandly as she no doubt listened to everything. Benedict's golden hair gleamed from across the room, but he was too far away for her to reach him through the crowd.

"Oh, Miss Flowerdew," Lady Crosbie called. She sat on a settee in the corner, her pale-gray silk skirts fluffed around her, surrounded by attentive admirers. "Tell us, what did you really think of my little shop? A few people doubt I could manage such a place! But I know you have the best taste, just look at your wonderful little pendant." She glanced around at her friends. "Miss Flowerdew was so kind as to visit my tiny place in Cairo. I wish I could have temped her with more than that bracelet, but I have nothing as fine as her Bastet."

Flora reached up to touch the cat, feeling it warm to her hand. "And I wish I could afford something very large and grand, like your beautiful wares, Lady Crosbie. I adored the statue of Anubis. But my reticule is wee and holds few coins."

Melanie laughed, and wafted her silk fan in front of her face, catching her glossy curls. "Oh, I do hope I have something for every variety of pocketbooks. I only want to bring a touch of beauty into the world, even if they are replicas."

"The style of the ancient Egyptians is surely timeless, no matter when an object was made," Clara Lewis-Clunes declared, as she drew closer to their little group. She did not wear her Egyptian collar, but a strand of pearls with her crystal-beaded pink gown draped across the bodice with elaborate folds of creamy tulle.

"You are quite correct that it's beautiful, no matter when it was made," Flora said. But the real thing surely held far more monetary value. She wished she had a more educated eye, to know whether Lady Crosbie's shop did indeed hold copies. She resolved to ask Monsieur d'Etrages about the bracelet she wore, once they met again at the Temple of Nephthys. "You do have excellent taste, Lady Crosbie."

Melanie laughed. "No, not at all! I only know what I like to look at. If people do agree with me ..."

"And how could they not?" Paul Lewis-Clunes leaped in to compliment, as his wife frowned at him. He did look so different from his rather dour self as he leaned closer to offer Melanie a plate of delicacies. Another illicit romance in the air?

"Shall I fetch you a fresh glass of wine?" Richard North asked, edging Paul away. He stood near her shoulder, quietly attentive.

"Oh, Richard, you *are* a dear," Melanie sighed. "It is so nice to be *seen* at last, not disregarded as if I was not even there! A glass of wine would be most restorative indeed."

Flora realized she needed a breath of fresh air after all the chatter, the heady scent of the flowers in the warm salon. On deck, she glimpsed the glow of a cigarette tip, and moved closer to see it was Elspeth's maid, whom she'd glimpsed on the ship. She was laughing with someone, a man in a white robe and shadow-darkened turban, a man who seemed familiar to Flora. Could it be the man who had talked to her in the dining room, begging her help? When she hurried toward them, though, he ran away, leaving just the girl.

Flora took her own cigarette case from her truly tiny reticule, and lit it as she studied the night sky that stretched above the river, trying not to let the maid know she'd seen her talking to the man.

"I don't think I've ever seen anything so beautiful," she said truthfully, waving her cigarette at the eternal sky around them, so seemingly silent and peaceful.

"It's all right," the maid scoffed. "You should see the sky in Devon in summertime."

"That's where you're from? How ever did you end up here?" Flora held out her case, and the maid took three. "I'm Flora, by the way. You work for Mrs. Rosse? That should be interesting." That would explain how the girl came to Egypt, and was not easily impressed by quiet beauties. And suddenly Flora realized she hadn't seen Elspeth in a while. Where could she have gone?

"Aye, for five years now. She's a hoot and scream, it's true, but she pays well, and doesn't mind what I do in my own time. And aye, I'm from Devon. Farm family. I jumped at the chance to see a bit of the world."

"And that's where you met Mrs. Rosse?"

She shook her head. "I worked in Kensington, in a rotten sort of house. So-called gentleman and his pasty-faced son chasing after the girls at all hours, the mistress pinch-mouthed and stingy."

"I know just the sort of place you mean," Flora murmured, thinking of the long-ago days she'd had to work as a scullery maid before she found the theater. Vile stuff. "Mrs. Rosse lured you away?"

"I liked to go to the British Museum sometimes, get away from it all. Saw her there once in a while. Those turbans of hers!"

"She is most—noticeable."

"Well, she saw me looking at the mummies, and she actually talked to me! Told me all about them, how they were made, the treasures they were buried with. Finally, after a few times, she said she was going back to Egypt and would I like to come. I never looked back, I tell you."

"She seems like a good person to work for. Never dull," Flora said, wondering if this girl knew more about Elspeth's love for Sir George and belief in their reincarnated passion.

"She's that. Dotty, sure, but nice." She put out her cigarette and glanced at Flora, until Flora gave her another. "Have you known her long, then?"

175

"Not long at all. But I am a little dotty myself, so I quite liked her from the first."

The maid laughed. "You don't look it. Dotty, I mean."

Flora laughed, too, and fluffed at her plain blue taffeta skirts, remembering the spangles and tights she once wore. "Not now, maybe. People do talk to you more if you look harmless at parties."

The maid's eyes narrowed through the smoke. "You a spy, then?"

"Not really. I'd be terrible at it. Just curious about Sir George's strange demise. Who wouldn't be?"

"That was a rum thing, no doubt about it." She shook her head sadly.

"He was friends with Mrs. Rosse, wasn't he?"

"Sometimes." If she really did think Flora could be a spy, she did seem to trust her anyway. "He and Mrs. Rosse used to have some right carryings-on about how much they hated thieves and smugglers here! Like playing whack-a-mole at a village fete, it sounds like, villains always popping up all over the place."

So did that mean Elspeth did not consider her lover-through-the-ages a thief? "I would imagine it would be. I see so many antiquities for sale, here and in England. I'm sure a man like Sir George, who everyone says was such a dedicated scholar, wouldn't be happy about it. Was there anyone in particular he didn't like? That he suspected of theft?"

The maid frowned in thought. "You think it had something to do with him ending up in that mummy case, then? Blimey. Could Mrs. Rosse be next?" She was quiet for a moment. "I never heard a name. But I know there was someone in particular he suspected lately. Used to call them—oh, what was it? *Haraami*, servant of Thoth."

"*Haraami*?" Flora thought over some of the suspects in her mind, wondering who could match such a description. Thoth was the god of wisdom, writing— and sometimes of thieves.

"Don't know what it all means. And I'll tell you something else, something Mrs. Rosse isn't happy about at all."

"What is that?"

"She says she knows of someone misusing ancient rituals for the gods! She was absolutely raving about that last night."

"I imagine she wouldn't keep quiet about that." Flora was sure Elspeth was most strict about the gods' rituals.

The maid giggled. "Not her. She also thought Sir George had another woman. And after she came through all those lifetimes to find him again!"

"Did Lady Crosbie know, too?"

She shrugged. "All she seems to think about is that shop of hers, and parties at Shepheard's. I doubt she'd notice. But Sir George *was* handsome, I'll give him that, and had such nice manners. Always had time for a chat with anyone, even a maid like me. I wouldn't be surprised he had another lady on the go."

Flora wondered if maybe she was looking in the wrong direction, thinking Sir George had been killed because of professional reasons. Maybe it was personal. Maybe it was run-of-the-mill jealousy, if he did indeed have lots of affairs. She remembered the gossip about James and Clara Lewis-Clunes, among others. "You've been visiting here for a long time with Mrs. Rosse."

"Sure." A passing crewman called out a greeting to her, and Flora recalled she'd been talking to the familiar-seeming man.

"You must know everyone very well. Like the crew of this boat, maybe."

"Mrs. Rosse has hired the *Falcon* before, sure. I met a few of them who are always aboard." She scowled. "Nothing wrong with that!"

177

"Not at all. Many of them are quite handsome, I agree." Flora offered her another cigarette. "That man you were talking to earlier, is he a regular on the crew?"

The maid still seemed suspicious. "Not him. He worked on one of the digs, I think. Lots of questions. Just like you."

Flora laughed, thinking of a cranky old matron at the orphanage who told her she chattered too much. "Too true. I've always liked a chat." She stayed for a few more moments, gossiping about the people Elspeth knew. When she excused herself to retire, she took a little detour to the small salon used by the crew, but she didn't see the man who wanted her help there. Everyone there fell silent, watching her curiously. She flashed a quick smile, and rushed to her cabin. Somehow, a warm wave of relief washed over her as she locked the door behind her.

~

Stay with me. Wait for me ...

Flora was jerked out of a dream-world, a vision of the reflecting pool under the moonlight, a whisper on the wind, by the clatter of running footsteps on the deck outside, a muffled shout somewhere beyond. She sat up in her berth, blinking and disoriented, still half beside that pool under the sparkling stars, half tucked under her tangled blankets. Mary snored in her own berth, having taken the sleeping draught, and seemed to hear nothing.

Flora shook back her tangle of hair and climbed down from her pillows. Chou-Chou, tucked up on her cushion, sat up and growled at the closed door.

"I know, sweetikins, I know," Flora murmured. She wrapped her dressing gown around her shoulders and pulled open the door.

It was definitely still deepest night, the over-arching

178

darkness lit only by bobbing lanterns, but the deck was lively with crew members dashing around and passengers peeking out of their doors.

She pushed out into the crowd, Chou-Chou close at her heels, until she scooped the little dog up. They were carried along to the bow amid panicked shouts. Flora peeked over the railing to see someone fishing through the water with a hook-like device. A pile of sodden fabric lay on the planks, topped by a red turban. It looked like the man who'd been talking with Elspeth's maid.

"What happened?" she gasped.

"Someone fell overboard," the man next to her said, staring down into the river. "Akhmed over there was on night watch, and saw whoever it was floating."

"Did he hear or see anything before that?"

The man shrugged. "A shout, he thinks."

Flora glanced back at the discarded red turban. Could it really be the man chasing her in the souk, and then lurking on the *Falcon*? Was this a suicide? Was he *pushed*? Shivering in the warm breeze, she tugged her dressing gown closer around herself and Chou-Chou.

"Do they know who it is?" she asked, but the man shook his head.

"Flora!" Benedict pushed through the gaping crowd to take her arm. His brow furrowed with worry, as if he knew how she really fared even when she pretended she was quite fine. "Are you all right? They said someone went overboard. Anyone we know? Where is Aunt Imogen?"

"I don't think it's anyone we know." She nodded at the turban. "Maybe it was a crew member?"

A cry went up, and a bundle was hoisted up on the hook. As it was dragged up over the railing, Benedict's hand tightened on her arm, holding her steady. "Maybe you should look away ..."

179

She gave a hoarse laugh. "Oh, Dukie, surely you know me better by now?"

He laughed, too. "Indeed I do."

Flora noticed the drowned man's striped robes, blue and white, just like in the souk. "I think maybe, just maybe, that was the man I saw before."

"Where?"

"Talking to Elspeth's maid here on deck earlier this evening." She didn't yet mention the souk. She wasn't at all sure it was the same man, just from the clothes, and she didn't want to sound more delusional than she feared she already did.

The cloth was pulled back from his face, and she fell back with a gasp. "I know him," she whispered.

"Who is it?" Benedict said, leaning in for a closer look.

Flora peeked again. That turban, the hawk-nosed face ... "He was my ship's steward on the journey to Egypt." And he was Assim, the foreman's, brother. Why had he been following her? What did he want? And why was he dead now?

A sharp scream pierced the night air, above the other commotion. Flora spun around to see Lady Crosbie, swathed in satin and swansdown, her hair tumbling over her shoulders, face pale.

"That man was trying to kill me!" she moaned, right before she fell to the deck in a swoon.

Fifteen

F lora leaned on the railing, watching the river banks glide past, green and peaceful. After all the chaos of the night before, it all seemed too bright and tranquil. She thought of all the turmoil and villainy the river must have seen over thousands of years, all of it covered by the lapping waves, the monumental temple statuary shrugging at it all.

Her head was whirling with questions. Why was the ship's steward following her about? What had gotten him shoved overboard? Did his brother, Sir George's trusted foreman, have anything to do with it? And why would Melanie Crosbie declare he was trying to kill her? She'd said so little after Richard North revived her from her swoon, just crying and panicked. Maybe the man was set to kill all the ladies of their little group, or something equally penny-dreadful-like.

And why was a dream cat following Flora around? Chou-Chou hated cats, though she seemed to pay this spirit one no mind. Maybe it was down to the pendant. Lots of people did seem strangely interested in it. She reached up and touched it where it lay under the lace edging of her shirtwaist, and wondered why Jacques gave it to her in the first place. What did she really know about him? About any of them?

"Flora, my dear," Imogen said, coming to stand by Flora at the railing. She held out a cup of tea as Benedict came to her other side and gave her arm a reassuring touch. His smile was crooked, worried as he looked down at her, and she tried to smile brightly back. She feared it wobbled a bit.

"How are you this morning after last night's dramatics?" Imogen went on. "I thought we were at Drury Lane! Here, do drink this up, it has a bit of stiffener added to it."

Flora took a grateful sip, as she'd been unable to take a single bite of breakfast, and nearly fell over choking. It certainly had more than "a bit!" Trust Imogen to know what was needed at any moment.

They went to sit on a row of deck chairs, Chou-Chou clambering up on Flora's lap, watching the river banks float past in silence for a moment. A crocodile slid from the sand into the water, silent and dangerous.

"It certainly was rather strange. It all felt like a dream," Flora said, stroking Chou-Chou's caramel-colored fluff, as the Pom's eyes seemed to narrow in thought. "Why was the ship's steward sneaking about here? I think—yes, I think I saw him before, as well. Following me in the souk the day I went to Lady Crosbie's shop."

"Flora!" Benedict cried. "Why didn't you tell me this before?"

She glanced up at him, startled by the intensity of his face. "Oh, Dukie, I've been doing everything on my own for a long time," she protested. But to be honest, she felt a warm little glow at thinking maybe she didn't have to do things all alone right now. She had people she could trust. "And I didn't want Lady Crosbie to find out, I wanted her to feel at ease, open to girlish chatter with me. She couldn't do that if she thought I was on my guard, that someone might be watching us both.

182

Nor would she if there was a Viking glaring over my shoulder at the time, sweet as that is."

Benedict gave a smug, pleased little smile. "You think I'm like a Viking?"

"You know you are, darling," Imogen laughed.

"Yes," said Flora. "Big and blond. They should have called you Rollo instead of Benedict."

"Your father did once visit Svalbard, I think," Imogen added. "But right now we must concentrate on *this* ancient place. Do you remember anything at all suspicious about this dead steward, Flora?"

"Not on the crossing. He did seem to have lots of information about the Temple of Nephthys. His brother is Assim, Sir George's foreman, so I didn't think that was so strange at the time."

Benedict frowned. "As far as we know, Assim moved from the Temple of Horus to Nephthys, and isn't onboard the *Falcon*. Could he have done this to his own brother? Or set him to follow you for some reason? Maybe he was in England with Sir George."

Flora frowned. It seemed logical that he could have been the one who put his brother up to this, but ... "We do need to find out more about him, about his role in the work at the temple, how he and Sir George got along."

"He seems to admire Sir George, to approve of his working philosophy, but who knows if that is the truth?" Imogen said. "And what about Lady Crosbie? She seemed quite distressed last night, and it was her shop this man followed you from, Flora. What exactly did you see there?"

Flora closed her eyes and imagined she was back in that shop. The scarves and robes, the statues and mosaics, the jewelry, like the beaded cuff Melanie gave her. "It was quite lovely, really. Very bright, full of beautiful things well-displayed. She seems to know what she's doing when it comes to her business. She said the items were just copies ..."

"Do you think that's true?" Imogen asked.

"I don't know enough to tell." Flora gave a frustrated shrug. "I do like shiny things, but I don't yet have a keen eye for antiquities. I did come away with a bracelet—I thought I could have someone like Jacques take a look at it."

"Georgie would not have approved of his wife selling antiquities," Imogen said. "Even if practically everyone in Egypt does it. He was a stickler for preserving artifacts."

"So I've heard," Flora said.

"But would she have murdered her husband to keep her shop open? I have a hard time seeing that," Benedict asked doubtfully.

Imogen patted his hand. "My dear, gallant nephew. You cannot imagine the lengths we women must go to sometimes to claw back a tiny shred of independence. But does Melanie have it in her? She seems so sweet and fragile. Just like Georgie's first wife ..." Her words trailed away, and Flora knew they all thought of the rumors about Sir George's first wife and the manner of her death. What if something in that past had come back now to hurt Sir George? Or what if James or someone like him harbored grudges from those long-ago events?

"The shop was very pretty, just the sort of place to be prosperous, catering to wealthy tourists and such," Flora said again. "Could such a—a *fluttery* person really manage a business so well? But her assistant, whom you met here on the *Falcon*, does seem very devoted ... maybe he does most of the work. She seems to maintain a regular customer base, like Clara Lewis-Clunes."

"Ah, yes. Clara Lewis-Clunes," Imogen said. "Now *there* is a woman who could do with more independence, more of her own interests."

"What would she have to do with the steward,

184

though? And why was he skulking in the souk, and here on the *Falcon*? Was he following me, or Lady Crosbie?" Flora murmured. "It's all very frustrating."

"Look, there is the temple!" someone farther along the deck called out, and Flora hurried back to the railing to watch as the temple slowly moved into full view. As soon as they docked, Theo Ottway hurried aboard, searching for her eagerly, as Benedict scowled at his puppyish enthusiasm.

"Miss Flowerdew!" Theo cried, hurrying toward her with a brilliant smile. "What do you think of your first glimpse of the Temple of Nephthys? I hope it doesn't disappoint."

"How could it, Mr. Ottway?" Flora whispered, still watching the temple, enraptured. "But what of you? I know you've been thinking of this place for so long! Has it lived up to your expectations?"

His freckled face shone. "Oh, it has been most glorious. I've already learned so much! If only Sir George himself was here to teach me all he knows. I did long to work with him ."

"Perhaps *you* will be the Sir George of your generation, my dear boy," Imogen said kindly.

Theo beamed. "Do you really think I could?"

"You've been studying and working so long, Mr. Ottway," Flora said. "And I have the strong feeling there are still many secrets to discover here ..."

As they stepped off the gangplank of the *Falcon* and made their way along the path leading up to the Temple of Nephthys, Flora tilted the narrow brim of her hat to her eyes to shade them so she could examine it in all the white-gold glare of the sun. The walls seemed to shimmer, like a thousand diamonds, and all was timeless and serene. She could definitely see why Sir George, and so many others, were devoted to it all. It was a gloriously magic feeling, a sense of being tossed back through time. Maybe Elspeth had a point after all.

Paul Lewis-Clunes waited for them, but his wife was nowhere in sight, nor was James Crosbie. Lady Crosbie, resplendent in black-and-white lace ruffles, a silk parasol over her head, held onto the arm of her attentive clerk Thomas, who led her into the shaded interior.

Richard North came out to greet them as well, and fell into step beside Flora. "What do you think of it all, Miss Flowerdew?"

"It's like something I read about in novels, not something real," she answered. "So astonishing."

"It has been a great find, sure to be one of the most legendary in the history of archaeology. And the village of Al-Fashn is just behind that hill. Hopefully we can begin further excavations there this winter. The people who worked on the temple once lived there, just as they do now; I'm sure there would be much to find, new places to put one's stamp on. I fear Sir George wasn't quite as interested in such an expansion, even with his love of history."

"I do wonder why. There must be such fascinating stories to discover there." Flora studied the temple ahead, and remembered hearing about arguments over who would take over this site now. Who would get to decide what happened? "Are you taking over the dig now, Mr. North?"

A frown seemed to shadow his face, quickly covered by a pleasant smile. "I should certainly like to, and I feel I must be the natural choice. I worked with Sir George for a long time, and have many ideas of areas that could still be recovered. The sarcophagus was merely the latest discovery! But we shall have to see." He took her arm to help her over a pile of stones. "If only George had listened to me ..."

"You did not feel your expertise was appreciated as it

186

should be? I'm sure such long devotion to this site must count for a great deal." Or maybe he meant he tried to warn Sir George about dangers? He'd been at the British Museum, after all.

Richard leaned closer, seemingly eager to make confidences. "I would certainly hope so." They stopped in a patch of shade, watching the activity just ahead, white-robed crew removing baskets of earth, sifting, cleaning, sorting. "Sir George was a man much blessed, who I fear couldn't always see his own clear path. He had his own ideas about how the digs should progress, and had no use for conventional, educated wisdom."

"And you were not as—blessed as you deserve?" Flora murmured sympathetically. "How terribly unjust!"

He laughed and scuffed his dusty boot through the pebbles, embarrassed. "Oh, Miss Flowerdew, how kind you are. We archaeologists and historians can be a viperous lot! Always scraping for the best sites, quarreling over conclusions. You must take no notice of me. I just feel so very deeply about the temple. Feel I owe those who once lived here to find their stories once again."

"I do understand that so well." Flora thought of the ghosts that appeared in her séance room, all eager to have their tales heard, though usually their stories were not that interesting. But sometimes you encountered some real drama. She glanced over her shoulder, and saw Lady Crosbie walking with her clerk, Thomas holding a parasol over her. Melanie looked beautiful indeed, her lace veils fluttering. Richard watched her too, longing writ large on his face before he covered it.

"It seems Sir George's personal path was blessed, as well," Flora said. "After being so sadly widowed twice, to find true love once more!"

Richard scowled. "He did not appreciate Lady Crosbie as he should have, I fear. Such a sweet lady, so soft-hearted! She is very brave now to embark on life alone."

Flora wasn't too sure about Melanie's 'bravery,' but she certainly did sense hidden depths to the lady, just as there were with everyone here in Egypt. Shadows amid the brilliant light.

A group of villagers passed Flora and Mr. North's shady spot, and Flora suddenly had the prickly sense of being watched. She glanced over at them, and found two of them staring at her very closely. One of them pointed at the wave of her red hair that had escaped its pins and trailed below the edge of her hat.

"Daughter of Nephthys," a murmur went up, and Flora self-consciously tucked her hair up again. "What does that mean?" she whispered to Richard. "I have heard that said before."

Richard frowned. "It's your red hair, said to be the same shade as the goddess's. It is said, though there is no proof, that there was a cult of the goddess in ancient times, filled with secret rituals and magic. Sometimes I heard silly whispers that it has been revived in the present day. You should be careful, Miss Flowerdew. You wouldn't want to be part of their rites."

Flora shivered. "Rites?"

"Chanting, incense, maybe even sacrifices. Magic. But that was all long ago, you see it on wall paintings in the temple. I am sure they just admire your beauty now!"

"Yes, indeed." She took his offered arm and they continued to the temple itself, catching up to the others. She found them in the sanctuary chamber, where once the gods and goddesses had been served. It was a small space, but she could see it had once been sumptuously decorated with elaborate wall paintings. The *naos*, which Flora had been told was once the center of the space, the stone shrine housing the votive statue of the goddess, rose above all else, framed by carved pillars. The whole place seemed wrapped in silence, in divinity and mystery.

"Welcome, welcome, *mes amis*!" Jacques called, holding out his hands as he saw them coming into the room. A murmur of awe rose up, echoing off the stone walls, and Imogen and Benedict went to examine a painting of Nephthys spreading her wings. "You are all in for the most glorious treat here, I promise you."

Richard left Flora to go to Lady Crosbie, edging out Thomas, who glowered as Melanie giggled and laid her hand on Richard's sleeve, letting him show her to a stone seat.

"Mademoiselle Flora, you shall enjoy it here most of all, I think," Jacques said, bowing gallantly over her hand. "What do you think of it all?"

Flora glanced around. It was smaller than the last temple they visited, but prettier, more personal. She could almost sense it really had been built out of some strong emotion, some great tenderness. "Astonishing. More than I could have imagined. It's all so very elegant." She wished she could think of more to say to express what she felt in that moment, but there were no words. She could see why Sir George and others would devote themselves to it all.

"Come, come, let me show you more." He led her into a small side-chamber, where a torch cast flickering light over a wall painting. Flora was amazed—it was just like the card of the Tower, the winged goddess casting light down onto an altar. Red and blue and gold paint still clung to the outlines, to the dramatic feathered spread of the wings. And the fall of her bright hair over her shoulders, red curls.

"Daughter of Nephthys," Jacques said, and Flora could find no words to answer. After a long moment, they made their way through a doorway into a courtyard.

"The pool!" Flora gasped. It was like her dream: the

189

long reflecting pool casting moonglow back up onto the stone walls, the ring of palm trees, the sound of the wind overhead whispering to her.

She drifted through it all, and felt as if she was dropped into her dream once more, but this time it was real. All the details, the serene pool, the deep-blue mosaic tiles, the ring of palm trees and fruit trees, looked like the place she knew so well in her dreams. A feeling of longing swept over her. She couldn't help but wonder whether Elspeth had the right idea after all—they had lived here before, everyone knowing each other through the ages. It shed a new light on what Flora had to discover here, the villainy she needed to rout out.

At Flora's heels, Chou-Chou let out a low whine. Flora glanced down to see her dog staring at a shadowed corner. Chou-Chou's ruff of fur stood on end, as it sometimes did in seances. Flora studied the corner, half-concealed behind a crumbled statue of a falcon, but saw nothing, only the shifting shadows. Until there was the merest flutter of movement. A tail tip? Chou-Chou started to dart away after it, and Flora snatched her up before she could be lost in the depths of the temple.

"A beautiful spot, *non?*' Jacques said, as if he didn't notice Chou-Chou's little drama.

"Beautiful. I could stay here forever. I think in ancient times it must have been filled with bright colors." They walked on, and Jacques pointed out an inscription on the wall, just above a narrow doorway.

"*The reward you shall give me is a long life only at your side, with all else falling away into the waves of the river, the glow of the sunset.* Most unusual," he said.

They came to a low bench in the shade, and sat down for a moment. The chatter of the everyone else in the distance was indistinct, a low hum, and Flora could hear the lap of water in the pool, the breeze in the palm trees. Chou-Chou clambered up into her lap, still shaking, but calmer.

"I've received so many compliments on my amulet," Flora said, touching her fingertips lightly to the cat. It felt warm again. "I feel I should probably give it back. It must be quite valuable. Lady Crosbie even wants to buy it!"

Jacques looked shocked. "No, no, you mustn't sell it! And I would not take it back. It is meant to be yours. It must be with no one else. It will always give warning only to its true owner."

She wondered if that was what the pendant had done, warned her. "You are so kind to give it to me, then. I shall keep it close, I promise." Flora shook back the sleeve of her jacket to show him the beaded bracelet she'd received at Melanie's shop. "Can I ask you about this piece, too? I found it in Cairo, I know nothing about it."

Jacques took out his pince-nez and studied the bracelet closely. "Very pretty indeed. Quite well-crafted. See how the beads interlock here and here, forming this fine pattern? I think you did not buy it off a street lad."

"No." For some reason, she felt reluctant to tell him where she actually found it. "A shop in Cairo. Is it a real antiquity?"

He looked at it again. "No, though as I said it is a very high-quality copy. It would take much knowledge to get all these little details right." He took off his glasses and smiled. "I hope you did not buy it thinking it genuine?"

Flora shook her head. "I just liked it, and I wasn't sure. It was not expensive at all." So that was not a stolen item, then. She resolved to ask Jacques as soon as she could about local thefts.

They rose again and walked to the edge of the rise, looking down at the river in one direction, the old village in the other, clusters of low-slung, brown huts. In the other direction stretched green fields. As Flora examined the streams of people moving below, hurrying on their work, she felt a cold touch of frustration. Sir George had such a wide life, filled with people and overflowing with ambitions! Surely there were dozens of people who *could* have wanted him gone. Family, friends, rivals, enemies, old lovers like Imogen. Where should she even start?

On the other hand—how many of them could have been in England to do the killing and stuff him in the sarcophagus? Or have connections to help them? Richard North had been there, but had seemed truly shocked at the events at the museum, and declared he had an alibi.

She noticed Assim moving through the crowd, taller than the others, dignified and unhurried. She had to ask him about his brother, but for some reason he always made her feel so nervous. Almost as if his quiet demeanor meant he was looking into her thoughts. He'd been with Sir George for so long ... what secrets did he carry with him?

"It looks as if the work is certainly going fully ahead, even without Sir George," she said.

"*Certainment*. Monsieur North has put himself in charge for the moment. He is not as knowledgeable as Sir George, of course, but he has worked here for some time and can make sure the work proceeds smoothly. An abandoned site, especially one that has proved as rich as this temple, is very vulnerable."

"There have been many thefts in the past?"

Jacques laughed. "Everywhere, *ma chere*! From ancient times until now. This place has been more secure than most. Sir George was much respected, and much feared. He had no patience at all for looting and pilfering, and would immediately dismiss and prosecute anyone he found engaging in such deeds."

So anyone Sir George had punished for thievery could also be added to the list of suspects. "His crew seem to be working hard for him even now."

"*Oui*. As I said, he is a man who inspired loyalty. Most of his people have been with him for years. He demands hard work, careful work, but pays very well, and is always willing to step in to help someone who gets into difficulties."

Flora studied Jacques, wondering what he really thought of Sir George. He did sound like he admired him. "I have the feeling, monsieur, you must have done the same when you were working your sites."

He smiled. "I did try. A loyal crew is worth more than diamonds in such work."

"Sir George had the same workers every season?"

"I would think so, yes. A leader who acts with respect and pays well—they would line up to return to him. Not to mention the bonuses he awarded when significant finds were made! More lucrative than stealing. He worked everyone hard, but he worked twice as hard himself." Jacques gestured to the busy field below. "Excellent for the temple, yes, but not so easy for his personal life."

Flora thought of Lady Crosbie, her seeming grief. "His wives, you mean?"

"I fear the first Lady Crosbie, James's mother, was not a happy woman. But they seemed devoted to one another, they married so young and worked together here and at other sites. The current Lady Crosbie ..." Jacques smiled and shook his head. "Well, you have met her. Lovely, of course, but they surely had little in common."

"And do you know much about his foreman, Assim? They say he has worked here for a long time."

"Monsieur Assim. Well-known in this work, *oui* ... many would like to steal him away. He started as a boy, carrying away buckets of dirt for sifting, things like that. He's been here at the temple since Sir George discovered it. I've never heard anything bad about the man." He glanced down at her. "Why, mademoiselle? Do you suspect him in this terrible business?"

"I hardly know enough to suspect anyone at all. Or maybe everyone?"

"Egypt is a complex world, *ma chere*. Just be very careful where you step." He pointed at the amulet. "She will help you, if you let her."

She thought of the "Daughter of Nephthys" business, the glimpses of cats. "Because I have red hair?" she said with a laugh.

But Jacques did not laugh. "Not just that, though people here will think that most special indeed, as you have seen. Because there are such webs of secrets here. Secrets, and that most powerful thing of all—money. Any questions that ripple the surface ..." He shrugged.

Flora nodded. She knew all too well the strength of secrets and wealth—and position. The great lengths people would go to in order to protect them. "I can take care of myself, monsieur."

"I am quite sure of that." He took her arm, and they walked on. "Now, see this statue? The very red-haired goddess! You do look much like her ..."

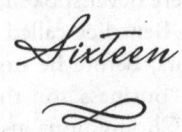

Sixteen

"Oh, Flora, my dear, you must hear about this! I have been reading about the ancient rites of Nephthys, which were once performed here in this very place," Imogen called to Flora. They had decided to stay lodged aboard the *Falcon*, and Imogen was ensconced in the salon with a stack of books as Mary tidied around her, and Benedict played fetch with Chou-Chou on the deck. "The rites of Nephthys involved evoking the journey to the afterlife, going into darkness and being reborn. Being concealed in darkness, with veiled acolytes purifying all with incense, until one is thrust back into light. Red-haired acolytes were the most sought-after, as were young women with red hair to be reborn."

"Sounds spooky to me," Mary called.

Flora sat down across from Imogen, giving up on doing anything useful for the moment. She felt so strangely restless. "Sounds fascinating indeed. I'm glad to hear my hair was once not quite so unfashionable as now."

Evie didn't glance up from the notes she was jotting down at the table across from Imogen. She'd decided after the story of Sir George was revealed, she would try a series on excavations in Egypt, the dangers and dramas of it all. "This world needs more goddess rites, if you ask me. Men have made such a hash of things."

"Truer words were never spoken," Imogen said.

"I do protest!" Benedict called from the deck beyond the open doors, before he urged Chou-Chou to hurry up with her "business" on the papers laid down for the purpose. Chou-Chou just wanted to keep running.

"Not you, of course, my darling," Imogen added. "Maybe if you had red hair, Bennie, they would have let you into the temple anyway."

"If you had lived back then, Flora, you could have ruled them all," Evie said. "Sat about in your temple like a Delphic Oracle, and told everyone what to do. Led all the rituals."

Benedict leaned in the doorway as Chou-Chou sat on his foot. "They could have done a lot worse than trust Flora's say-so."

Flora laughed. She thought of the fortune teller in the souk, telling her she had to utilize her great powers.

"Indeed so," Imogen said. "Some of these pharaoh chaps were utterly appalling. Whipping, cutting off hands and noses, all sorts of things. I hope this temple was something of a refuge. I only wish dear Georgie could have finished his work here."

"It does sound as if his scholarship was quite exemplary." Flora told them about her conversation with Jacques, what she'd learned about Sir George's honesty, his battle against theft and looting.

"That darling man," Imogen sighed, with a sad shake of her head. "Such strong convictions, such dedication to history. How hard he fought!"

"So you think he was killed for opposing art theft?" Benedict said.

"It does seem likely to be one solution," Evie said. "Think of the Beaton case in Karnak all those years ago!

That man was coshed over the head and dumped in a tomb for daring to stop thieves."

"But surely it also could have been something more personal," Mary said. "Maybe someone who knew his unhappy first wife wants revenge for his treatment of her? Or he was having an affair now, and a husband wasn't happy—that happens all the time! Or he angered his wife. Or Mrs. Rosse wanted to hurry up their next life together."

"I can see where Lady C might be unhappy," Flora said. "She seemed irked that he didn't have much time for her. But she was here when the body was found, not in London. And could she have done the murder, physically? She seems ..."

"Delicate?" Imogen snorted. "Flora, my dear, you know as well as I do what sort of person Lady Crosbie is. Spoiled, fond of her own way. Being delicate and ill is a good way of gaining a modicum of the power we are denied as women."

"What sort of man would want the woman he loves to feel ill?" Benedict asked, a puzzled frown on his handsome face. "I would go to any lengths to help her."

"That is because you are a kind and reasonable person, darling boy, and that is quite rare," Imogen said. "You can see other people's point of view, and you know that 'other people' includes women. Some men think they want a woman who is helpless and uncertain, who depends on them utterly. They don't like to be opposed, or even disagreed with."

Benedict kicked out at the edge of the rug. "If that's the case with the Crosbies, then I can definitely see why Lady C would get tired of having to pretend to swoon to get her husband's attention, and decided he wasn't worth the trouble."

Flora laughed. Benedict really was an unusual man, a man of sensitivity and good heart. "But she would still have to get to London, kill him, stuff him into the sarcophagus, and get back to Cairo before anyone noticed. I do think Sir George's battle against theft seems a likely motive, but that would leave us with hundreds of suspects."

"We could get Chou-Chou to help," Mary suggested. Chou-Chou glanced up from licking her paw, her eyes crossed.

"Or maybe not ..."

~

If the Temple of Nephthys had been stunning in daylight, it was absolutely magical in the night. Flora froze as she stepped out of the barque to take it all in, the flickering torches turning the brown stone walls pinkish-coral, the moon sliding high into the dusty-black sky. Flora had been so excited when they received an invitation to a ball at the Temple, a "celebration of Sir George's life." It was even more beautiful than she'd imagined.

"I can see why Elspeth Rosse thinks she's been here before," Benedict said, as he came to Flora's side. His expression as he took it all in was as awestruck as she felt. "It's like something in a painting, not real at all. I can't believe we're here to see it for ourselves."

"I know. I've felt like I'm in a dream ever since we got to Egypt." And part of the dream was being so close to him.

"Come along, my dears," Imogen called, as she floated up the pathway ahead of them. The lace and satin ribbon train of her sapphire-blue gown, dotted with crystal stars and pearl moons just like the Egyptian sky, twisted behind her, leading them onward.

Benedict smiled his crooked little grin down at Flora, that dimple low in his cheek flashing. It always made her feel ever so slightly weak in the knees. He offered his arm, clad in impeccable evening black wool. "Shall we, then?"

"Thank you, Dukie." She slid her hand over his sleeve, feeling the flex of his arm under her gloved hand. They joined the stream of people, clad in finely tailored evening suits and silk gowns that would rival any ballroom in London, that flowed along the pathway between the flickering lights. Their steps were lined with more torches, held by people in delicately pleated white robes, and the strains of music beckoned them forward. The flames touching and then flickering away from the faces of the statues made them all appear to be alive, watching, judging, seeing the ribbon of constant life move past. For a moment, Flora felt quite dizzy with it all, and the scene turned blurry at the edges, fading into something else entirely. Just like in her dreams, the temple was no longer crumbling, but alive with color and emotion.

"Miss Flowerdew," Theo called, and Flora turned to see him hurrying toward her, his face alight with eagerness, though his hair was as tousled as usual, his suit a bit askew. "How wonderful to see you here again! How are you finding our little temple, then?"

She tilted back her head to study the inscription about the reward of long life "only with you." Though she knew the Temple of Nephthys was "small" compared to the Temple of Horus, it was such a glorious jewel box that word could never encompass it.

"Astounding," she said. "No wonder you were so happy to obtain this position! I can see why anyone would keep returning, lifetime after lifetime."

"You have been talking to Mrs. Rosse! But I can see it has captured you, too." He frowned as he studied the merry gathering, the lights and music and jewels. "Though I must say the festivities must have been better millennia ago. This music sounds all wrong! I'm sorry you must see it in such a garish fashion."

"When the goddess awakens again, it will be as it should be once more," Elspeth Rosse said.

Theo's frown deepened, as if he did not approve of Elspeth's theories, but Flora smiled as she turned to her. Elspeth did look entirely resplendent, in robes of deep garnet-red and gold, a tall turban of gold-and-silver dyed ostrich feathers crowning her. "I do think the world could use more goddess energy now, Mrs. Rosse."

"Right you are. And I hope you will join our little rites when the time comes."

"I am sure Miss Flowerdew has no time for such things," Theo said sternly.

"Nonsense!" Elspeth barked. "She is just the sort of spirit to appreciate such transcendent things."

Flora wasn't too sure about it herself, not if these rites included going into the afterlife and being reborn. "When the time comes for what, Mrs. Rosse?"

"Oh, do call me Elspeth. I know we are great friends now." She took Flora's arm and led her toward the temple, away from the sputtering Theo. They moved through the columned doorway into the hypostyle hall, where the crowd flowed between the carved columns. Elspeth took a goblet from a passing footman and handed it to Flora. "You deserve so much better than a red-faced clerk with no imagination. You deserve your own pharaoh."

Flora thought of Benedict's merry smile, his laugh, the glow of his golden hair. "Your lips to God's ears," she murmured, and took a long sip of the wine. She choked a bit on the spiced heat of it. "What is this?"

"Delicious, isn't it? An ancient recipe, *nebit shamsi*. I am so pleased they're serving it tonight instead of insipid champagne. At least they got something right." Elspeth glanced around at the well-dressed and bejeweled visitors. "The time is surely coming for Nephthys to rise again. She will need your power, and drinking the *nebit shamsi* will help strengthen you."

"My power?" Flora nearly snorted in disbelief. If she had power, she'd never have been a helpless child in the orphanage, never put up with old men's pinching fingers at the Follies, never been hungry.

"You must sense what is awakening inside of you, here at the temple. Your hair has always been a sign of your destiny, along with your inner fire! You are a daughter of Nephthys, as I am." Elspeth waved her arm at the chamber around them, her trailing green satin shining like a snake. "I must join my pharaoh soon enough ... someone will have to take my place to defend this place."

Flora was very sure she'd never be a replacement for someone like Elspeth. Like Imogen, she was completely free and unafraid to live her own life. But she remembered what Mary had said in a passing comment, that maybe Elspeth wanted to hurry along her next life with her pharaoh, aka Sir George. With that glint in her eye, Flora realized she would never put much past Elspeth. "But I have to go back to England soon. Surely someone else would be better suited to, er, *goddess* things." She glanced around the crowd, and noticed a woman who was also clad in silk robes, these woven with a pattern almost like watercolors, a river and swaying trees in pale greens and blues that set off her light blonde hair. "That lady, maybe?"

Elspeth frowned. "Not *her*. It needs exactly the right sort of person."

Flora studied the lady with more interest. She did like people who were "not the right sort," no matter where she found them. "Who is she, then?"

"A Mrs. Herbert. She supplies shops in Cairo with —things. A sort of middleman, you might say. Calls herself an *importer*." Elspeth snorted, as if she knew "importer" encompassed so many things.

Flora wondered if Mrs. Herbert ever worked with Lady Crosbie's shop. She thought she'd heard the name before, but was not sure where exactly. Elspeth drew her deeper into the temple, and Flora soon found her goblet empty. The torches flickered and blurred, and the figures in the faded wall paintings seemed to shift and dance. Could the drink be making it look different? She did always try not to get tiddly, it led to such trouble.

"What is that?" she asked, drifting toward a darkened doorway that seemed to emit wafts of smoky tendrils. It was half-hidden behind a statue, and was locked.

Elspeth tugged at her arm to draw her away. "It was once storage for the temple's priestesses. Unguents and incense and such things. I believe George used it for artifacts before they were packed. Dirty, moldy place now. You must see this over here instead ..."

Elspeth led her toward another statue of Nephthys, this one with her wings outstretched, though one was broken off. But she was soon called away by some friends, leaving Flora to look around alone for a moment. She glimpsed Assim leaving the chamber.

"Mr. Assim," she called, trying to catch up to him. Her tight satin bodice and stylish slippers slowed her down. But he slowed his steps and glanced back at her with his usual unreadable expression. "I wasn't able to say earlier how sorry I am about your brother. He was my steward on the voyage here."

He gave a little bow. "You are very kind."

"I was surprised to see him here."

"We were not close. We had differing opinions on many matters."

Such as theft? She couldn't picture the dignified Assim smuggling artifacts. "Matters?"

Assim sighed. "I fear my brother saw our heritage here as merely a way to ensure his own monetary fortunes. He was blind to the forces of the past, and I knew it would go poorly for him in the end."

Had Assad been a smuggler, then? And he *had* been in England. Maybe he was trying to get away from it,

202

and that was what he needed her help with aboard the *Falcon*. Whatever it was, she was rather amazed Assim would be open about it now, given his usual reticence. "It would indeed be a terrible thing to mar such beauty as this," she said gently, gesturing at the statues around them. They had sat there for thousands of years watching the world go by. She could see why someone would be determined to keep it that way.

"Beautiful, yes, but that is not its only value. It is our history and heritage, the legacy our ancestors entrusted to us. Sir George wanted to preserve that."

"And that is why you worked with him for so long."

"Yes. I, too, know the tragedy of such losses. They can never be replaced." They walked together out into the night, looking down at the torches that led up to the temple, the glorious star-lit sky above.

"It must have been so shocking for everyone here, what happened with Sir George," Flora said.

"He did not even tell us he was going to England. He merely said he had business in Morocco, and I should carry on the work for a few weeks. He usually confided in me. I knew he meant to find ways to secure the artifacts, but ..."

"The sarcophagus was a most significant find, I am sure."

"Yes. Burials in such temples are rare. It was surely meant for someone of great importance. It was a great day indeed when it was uncovered, but it had only given us a fraction of the information it surely could have."

"From what I have heard, Sir George was most revered in his profession."

"Very respected, yes, and with good reason."

"Then who would ever want to do such a shocking thing?" She thought again of the overwhelming scope of it all, the many, many lives Sir George and his work had touched.

"He never backed away from a conflict when it came

203

to his convictions, mademoiselle," Assim said severely. "But for those of us who worked here—we will see his work go on. We will see his spirit at rest. Whatever it takes."

Assim was called away, and Flora tiptoed to the storage room door and peeked inside. A ray of light fell over the stack of crates, and she studied a peeling label on one of them. *Muslin, blue*, it said, and she wondered at the elaborate curlicues of the ink.

A burst of laughter nearby pulled her away from the crates. She didn't want to be caught there, not without a good explanation for snooping! She had no idea whom to trust yet. She hurried back to the party, and took a glass of wine from one of the waiters.

As she sipped at it, she studied the party. A dance floor had been cleared in the hypostyle hall, the string quartet playing a fashionable waltz. Lady Crosbie danced with James, but neither of them looked terribly happy about it. He scowled as she spoke to him quickly, whispering, her brow furrowed, and Flora wished she was closer so she could hear. The Lewis-Clunes also didn't seem to be having a great deal of fun; Paul tried to take the almost-empty glass from his wife, and she shook her head fiercely. She turned away from her husband to take another drink.

Ah, the bliss of marriage and family, Flora thought wryly. She pasted a smile on her face as Theo Ottway came toward her. "Would you care to dance, Miss Flowerdew?"

Flora studied the party, the music and flowers, the unreality of it all. She doubted she would find out more that night, but maybe Theo had some new ideas of the journal. "Thank you, I would love that."

Seventeen

I have seen many curses in my work, carved in stone and written in papyrus, and never have I given a single one credence. But after seeing what has happened on the site, the loss and accidents, it seems someone is unhappy with us. It is something unspeakable. The gods do not favor us now, we have insulted them ...

Flora thought of the strange passage she had just read in Sir George's journal, and it made her shiver. The gods were insulted. By theft? By the rituals Elspeth said someone was misusing? She paced the length of the reflecting pool and then up the other side. The party had dwindled at that late hour, and she could hear only faint laughter, tipsy laughter. She was alone in the magical courtyard, but it felt as if someone watched her.

She remembered what Theo said. Sir George had said he discovered something "unspeakable." Elspeth's maid said she was angry because someone was making a mockery of rituals in some way. What did that mean? If only she could read the hieroglyphics for herself, or was more versed in Egyptian mythology like her old acquaintance Madame Eglantine, one of her teachers when she first went into mediumship. Egyptian magic was all the rage among mediums—maybe she really should expand her business a bit.

205

She studied the inscriptions along the walls, lit by the glow of the moon and the flickering torches. She noticed a wall painting, faded and flaking, a mere shadow but enticing. A woman with flowing hair beneath her headdress, clad in a diaphanous robe, stretching out an arm bedecked in bracelets to a man whose face was partially chipped away.

She gathered up her ruffled skirts and climbed up a pile of boulders, trying to see it better. *Oh, Daughter of the gods, protect us here ...*

As she traced her fingertips over the ancient lines etched in the stone, something warm and soft brushed against her ankles, almost making her topple over. She braced herself against the wall and glanced down, just in time to see a slim black tail vanish into the night. Her amulet grew warm against her throat. A warning? A flash of protection?

She felt as if she'd tumbled down into her dream again, the pool made new, the night soft.

"It is the last time," she heard a man say roughly. For an instant, she thought it was another dream, but the low, tight tones were real enough. "I won't take any more of this!"

Flora shrank against the wall, peeking out toward the moon-rippled pool and praying she wouldn't be seen.

It was Paul Lewis-Clunes, standing with a woman beneath a stand of palms, leaning close to each other. But it wasn't Clara. It was the woman who supplied the shops, Mrs. Herbert, in her watercolor robes. Their voices were soft, intense, but they echoed against the stones.

"There is nothing to worry about now," Mrs. Herbert said, with a dismissive flip of her hand. The light caught on the jeweled rings stacked there. "All is clear before us. This will be the last, I promise."

"I have heard that before!" Paul snapped in a quivering voice. Was he frightened of something? "Why should this be an end to it now?"

"Because there are many strangers around, as you well know, Paul. The temple isn't a quiet little backwater now. Our efforts to be rid of them have not worked, as you well know. We must move on."

Paul ran a shaking hand through his hair, leaving it untidy, which seemed most odd indeed for him. "I told you that wouldn't work. He can't be trusted."

"Lucky he tumbled overboard, then, hmm?" She laughed, and Flora was sure Mrs. Herbert must mean the man who had chased her through the souk, who died on the *Falcon*. Assim's brother. Had he been trying to scare her, be rid of her, then? "We've outgrown this place, anyway. The leader Hatshepsut is right about that. After this, we shall be gone."

"Gone where?"

"You don't need to know that yet." She curled her hand into his sleeve, crumpling the fine wool. "You aren't losing your nerve? We need you now."

"I just don't like it. I haven't for some time, not since the expansion."

"So stolen jewelry was fine, and this isn't? You *are* losing your nerve. Remember what happens when you do." Her hand tightened, and he winced. "It is all in service to the goddess. You know how great her demands are."

"The goddess?" He laughed, high-pitched, broken off on a yelp. "In service to people like my wife, you mean."

"You married her, knowing of her commitments. Face it, Paul darling, no one else would have had you."

Flora almost gasped at this little bit of juicy gossip. She'd been sure the Lewis-Clunes marriage was not all it should be, of course, but this sounded rather extreme. What did it all mean? Something brushed against her ankle again, a soft "mrow" sounded, and she didn't dare breathe. She silently willed them to keep talking.

"Just this once, it must be done," Mrs. Herbert said cajolingly, her hand turned caressing. "We have to make the move at once. Now, come along."

They linked arms and turned toward the temple doors, while Flora cursed, burning with curiosity. She hadn't really suspected Lewis-Clunes of real mis-doing —he seemed priggishly devoted to his work, and his wife empty-headed and dissatisfied. Yet another lesson in not jumping to conclusions about people; they were ever strange and changeable. Had they killed Sir George, then? How? And what was going on here with the "goddess?"

When she was quite sure they were gone, she carefully climbed down from her perch and shook out her skirts. She glimpsed a pair of jewel-green eyes blinking at her from the darkness. The appearance of a cat protector just seemed like one more strange discovery in this place.

"Are you coming, then, Bastet?" she said, but the eyes vanished. She was on her own for the moment.

She followed the path Paul and Mrs. Herbert had taken, through the doors and back into what was left of the party. She didn't see Melanie Crosbie, James, or Clara Lewis-Clunes, or even Benedict, Evie, or Imogen. She would have to tell them what she'd just heard. She wanted to poke around a bit more near that tunnel entrance, but Richard North was there, casually sipping his wine but keeping a watchful air as people moved past him, subtly steering them away.

A conspiracy, then. Was it only North, the Lewis-Clunes, and Mrs. Herbert? What was hidden in there? More stolen art? Yet Assim had hinted there was more to it all. More demands from the goddess, maybe.

She knew there was no way she could get in the tunnels right now, just waltzing in past North. There had to be another entrance somewhere, surely. Temples and tombs all seemed to be built like mazes. Perhaps Sir George's journal held a guide. She knew she also couldn't ask Theo, though, despite his seeming passion for her; she couldn't trust anyone right now. Who knew how far this goddess conspiracy spread.

She saw North glance toward her. She carefully backed away, keeping a sharp eye on the tunnel door behind him. But she should have looked behind her, too.

"Are you searching for something, Mademoiselle Flowerdew?" Assim asked, perfectly toneless.

Blast, Flora cursed at herself. What a wretched detective she was! She turned and smile her brightest "what, little innocent, silly me?" smile that usually could fool almost any man at all. Assim did not seem fooled. He folded his arms as he watched her, one eyebrow arched. What did he really know about his brother's work?

"Just so curious about this beautiful place, like everyone else," she said lightly. She strolled away, hoping he wouldn't notice her interest in the tunnel door. "I'm astonished by every inch of it!"

He fell into step beside her, as she had hoped, and they moved further into the sanctuary. Any chance of a peek at the tunnels now was gone. For the moment.

"You should be most careful in this area," he said. "It is only partially excavated, as you can tell from this rubble, and it's easy to be lost here for those who are not expert in its secrets."

So many such spots, a person could be lost in them and never found again, until they were as dusty as the mummies. Flora shivered at the thought. "I am sure Sir George knew every inch. Did he excavate the tunnels beneath the main rooms himself? That must have been frightening."

Assim didn't even blink. "Tunnels?"

"For storage, I hear. I only glimpsed the entrance."
She smiled wryly. "But I am an avid reader of a certain
type of book, Mr. Assim. Gothic novels and such. I
daresay it would be a perfect place for rituals and sacrifices and such, or that's what would be in a fictional
tale."

"We are not a tale by Starkey, mademoiselle. This
work is far more dull."

"That's too bad." Flora glanced around, trying to
pretend she wasn't all that interested in tunnels anyway.
"Where was the sarcophagus found? No one has said in
our tours of the temple."

"Sarcophagus?"

"The one where Sir George was found," she whispered. "Shocking! I was there, you know, in the
museum."

Assim said nothing, but led her around the edge of
the main sanctuary to a smaller chamber she could tell
was tucked just behind the pool. There was no roof, and
the surface was still covered with the rubble of removal,
but somehow she knew how it would have looked when
whole and new. Paintings on the walls, the scent of flowered oils in the air.

"It was found just there," Assim said, gesturing to
an empty niche carved with signs of Nephthys and Anubis. "It was certainly one of the largest finds, and intact,
in beautiful reddish stone. It had been opened at some
point, the mummy and canopic jars, along with the expected amulets and charms it was believed to once hold,
were missing. . The inscriptions led Sir George to believe
it might have been the priestess here, daughter of the
pharaoh's official."

Ah, Elspeth's previous incarnation, seeking her
pharaoh-love. "Maybe she flew free to find her true
love," Flora sighed. Assim ignored her. "I would not
have thought Sir George would want it moved."

"He did not, not yet. He was adamant it should be

studied thoroughly in situ first. If items are moved too quickly, all invaluable historical information can be lost."

"So how did it end up at the British Museum?"

Assim shrugged. "Sir George suddenly changed his mind. He said he would accompany it to London, alone, along with some other finds. He would hear of no opposition. He did finally agree that Mr. North could go, and Mr. Lewis-Clunes followed without permission. Perhaps the Egyptian Museum wanted to be sure they knew what happened to it."

So, North and Lewis-Clunes had seemingly been the only ones in England. Maybe one or the other had done the ultimate deed for the "goddess." But how, when? "You did not go, then, Assim?"

He turned his head away, still expressionless. "I was forbidden by Sir George. He said someone must watch over the site."

"Mm-hmm." Flora knew a non-answer when she heard it. But she also knew she'd never get anything out of Assim he didn't want to share. At least she knew a few of the English crew had been in London at the time.

"So you don't know of any goddess rites here?" she asked, switching directions. "Sounds like fun to me, I might want to give it a try."

Assim snorted. "Nothing of the sort, mademoiselle. This is a place of serious scholarship."

"Nothing untoward at all, then?" she coaxed. "I hear that theft is rife at such places. Fighting off villains sounds exciting. And maybe there are other crimes?"

He scowled, and she involuntarily fell a step back. He looked quite fearsome in that moment. "Sir George was known to have no tolerance whatsoever for such things at his sites."

"Sir George maybe. But what about everyone around him? He couldn't be everywhere at once." And it was Assim's brother who chased her. Until he fell, or was pushed, into the Nile.

"The human soul is greedy above all else, mademoiselle, as I fear you must know," he said. "It was ever thus. We must always be on our guard against it. Now, come along. The night grows late. Your friends will be waiting for you, and it's not safe here in such hours."

Flora thought of Benedict, Evie, Imogen, and knew she could trust them to be on watch elsewhere that evening, taking in every clue they could. She took one more glance around the chamber, moonlight filtering through the lost roof onto the empty niche. It felt as if someone watched her there. "Yes, I'm sure it's time we found our rest," she murmured, suddenly anxious to be anywhere but there.

∼

Back aboard their lodgings at the *Falcon,* tucked into its cozy salon with her friends, Flora felt like she'd moved into a whole different world. Soft lamplight, easy laughter among friends, comfortable dressing gowns, a plate of delectable sweetmeats and pots of tea as they talked over the party. Mary relayed gossip she'd heard among the staff; Benedict relayed the gossip he'd found out from some young debs from Cairo he'd danced with.

"We just need to get into those tunnels," Flora muttered. She reached for a brass bowl of sugared almonds and popped one in her mouth to chew thoughtfully. She'd told them about Paul and Mrs. Herbert, their schemes for the "goddess." Surely there was something stashed down there!

"It might just be a ruse to lead us in the wrong direction," Imogen speculated. "These mysterious-sounding tunnels usually just turn out to be little dusty cupboards, nothing like in novels."

"Did you manage to glimpse anything at all in there, Flora?" Evie asked, scribbling in her notebook.

"I only started toward them, North was standing there for the longest time, and if he really is involved in something nefarious, I didn't want to rouse his suspicions," Flora said. "But earlier I just saw some crates. And dust! But there was ..." She paused for a moment, trying to visualize that little room, remember what she really saw there. *Something* was bothering her. "There were those crates all stacked up. Not strange at all, if it's really storage. But the—yes! The writing on the labels looked familiar somehow. Looping and curly. Oh, if we just had time for a proper lookie-loo. It would be the perfect place to stash things being smuggled out, with Sir George out of the way. He would never have countenanced stolen jewelry."

"Or more," Imogen said darkly.

"More?" Benedict asked.

Evie took a long drag on her Turkish cigarette. She'd gotten way too fond of them lately. "Drugs, you mean, Imogen? That's always a problem here, it's a prime place for smuggling to get around the taxes. Get something strong enough, and you'd be seeing the goddess for sure."

Flora flopped down on a settee, and Chou-Chou tumbled down on top of her. Benedict, sitting on the carpet nearby, leaned his head back against the cushions. She had to resist the urge to reach out and stroke his golden hair and forget everything else. "Drugs *and* art! And any, or all of them, could be in on it? Eek. We might as well go back to England."

"Now, Flora darling, where is your usual fighting spirit?" Imogen said. "We have figured out puzzles before, we'll do it again. Ben, dear, bring some paper over to that table and we'll make a list, see it all laid before us in black and white."

"You and your lists, Aunt Imogen," Benedict moaned. He tugged at his cravat to loosen it.

"You know I am right. Organization is the key, just like in party planning." They pulled themselves up from their nests and made their way to the round dining table, Chou-Chou on Flora's lap as Evie passed out pencils. "Now. Anyone here could be a suspect. Whom do we have? Start at the beginning, leave nothing out."

Evie duly jotted down *Number One*.

"It's hard to know where to begin, isn't it?" Flora said. "Sir George did have a complicated life."

"Anyone with a life worth living is complicated, darling," Imogen protested. "Otherwise, one is just plodding along through the day!"

"No one could ever say that about you, Aunt Imogen," Benedict said.

"We could start with Lady C, I suppose, though she doesn't seem very scheme-y. But maybe that's part of her plan," Flora said, watching as Evie wrote *Lady Crosbie— Melanie*. "She feels she was quite neglected by her husband, despite her delicate health, and has devoted herself to her shop."

"Which may or may not deal in stolen antiquities," Evie said.

"Georgie would have been furious indeed if his own wife peddled in stolen art," Imogen declared.

"She did want my cat amulet rather a lot. And I showed Jacques the bracelet she gave me from her shop. He says it's a copy, though a good one," Flora said, touching her necklace. It was cool now. "But there were dozens of things displayed there, it would be easy to mix real pieces with false. If she was lonely, neglected, she'd surely have even more freedom to manage her own work ..."

"Plus Mr. North and that clerk of hers seem potty about her," Mary said. "Maybe she had someone else!"

"Or, knowing a bit more about her now, she might

214

have thought another match more advantageous for her at this stage of her life," Imogen said. "Such women often do."

Mary leaned closer, and added quietly, "I was talking to one of the maids back at Shepheard's. She said she'd heard that Sir George was visiting a solicitor about a divorce."

"Divorce!" Flora gasped. Even Imogen and Evie, usually utterly unflappable and worldly, looked startled. A divorce was easier to obtain now than it had once been, but it was still labyrinthine and difficult, and quite scandalous.

"The maid said everyone thought Lady Crosbie was having a ding-dong with someone else, and maybe Sir George found out about it. But she didn't know any details, or even if he'd really gone to a solicitor." Mary looked quite disappointed at such lack of juicy additions.

"My heavens," Imogen murmured. "Marital infidelity and discord on top of everything else. Maybe Lady C thought she'd get more as a widow than as a divorcee. It must have been rather extreme if Georgie was truly thinking of a divorce—he was not a jealous sort, and devoted to his work above all else."

"But could she have done it? Physically?" Benedict said. "She's very slim, and not in robust health. Even if she could magically get to London and back here so quickly, how could she kill him there and dump him in that sarcophagus?"

"Perhaps with half the archaeological profession in love with her, it would be easy enough to entice someone else to help her," Imogen suggested dryly.

"There have been other rumors of romantic dalliance, too," Flora said. "Paul Lewis-Clunes and that Mrs. Herbert looked rather cozy, for instance! I suppose in such a small world, it's quite inevitable for everyone to fall in and out of romances. Why, when I worked at the Follies ..."

"Yes?" Benedict and Evie asked eagerly. Flora hardly ever shared her theater tales, and she knew her friends would love some of the more colorful happenings. But that life was behind her. "What happened?"

Flora felt her cheeks turn heated, and took a quick gulp of wine. "Not important now. But I heard James might be in love with Clara Lewis-Clunes, or maybe even with his own stepmother."

"James?" Imogen said with a laugh. "That boy would hardly say *boo* without permission."

"He's hardly a *boy*, more a middle-aged man," Benedict said. "And he isn't nearly as successful as his father in their profession. It must be hard to always be overshadowed like that, never fully having his father's approval or professional respect. Maybe he thinks he could prove himself if he took over the work at the temple. And remember the rumors of the death of Sir George's second wife? What if James blames him for what happened to his mother?"

"Would the work really be his?" Evie asked. "Richard North seems to stand ahead of him, and he could be in love with Lady C. Professional ambition and love all in one. He does seem a strong candidate to me."

"Mr. Lewis-Clunes might want the work, too," Flora said, thinking of him whispering at the pool with Mrs. Herbert. "He is much clumsier in his professional striving than Mr. North, but seems just as passionate. And he and his wife don't seem to have a harmonious union."

"Speaking of love," Evie said, "Elspeth Rosse could be angry that her great passion through the ages isn't working out as she believed it should. She doesn't seem to be someone who would appreciate her plans being thwarted," Evie said. "Surely she could do murder for the sake of being reunited with her pharaoh."

Flora considered this. She liked Elspeth very much, liked her free spirit and sense of adventure, but Evie was right that she seemed quite devoted to her ideas of eternal love. "I do have to admit that she has a rather ruthless determination when it comes to her ideas of love beyond time. *And* she was in London. If she thought Sir George was leaving his wife for yet another new love ..."

"But maybe if he was alive, he would have married Mrs. Rosse at last?" Mary suggested. "Seems better to hope than be done with it forever."

"Unless he really had set his sights on a new bride altogether," Imogen said.

"Just like a man," Evie scoffed. "No sense of loyalty."

"Hey!" Benedict protested.

"Not you, I'm sure, Dukie," Flora soothed.

"There are those rumors of the second Lady Crosbie's suicide," Imogen said, with a sad shake of her head. "It was a shockingly short space of time before he married Melanie. Men do tend to fall head over heels so very early. Maybe we *do* come to James again. Maybe he wanted to avenge his mother."

"Or he was another who loved Melanie himself!" Mary cried. She always did land on impossible passion as the most likely answer. And Flora had to admit she could be right—it was nearly always love or money. Or the need to maintain respectability at all costs.

"As fascinating as all this is," Imogen said, "I tend to think matters here are more likely for professional reasons, for greed—maybe mixed in with a soupcon of romance to give it just that lethal flair. There are riches to be found in Egyptology for the unscrupulous."

"Theft is rife among art, you are right. And here it's many a family's very livelihood, and has been for thousands of years," Benedict said. "I remember Sir George telling me tales of the looting of the tombs when I was a boy. And he was adamantly against it all. That would be enough for many to be rid of him."

"He was fearless for his principles," Imogen said, dabbing at her suddenly-damp eyes. "He would never have heeded the danger to thwarting such people. Yet would it not have been easier to shove him into a pit here, loosen a boulder to crush him or something? Someone like that foreman of his, Assim, someone always on site, could have done it very easily back then and declared it all an accident."

Flora tapped at her chin in thought. "Even though Assim was the brother of the man chasing me in the souk, and he's maddeningly unreadable, I just don't get the sense he would have done something like this. He seems quite devoted to the work, to the idea of history here. His loyalty to Sir George and the work here seems quite genuine."

"Assim does have a reputation for always having Sir George's back in this work, that is true," Imogen said. "He is just as much against the looting of the art. Other teams try to lure him away, but he has never left."

"What about Monsieur d'Etrages?" Benedict asked. He pointed at Flora's amulet. "Is he into the black market for art?"

Flora felt quite protective of her new friend. "I am sure he would not! And he is retired now, he's just a scholar. He does seem very interested right now in some kind of goddess, as is Elspeth. And everyone else, I guess. They all talk about it a great deal, and there's something about my red hair. It seems a thing of great interest around here."

Benedict gave a worried frown, and gently touched her arm. "Flora. I hope you're always on your guard here. We all worry so much about you, especially after what happened in the souk."

Flora felt quite a warm glow at the feeling of no longer being alone. She'd fought through a cold world on her own for so long, and the idea that she didn't have to now was so alluring, so frightening. So—nice. "Surely I'd be the last one chosen for a ritual sacrifice or some such nonsense! And I have the feeling sacrificial knives and anointing oil isn't what's stored in the tunnels at all. I just wish I could get a nice long look at those crates!" And listen more to Mr. Lewis-Clunes and Mrs. Herbert in their whispered conversation.

"You aren't going in those tunnels by yourself," Benedict barked. "Never!"

"I'm not as silly as all that, Dukie, give me a bit of credit." Her face did feel rather warm when she recalled she had indeed gone off to the souk alone, and been chased. But that was then. "I've learned my lessons. I'd bet my last sixpence it is art in those crates, headed to market. But where did it come from ... who is really in charge of it all?"

"And maybe more, don't forget," Evie said. "I was chatting with some journalists back in Cairo, seeing how they run their papers here. My, but they love to natter on! Not at all like purse-lipped London reporters, guarding their stories like mother falcons. They told me about the drug smuggling problem that's going on now."

"It must be very lucrative indeed," Flora said. She remembered her theater days—all the girls with their syringes and little silver boxes in the dressing room. It was easy enough to get the cheap stuff, rough and quick, but what if someone had *finer* tastes? It would have to come through someone who took their own cut.

"They come from India and Afghanistan, get packaged and shipped out from sites here along the river," Evie said. "Silks and spices and art are good places to hide them. You get around the taxes importing them aboveboard would incur, and your buyer gets a better quality than at the corner apothecary. Sir George doesn't sound like the sort to have any patience with such matters."

"Not at all," Imogen declared. "He detested such things. Said even laudanum ruined lives, and should be banned from apothecaries, much less stronger stuff like heroin. If someone really is using the temple to smuggle drugs ..."

They all stared at each other in horror. "Then anyone who stands in their way could be the next to die," Flora whispered.

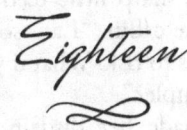

Eighteen

"**E**vie! Are you awake?" Flora whisper-hissed as she knelt beside Evie's berth. It was very late, the night beyond the window deepest purple-black, barely touched even with starlight. But Flora couldn't sleep until she found a few answers, and she *had* promised she wouldn't go anywhere alone.

Evie, though, always slept like a log, whenever, wherever. She shot up straight, her cropped auburn hair standing on end, cheek creased from the pillow. But if she slept easy, she also woke instantly. Her eyes widened. "Flora! Are you ill?"

"Not at all. I just have a strong sense we should take a peek in those tunnels at the temple, before someone empties them."

Evie might like her sleep, yet she loved adventure even more. She leaped out from under the bedclothes and reached for her clothes scattered on a chair. "Just a quick peek, right?"

"Absolutely."

Fifteen minutes later, they were dressed in sensible split skirts and jackets with pockets copious enough for a few supplies. Including folding knives and water canteens. Lanterns were found, and the barque unmoored.

Evie found a crowbar on the deck and took it in case it might be useful.

Chou-Chou whined imperiously, trying to catch Flora's hem in her sharp little teeth, but Flora firmly shut her back in the cabin. "I am sorry, lambikins, but you are too precious to risk. What if you're dog-napped, or get lost in the temple?"

Chou-Chou made her disdain at such a notion clear, scratching at the door.

"And don't tell Benedict, either!" Flora added. "We'll be back in two shakes."

Flora and Evie quickly scrambled into the little boat, and Evie rowed them to the shore where they started the climb up to the temple. At that hour, with no workers or party goers, it was a very different atmosphere. Dim and ghostly, as if the ancient spirits were in charge again. Flora wondered if this was really such a good idea, but they'd already come so far. She *had* to find out what temple shenanigans got Sir George killed and stuffed in that sarcophagus.

And she was quite determined that wouldn't happen to her.

They lit the lanterns and climbed quietly toward the silhouette of the temple, shadowed by the moonlight. The clouds slid around its silvery glow, making shifting movements on the crumbling stone walls. A single bird cried out somewhere in the distance, quickly silenced.

Flora's high-kicking dance days were far behind her, and she found herself a bit out of breath as they scrambled upward, as fast as they could. Evie, however, accustomed to chasing criminals through narrow, mucky lanes so she could write about them, loped ahead.

"Oh, do wait," Flora gasped.

Evie laughed. "It'll be light in a few hours! You don't want to get caught here, do you? Come on, slowpoke."

Once they passed the entrance pillars and stepped into the first chamber of the temple itself, everything changed in an instant. The night breeze turned dusty, scented with the faint memory of incense, the wind echoing against the stone walls. It felt like someone was watching. Flora almost held her breath as they moved into the sanctuary, between rows of cracked statues that studied their every movement, no doubt wondering what strange errands humans were on now. One of them even seemed to turn a bit when a beam of lantern light hit his hawk-nosed face, and Flora told herself sternly not to be so silly. She'd thought just two people would be more stealthy than a group, but she was starting to rue not bringing Benedict along.

Or Chou-Chou. The Pom was sure to winkle out the suspects.

The only sounds there, deeper into the ancient portals, were their boots grinding on rubble underneath, and the soft skitter of small, nocturnal creatures. They went into the libations room, lanterns held high to peruse the faded inscriptions. One statue Flora had never noticed before stood guard beside the door to the tunnels. She wasn't sure how she'd missed it; he was quite a looker. Maybe he was Elspeth's pharaoh. No wonder she sought him over the centuries. He was quite a looker, with those glass-sharp cheekbones and fine nose.

"What a dasher," Evie exclaimed.

Flora laughed. "He must be a veritable Adonis for *you* to take notice, Evie."

Evie gave a little snort. "I'm not blind, am I? I can appreciate a bit of beauty as much as anyone, even one with a male appendage. Who is he? I hadn't noticed this statue before."

"I'm not sure. I wondered if it was Elspeth's pharaoh, the one the builder's daughter was so in love with."

"He must be guarding something important." They found the door to the tunnels tucked away behind the pharaoh's stone shoulder. It was barred now, though, with empty crates stacked in front of it. They went to work clearing it away, and Evie managed to pry it open with the useful crowbar. The waft of dust swept out, swirling around them, bringing the scent of old flowers. Flora tucked her scarf around her nose and plunged ahead. Their lantern light ducked and bobbed on the rough walls, making the figures in the wall paintings bob and weave, vanishing and reappearing.

The crates were at the back, moved into a small, roughly round chamber. Someone had been working fast. Flora imagined she could still smell the rich oils and incense once stored there for the temple priests, spicy and flowery.

She stooped to examine one of the peeling labels. The words had faded, the paper curling at the corner, but she could make out the shape of the letters. Just as she'd remembered, the curls and loops of the writing looked familiar. "I am sure I've seen this."

Evie studied it over her shoulder. "Maybe you saw it on a crate back at the British Museum? Or on the docks?"

Flora considered this, and shook her head. And the writing in Sir George's journal was very stark, no curlicues. This was ...

Then she remembered, a flashing image in her mind. "The boxes in Lady Crosbie's shop! But I don't know if it was her or her clerk who wrote them. Which of them is involved? Or both of them?"

"Typical that it would be the spouse," Evie said. "Shall we take a peek inside?"

"I think we have to, after all this trouble to get here."

Evie pried open the lid, and they tossed aside wads of excelsior and woolen batting. Beneath were smaller boxes. They held just the sort of thing Flora had seen in the shop—jewelry, little carvings, silk slippers, bracelets like her beaded cuff. Polished incense pots inlaid with mosaics in once-bright blue and red. Flora had the sense these were not copies. She had learned a few things from Jacques and her own readings, the consistency of materials, the patina and craftsmanship. Copies could be excellent indeed, but there would be a few flaws every time.

"Flora," Evie whispered. "Look."

Flora peered at where Evie was emptying another crate. Evie held up a canopic jar, but it didn't hold just gray dust. It held little packets of brownish powder. "Raw opium?"

"A great deal of it in here. It would save a hefty sum in import tax if it slipped out like this. No wonder Sir George was angry, if his temple was used to cover such a scheme."

"And no wonder Lady C and her friends would go to such lengths to hide it from him."

"Who else would you say is involved?" Evie whispered.

"It could be anyone here. With so much at stake, antiquities *and* smuggled drugs ..."

"Awfully bold of them to stash it right under Sir George's nose, if they were using the tunnels back then."

"Maybe they thought it would be safe here until he got back. Or maybe"

They exchanged wide-eyed glances. "Or maybe they knew he wasn't coming back from the beginning."

So nothing to do with mysterious, cursed artifacts or reincarnated pharaohs. Just common, grubby, ordinary theft. But why? Surely Melanie Crosbie had everything! A rich, respected husband, a shop, admiration, beauty.

But Flora well knew that women, as much as men, could want much more. Could want power and wealth, freedom to make their own choices in life. Maybe Melanie Crosbie wanted to use the brain under her glossy curls as much as her beauty, wanted a way out of boredom. Had she turned to criminality to do that?

In the tight, astonished silence, Flora suddenly heard something. A light, steady scratching, sort of like

Chou-Chou back on the boat. It was impossible to tell from where it emanated—it seemed to bounce off the stone walls and low roof.

"Do you hear that?" she whispered.

Evie, usually utterly unflappable even when faced with blood and body parts, went a bit pale under her freckles. "Could it be bats or something? I do hate bats."

Then there was a distinct and mournful "mrrow" from behind one of the walls.

"The cat!" Flora gasped. Her magical cat, the one that kept appearing and vanishing. It had to be. Or rather, it didn't *have* to be, it could be any cat at all. But she had a tingly feeling it was a cat she knew.

"Cat? Flora, have you lost your mind? Not a strange thing to happen in a place like this, but ..."

Flora ran further into the tunnel, thinking she had to find the cat. The cat, who had led her out of danger in the souk and on the boat, was in trouble somewhere in the temple.

"Flora!" Evie called, but she followed.

Up ahead of them, in the narrowing corridor, Flora was sure she glimpsed a black tail swishing and vanishing. But it was a real cat, not just a ghost she sensed.

"We call on thee, oh goddess, to lead us out of the darkness! To guide our path through the next life, to show us the light ..." She saw a flash of bright cloth behind a tumbled stack of crates, green embroidered with gold. She was sure she'd seen that color before. She pushed aside a crate, and saw Elspeth crumpled on the ground. Her turban had tumbled away, and her graying reddish hair fell over her brow, streaked with blood. Flora, horrified, was sure she was dead, until there was a low moan.

"Elspeth!" she cried. She fell to her knees beside the woman, trying to help her up from the cold floor. There was gash on her forehead, clotted with blood. "Elspeth, can you hear me? It's Flora. What happened here?"

Evie quickly took out her canteen and a handkerchief, dampening it to press it to Elspeth's head. Elspeth blinked at the glow of their lanterns.

"Oh, my dears," she croaked. "You must leave, go at once! I will find a way to get away, they think I'm unconscious here and have forgotten about me. Maybe they think I am dead!"

"Dead?" Flora whispered, checking to make sure Elspeth didn't have other injuries.

"They call themselves Daughters of Nephthys. But they are phony! They care nothing for the ancients. They would not accept the goddess's help. They use it only to cover their evil deeds." She took a torn piece of paper from inside her robes. "I found this when I followed them, and thought to take it so everyone could know the truth."

Flora took the crumpled document and studied it. "A petition for divorce?" So the rumors Mary heard were true. Sir George had tired of his wife.

"From my darling pharaoh to that viper. I found them hidden beneath a desk in her lodgings. I knew that marriage was a dreadful lie. She must have found out his plans and decided to do away with him sooner rather than later. She is nothing here without his renown! He must have known she was untrue to him."

Flora thought Sir George didn't exactly sound like a shining Galahad, either. Marrying his wife and then ignoring her. Sneaking off to get a divorce petition. Unless he'd known about her secret work, about her flirtations. But more than infidelity, Melanie seemed to have an illicit business to protect. It all made sense. But how did she do it all? And what was this Daughters of Nephthys business?

That faint chanting sound grew louder, seeming to echo around them.

"That is them now," Elspeth muttered. "Their so-called rituals. You need to leave now, my dear! They have been watching you. Your hair, you see. They need you."

Flora touched her amulet. It was cool. Where had the cat gone? "Evie, get Elspeth out of here. I'll be right behind you."

She rushed ahead into the tunnel, leaving Evie calling after her. It felt as if she was under a spell or something, compelled to move forward, her feet pulled out beneath her.

At the end of the winding passage, she came to another room. It was long and narrow, tables draped with white linen, shelves around the walls displaying statues of cats and goddesses with flowing, bright hair and outstretched wings. The air smelled of incense. It looked like a scene from the wall paintings of the temple, from descriptions of old ritual spaces in Sir George's journal. That mesmerized feeling grew stronger, hazier. She stepped into the room, and glimpsed a cat, sleek and dark, high up on a ledge. It watched her with glowing green eyes.

"Flora," she heard Evie call in the distance. Before she could reply, could spin around and flee, a stone door deep in the shadows scraped open and a row of figures in white robes appeared, like ghosts. The door behind her closed with a bang, and she glanced around frantically, her breath tight in her throat. She saw the only possible escape was through another tunnel at the back of the room. Piles of rubble cluttered its entrance, and it was dark in there.

She knew very well she should *not* hang about to find out what was happening. The haze that compelled her in there cleared in a snap.

"Daughter of Nephthys, you are here at last to join us," a man said, pushing back the hood of his robe. Richard North, Lady Crosbie's most attentive suitor. The man who had been at the British Museum. "You have come at last. We need your help to make this circle complete."

They gathered closer around Flora, blocking her in.

She glanced past them, that frantic heat rising up in her. She had to think carefully, stay calm. They said they *needed* her for something. Surely that meant they wouldn't just kill her immediately.

They all pushed away their hoods, and she saw Lady Crosbie; Mrs. Herbert the "importer;" Thomas, her clerk from the shop; James Crosbie, looking quite ridiculously sheepish; and shockingly, Theo Ottway. Theo, whom she'd entrusted so stupidly with the journal! Her people skills were surely slipping. But there was no Paul Lewis-Clunes, no Assim.

At the front of the chamber, on a raised dais draped in white silk, seated on a gilded Egyptian throne, was Clara Lewis-Clunes, clad in a purple robe, her hair loose and a tall, golden crown shimmering atop her head. She held up her arms and cried, "At last! Our rituals can now be complete."

"We greet you, Daughter of Nephthys," everyone chorused. If it hadn't been so frighteningly eerie, it would have been hilarious, like something at the Follies. But Flora was too frightened at being surrounded to laugh. "Come, join our queen."

"We need you to keep the fires alight, to show everyone here our power," Melanie said, her voice deeper than her usual fluting tones.

"If George had not opposed us, he wouldn't have ended up as he did," Richard said cajolingly. "I only pushed him when he demanded I give up the artifacts we had replaced with copies, not that anyone would have known."

"You *did* kill him," Flora gasped.

"No! It was an accident," he protested. "He came after me, and I pushed him away. He hit his head on the sarcophagus."

"And you thought you would just shove him into that sarcophagus rather than find help?"

"He was beyond help! He had insulted the goddess.

Now we must set it right," Clara cried. "Give us that amulet. Only we know where it should go now, how to use it. The old Frenchman was a fool to let it go, and Elspeth was a fool not to realize all this is only to reunite the goddess and her pharaoh! Please, help us, Flora, don't be like they were."

"We would never hurt you," Theo begged. "Please, Flora! Join us. Help us. Come, just have a sip of this wine ..."

"Oh, quit with the persuasion and cooing!" Richard snapped. "Just grab her! She'll have to help us."

Flora sensed someone coming up behind her, hands reaching for her, and she was launched into motion, her head suddenly clearing. She ducked and ran, searching for a doorway. Someone did grab her, and her old days of wandering the London streets came back to her. She kicked and slapped, evading capture, running onward. She glimpsed a door at the back of the room, behind the dais, only a crack, and headed toward it. She saw the cat's black tail, leading her onward.

A rough hand seized her arm, and she spun around, knocking from its plinth a statue that fell onto her pursuer. A shout and screams echoed, set off by a cat-ly howl. The cat edged the door open, and Flora followed, slamming the portal behind her. She knew it would earn her a few precious moments. She managed to snatch a torch just before she was shut in, and she plunged ahead into the tunnels.

"Wait for me, cat," she called, and a "mrrrow" answered in the distance. She followed it, trying not to think of snakes and spiders, trying to take shallow breaths of the ever-warmer air. She could hear nothing behind her yet, and she wondered if that ritual scene had been yet another dream. She could hardly believe ordinary, modern people would do such a thing, but there it was.

"Mrrrrow!" came a piercing howl, louder, more impatient.

"I'm coming!"

At last, she found another doorway, up a narrow set of stone stairs. She ran up it, her boots slipping beneath it. She wrenched open the door and tumbled out into the reflecting pool's courtyard. She tried to run forward, but her feet felt like they were tied down, heavy. Shouts rang out behind her, and she knew her time was growing short to escape. She gathered up every bit of her strength and dashed ahead.

Richard North burst out into the courtyard, Melanie close behind him. Flora stumbled over some rubble, and felt herself tumbling to the ground, felt the cold flash of raw fear, the longing to see Benedict and Chou-Chou again, to sit beside her own fire. For so many things! They were so near she was sure she could feel their hot breath on her skin. She rolled over, ready to kick, to hit and scratch, to do anything to escape.

But she did not have to. She glimpsed something on the roof edge of the temple, a glow of green eyes. There was a squeal, a scrape, and a statue of Anubis tumbled from above, black and massive, scattering stones in its wake. Flora heard a shout, a scream, and Anubis landed square on Richard North.

The air around her went hot and still, the stars blurring. "Bloody hell, I can't faint now," Flora gasped. But the world spun, and the darkness swallowed her up, Anubis reaching out for her in the endless night.

～

"Flora! Flora, please, *please* wake up!" she heard Evie pleading, as if from a great distance. She had never heard her friend sound frightened before, and she wondered vaguely what would happen to them if they were caught

231

by the criminals. She sat up, nauseated by a wave of dizziness.

"We have to get out of here," she gasped. Then she saw more people behind Evie, not Lady Crosbie and her crew, but Assim and some of his workers hauling away Richard North on a stretcher, and Theo Ottway loudly protesting his innocence, that he had been blackmailed. "You must believe me, my dearest Miss Flowerdew! I would not have let them hurt you!" More people flowed and scurried around the edges of the pool.

"What happened here? Are they found? The Daughters of Nephthys?" Flora gasped.

Something soft tapped her arm, and she looked down to see a small black cat brushing against her, staring up at her. The cat who led her outside. She scooped it up to hold it close, and found it was real and warm, purring against her.

"Elspeth bravely managed to get back to the *Falcon* while I followed you," Evie said. "I saw you run away from that robed band. How ridiculous of them, like the worst sort of penny-dreadful! You'd think they'd have some imagination at any rate."

"Flora!" she heard Benedict shout hoarsely. "You maddening creature. What were you thinking?" Before she could fully catch her breath, his arms were around her, pulling her into the sanctuary of his arms. His touch was fierce, almost desperate, as if he needed to confirm she was real—that she was safe.

Her cheek pressed against his chest, and she could feel the rapid, uneven rhythm of his heart beneath his shirt. "Are you hurt?" he demanded again, his voice raw, tinged with fear that still clung to his words.

Flora leaned against him, completely forgetting he was a duke and only knowing that he was her Benedict. She was safe with him. They were safe *together*. "But what happened? I think I fainted, or maybe I was hit, like poor Elspeth. We found the crates of antiquities and opium, and there was that gathering, and then—then ..."

She glanced around, at the pool, the moon, the temple, all the same as it had been for thousands of years. Not even their modern drama could change it. Not even the fake rituals of the goddess could alter it. "Then I woke up here, with you."

"Chou-Chou was howling so loud we woke up, and I knew something was very wrong," Benedict said. He held her close, enclosing her in warm safety. "Oh, Flora, what would I have done if you'd been hurt?"

"But I'm not, Dukie. I am right here. With you." She took his hand, letting him help her to her feet, letting him hold her steady. Followed by the cat, they made their way away from the temple, away from the past and into the present.

Nineteen

In conclusion, I must declare again you are the loveliest, kindest lady I have ever had the privilege to meet, and I can only fervently beg your pardon and hope that we will meet again one day. I will show you the man I can be, if you would only let me! I had nowhere to turn when the villains realized I cared about you, had become your trusted friend, and they attempted to blackmail me over an unfortunate entanglement. I vow to you I never betrayed a single confidence from you or from the esteemed Sir George's writings...

Flora sighed as she read Theo Ottway's tear-stained letter, trying to weasel out of being in trouble with the whole sad business, "entangled" with Lady Crosbie and her band. It was sad indeed, he had seemed a sweet lad, very helpful. If he truly had been blackmailed into helping their Daughters of Nephthys ring (and really, what did he have to be blackmailed over? Flora was aching with curiosity), it was a sad business. And if not...

That was for the courts to decide now. The Daughters of Nephthys, that ritual excuse for smuggling drugs and antiquities, the scheme that had led Sir George to his death, was over.

She glanced around the peaceful gardens at Shepheard's Hotel, where they had retreated after the killers and smugglers were taken into custody. The quiet shade beneath the palms and fruit trees, the waiters moving past with tea trays, the sound of a string quartet on the veranda, it seemed unreal. After the tumult of the temple, it was shockingly, deliciously quiet, a wonderful spot to kick her feet up on a cushioned chaise and try to make sense of all the recent drama. Flora had been under strict instructions from the hotel doctors to get some rest, but Imogen had gone off to explore more pyramids and temples, while Evie returned to London to write of her adventures and secure her promotion. Everyone was safe and happy at last.

She heard a low growl, which had become her constant background music of late. She turned to see Chou-Chou and the new cat, Thutmose, chasing each other around a horse chestnut tree. Until Thutmose leaped up into some unreachable branches to taunt poor, fuming Chou-Chou. Despite the growling and chasing and wrestling, they'd become good friends, curling up together on a cushion at night, watching the sunny world go by from windows and gardens. Flora wondered what would happen when they got back to cold, foggy London and there was nowhere for them to sun themselves.

She shivered just to think about it, dreading the smoky fireplaces and damp days, the people seeking the location of grandfather's lost cufflinks and such. She'd had too much fun in Egypt, danger and everything.

"Flora! My dear girl, how are you feeling today? Are you quite recovered?"

Flora turned from her squabbling "children" to find Elspeth Rosse hurrying toward her, clad in shimmering golden robes that sparkled in the sun. Behind her trailed her maid, the girl from the *Falcon*, carrying a stack of teetering hatboxes.

"I am feeling entirely fit and hardy, but my friends

236

insist I rest for a few more days," Flora answered, so glad to see Elspeth was also looking well, after getting coshed on the head by the killers in the temple and making her daring rush back to the *Falcon* to find help. The only sign of it all was a bandage on her brow, just beneath the beaded edge of her turban. "But I could certainly ask the same of you!"

"Oh, yes, I am quite well now. Just furious with myself that my efforts to stop that absurd Daughters of Nephthys claptrap went so awry. I always knew Melanie Crosbie was a bad 'un, and I was quite right." She gently touched the bandage, a wistful glint in her eyes. "How dare they so malign the ancient spirits, using them as an excuse for their criminal behavior! At least my darling love is avenged in this life. I can move on now, and seek my true destiny."

Flora studied the stack of boxes. "I see you're leaving Cairo, then."

"I am going to Baghdad, and parts beyond. I am being called into a new life." Elspeth patted Flora's arm. "And, if I may say so, my dear girl, you should do the same. There is a whole world to explore out there, filled with mystery and secrets! You have a gift, and you should not waste it."

Flora laughed, remembering the old fortune teller who told her the same in the souk. "Not much of a *gift*, if I can't stop myself from dashing into danger."

"You have courage. That can be tempered and controlled, but it's a vital trait to possess in this world. You should get out and see it! It needs more daring spirits like yours."

"I shall certainly consider it all," Flora said, thinking of how she dreaded returning to London. "Thank you so much, Elspeth. You have been a marvelous inspiration."

Elspeth gave her a quick, jasmine-scented hug. "Call

on me in Baghdad! We shall meet again." She pressed a card into Flora's hand and wafted away.

Flora studied the card, scribbled with the address of a hotel in Baghdad, and imagined it all. White minarets against a sun-splashed sky, gardens and balconies ...

Chou-Chou clambered up onto the chaise and curled on Flora's lap, staring up at her with wide, caramel-colored eyes as if she, too, wanted some new adventures. Even if they now included Thutmose.

"There you are, the troublesome trio," Benedict said, and Flora's heart went a little pitter-pattery at the sound of it, all sunshine and whiskey. He had stayed so close to her in her recovery, read to her, fetched her special sweetmeats from the souk, and she never wanted those days to end. It wasn't the moment for declarations or promises, and would never be, really. They were still who they were, with lives that waited for them in London. But as they sat there in the garden, as she remembered clinging to each other beneath the night sky at the temple, they both knew that this connection was something unique.

"We *are* troublesome, I know," she answered. He sat down beside her in an empty wicker armchair, his golden hair shining in the light. He looked tired, as she knew anyone would be after listening to a complex murder inquiry, but he was beautiful. "If it wasn't for us, you'd never have to go to such a beastly thing as an arraignment."

He took a lemonade from a passing waiter and gulped down a cool, invigorating sip. "It was rather uneventful in the end, nothing like chasing hooded villains through night-time temples, but it was interesting nevertheless. He told her the tale that had emerged, the Daughters of Nephthys that had been dreamed up between Melanie Crosbie and Clara Lewis-Clunes, who hoped to use their husbands' work to cover their smuggling. Richard North claimed the death of Sir George was an accident, while Melanie claimed he killed her husband to get his job, to use the Temple for his own ends and cut them out of the business. Sir George would never have allowed criminal activity at his dig; Richard needed him out of the way, and if he could not do it, Clara was sure she could put her husband in place there and use him instead. James claimed he did it all out of love for Melanie, and out of a desire to show his father he could outsmart him. When it seemed Assad, Assim's brother, would turn to Flora for help, after they had recruited him into their schemes, they killed him.

Now they were all most eager to turn on each other.

Flora thought it all over, the passion and anger and greed, the fury of it all. Just one more drama the temple had seen, one that would be forgotten soon enough. It all seemed so petty compared to the beauty of the centuries. So sordid.

But it was so wonderfully quiet there in the garden, with her pets and Benedict, the only sound for a moment the birdsong, the distant calls from the souk. Had the temple, the Daughters of Nephthys, really happened at all?

"And we got to stay here a little longer, didn't we?" Benedict said with a laugh. "That's not such a bad thing. This garden is like a paradise, isn't it? The temples and tombs, the palm trees and sunlight. I can't blame my father for preferring such a place to Thornhill."

"Even though it made your young life so lonely, Dukie?" she said, longing to take his hand, to erase those shadows of loneliness she could still see in his sky-colored eyes.

He drained his glass and set it aside, those eyes hooded, hidden. "That wasn't his fault. My life as Duke of Everton was always destined to be no fun at all, just as his was. But he was brave enough to break away."

"And left you with his mess. The bad finances, the leaking roof …"

He laughed ruefully. "I'm not so bad at clearing up messes. Might as well be me."

"I'll say you are absolutely right! You got me straight out of the soup there at the temple."

"Thanks to Chou-Chou howling the alert." He stroked Chou-Chou's tiny velvet ears, making her preen. Just like all ladies when he was around.

"Chou-Chou is a good one to have in your corner, but she'd have been able to do nothing without friends like you and Evie, and Mary and Imogen. I'm lucky to have you. I never thought I'd have a real-life *duke* being my white knight!"

He turned the force of his glowing gaze onto her, making her feel she could melt right into the grass. His attention was soft and unwavering. "I will always rescue you, Flora, if you need it. Just as I know you'll always rescue me."

His hand reached out, his fingers threaded through hers, holding on as if letting go might undo everything they'd just survived. She squeezed his hand in silent reassurance, and for the first time in hours, a faint smile touched his lips, radiating from his eyes to his whole face.

"How can we rescue ourselves now?" she whispered.

"Maybe the conundrum of Thornhill could wait on me just a bit longer, especially now there's a good agent in place," he said. He looked a bit—was it *shy*? Uncertain? It couldn't be, not her Dukie. But his smile was indeed distinctly shaky. "I thought maybe I'd like to see a bit more of Egypt. Even Morocco, or Turkey, or—anywhere, really. Walk in my father's footsteps a little."

So he would be gone? She wouldn't even be able to see him once in a while in cold old London? Flora tried to smile, to conceal her sinking heart. "That does sound lovely, Dukie."

"But I—I wouldn't want to see it alone. Would I?" His smile widened, turned hopeful at the edges. He must truly be looking forward to breaking away. "Maybe—that is, I thought, hoped ..." He ran his hand through his hair, leaving it tumbled and tangled. "I hoped you and Chou-Chou and Thutmose might like to explore it all, too. Gather up some warm sun, some adventures, to take back to England. No one does *adventure* like you, Flora. No one makes me feel so light and free as you do, so much—well, so much like myself. My true self, not the dukie—er, duke. You know me like no one else ever has."

"And you know me," Flora whispered. She felt something spark deep inside of her, something she'd thought had gone cold long ago. Was it—hope? He was right. He was not just a duke to her, and she was not just Florrie Gubbin. Elspeth had talked about true souls, and it seemed like it wasn't every day one could glimpse that fire in someone else.

"I do! At least, I hope I do. You are brave and kind, and so much fun." His hand tightened on hers. His expression suddenly surprised, earnest. "Traveling as friends, of course! I would never want you to think I am dishonoring you in any way. We can be ..."

"Whatever we want to be," Flora said, filled with hope.

That smile appeared again, warmer than the sun. "So you will go with me?"

"Of course I will. You don't have to ask me twice, Dukie." She glanced down at the crumpled card in her hand. "What do you think about Baghdad?"

Benedict laughed. "I think it sounds glorious. With you." He raised her hand to his lips for a long, sweet kiss, and Flora dared to hope that maybe this was only the beginning.

Also by Amanda McCabe

Flora Flowerdew Victorian Mysteries
Flora Flowerdew and the Mystery of the Duke's Diamonds
Flora Flowerdew and the Mystery of the Purloined Papers
Flora Flowerdew and the Secret of the Sarcophagus

Kate Haywood Elizabethan Mysteries
Murder at the Princess' Palace
Murder at Westminster Abbey
Murder in the Queen's Garden
Murder at the Queen's Masquerade
Murder at Whitehall
Murder at the Royal Chateau

Daughters of Erin
Countess of Scandal
Duchess of Sin
Lady of Seduction

Scandalous St. Claires
One Naughty Night
Two Sinful Secrets

Regency Rebels
Because of Miss Everdean
The Earl's Misplaced Bride
Delighting the Duke
The Earl's Second Chance

About the Author

Amanda McCabe wrote her first romance at the age of sixteen--a vast historical epic starring all her friends as the characters, written secretly during algebra class (and her parents wondered why math was not her strongest subject...)

She's never since used algebra, but her books (set in a variety of time periods--Regency, Victorian, Tudor, Renaissance, and 1920s) have been nominated for many awards, including the RITA Award, the Romantic Times BOOKReviews Reviewers' Choice Award, the Booksellers Best, the National Readers Choice Award, and the Holt Medallion. She lives in New Mexico with her lovely husband, along with far too many books and a spoiled rescue dog.

When not writing or reading, she loves yoga, collecting cheesy travel souvenirs, and watching the Food Network--even though she doesn't cook. She also writes as Laurel McKee. historical Elizabethan mysteries as Amanda Carmack., and Eliza Casey...

Please visit her at http://ammandamccabe.com